The Irish Inheritance

Martin Lee is the author of three previous histori-cal crime novels. This book is the first time he has managed to combine two of his passions - crime and genealogy - into one novel. It is also the first in a new genealogical mystery series featuring the investigator, Jayne Sinclair.

The Irish Inheritance

A Jayne Sinclair Genealogical Mystery

M J Lee

This book is dedicated to my grandfathers, neither of whom are alive at the moment. One of them fought for the IRA in both the War of Independence and the Civil War. The other fought for the British Army and the Free State Army.
They may have met, but I doubt it.

Also by M J Lee

Death in Shanghai
City of Shadows
Samuel Pepys and the Stolen Diary

Table of Contents

Chapter 1

The Dublin Hills. Ireland. July 8, 1922.

From a distance, it looked like a jaunt into the country-side for a picnic.

Three men, possibly friends, sat in the back of the Austin, chatting quietly. Two more men rode in the front. All except one were casually dressed in light jackets, open-collared shirts and sturdy boots.

The one exception was the young man who sat in the middle at the back of the car. He wore the uniform of a British officer: Khaki jacket, cavalry trousers and knee high boots, but no hat. He didn't know when his hat had vanished. He had looked for it before he got in the car but couldn't find it anywhere.

All knew where they were going except for the British officer.

'Well, it's a grand day for it,' said the man in front, O'Kelly was his name.

The sky was a bright blue, the sort of blue that occasionally comes along in April to chase away the showers and tempt people with dreams of summer.

'It is indeed,' said Declan Fitzgerald, one the men in the back, known as Fitz to his friends. 'I always love the hills above Dublin on days like this. It makes me think of fishing. Just sitting on the banks of the Erkne back home with a rod in my hand and the trout dancing in the stream below me, waiting to become my dinner.'

He nudged the man sitting next to him. 'Do you fish at all where you come from?'

1

The British officer snapped out of his reverie. He had been dreaming of escape. Imagining the door flung open and him running down the road, the wind rustling in his hair, his arms pumping him forward, away from the men who sat on either side of him.

'Well, do you or don't you?'

The British officer tried to focus on the question. The lazy heat of the spring day, the noise of the engine as it climbed the hill and the tight fit in the back of the small car had muddied his mind.

The other man repeated the question with a tone of exasperation in his voice. 'Do you or don't you fish?'

'No, not really. Not many trout streams in Bradford.'

'Is that where you're from, then?'

The British officer mimicked the Yorkshire accent of his youth, knocked out of him by the teachers of his public school. 'Sunny Bradford. Famous for wool, worsted, women and nowt else. A warm place despite the cold winds,' he added as an afterthought.

'Aye, sounds like Mayo, don't it, Fitz?' O'Kelly spoke again from the front of the car.

'I wouldn't know. Never been there.'

The driver changed down as the car climbed another hill, the engine making a high squeal as it argued against the weight of the occupants. Everybody inside had fallen silent, staring out of the window at the knee high vegetation, spotted with ferns and the occasional Mountain Ash. There were no people in the landscape, though. They had passed a few old stone walls, the remnants of houses abandoned in the famine and never inhabited again. But this wasn't an area where men lived or farmed anymore. Life was too tough here, too wild, even for the land-hungry Irish.

2

'Where are we going?' asked the British officer.

'Sure, we'll find out when we get there,' said Fitz adding a little laugh at the end of the sentence, making light of the situation.

'When will that be?'

'By and by.' This time Fitz finished his words with a small smile that said 'I'm not telling you any more, so stop asking foolish questions.'

'What time will we get there?'

Fitz turned to face the British officer. 'We're not allowed to tell you, you know that, but it's not far. So just sit back and enjoy the beautiful Irish countryside stretched out beneath you. Haven't your lot been coveting it for centuries?'

The officer, a captain, took the hint and stared out of the window past the man on his right. Silence descended on the car again, broken only by the whine of the engine as the driver changed gears to deal with the hills and dips in the road.

After ten minutes, when they had reached the top of one hill and were just about to descend into another valley, Fitz leant forward and tapped the driver on the shoulder. 'I think we'll stop here and stretch our legs, Davy, it's quiet enough.'

The driver changed down and the car whined to a gentle stop.

'Michael, will you take the prisoner off over there?' He pointed to a spot next to some rocks seventy yards from the road.

Michael took the officer's arm and urged him out of the car. The fresh air was a welcome relief from the staleness of the rear seat. Up above, a lark sang its song to welcome them.

'Michael, where are we going?' asked the British officer.

'I'm afraid, it's time.'

The officer stopped. 'But you said I was going to be ex-changed, I...'

'Orders have changed. I'm sorry.' Michael Dowling shook his head and held his hands palm upwards. 'There was nothing I could do.'

On the other side of the car, Declan Fitzgerald stepped out from the back of the car and inhaled deeply. 'Will you smell that? Nothing beats the smell of Ireland in the spring. Fresh as a cow's backside.'

He reached into his pocket and pulled out the Webley that had been sitting heavily there, revolving the barrel to make sure it turned smoothly. He had cleaned, oiled and loaded it the night before in preparation for today, but one more check wouldn't hurt anybody.

'Just let me run, Michael. Nobody will know.'

Michael shrugged his shoulders. 'I can't do that. I'm sor-ry.'

The officer looked over at the rocks. A narrow path cut into the ferns trailed down the hillside. If he ran now, he might get away.

'Don't stand here all day, Michael. Let's get it over and done with.' Fitz stood next to Michael now, the Webley pointing directly at the British officer. 'I'm fair parched and a drop wouldn't go amiss.'

He waved the Webley in the direction of the rocks. Michael Dowling reached out and touched the prisoner on the arm. It was a gentle touch but enough to let the man know there was no chance of escape.

The prisoner's body slumped, his shoulders forming a rounded bow and the chin sinking to the chest. 'You won't forget what you promised?'

'I'll return your things to your family.'

'Thank you. I have one last favour to ask.' He reached

4

into his pocket and pulled out a letter. Michael could see it was creased and smeared as if it had been opened and read many times. 'Could you send this too? I've meant to post it to his family but I've never had the courage.' He handed it over. 'He died next to me, a good man.'

'I'll send it on, saying it's from you.'

'Thank you.'

Fitz pushed the officer towards the rocks. 'Let's get it over with.'

The shove seemed to awaken the man. For a moment, Michael thought he was going to punch Fitz as his hands balled into fists, but the anger subsided as soon as it had appeared. The hands relaxed and he tugged the back of his army jacket down, straightening the collar. He strode over to the rocks, followed by Michael, Fitz and O'Kelly. The driver remained beside the car smoking a Sweet Afton.

The view from the rocks was breathtaking. A long valley stretched out beneath them, dotted with tiny houses. From each one, a trail of thin smoke rose to the blue sky. A chaotic pattern of black lines stretched between the houses. Some formed squares, others long rectangles. Most had straight sides but, here and there, a curved wall bent around a stream or ancient boundary.

'Will you kneel down and say your prayers?' said Fitz, more as a statement than a question.

The officer smiled. 'I don't believe in God. Not many of us do any more. Four years in the trenches can do that to a man.'

Fitz shrugged his shoulders. 'Well, say a few prayers anyway. You never know who's listening.' He pointed upwards.

'You will send my things to my family?' The British officer ignored Fitz and spoke directly to Michael.

He nodded. 'I've got the address.'

The British officer dropped to his knees. Despite himself, he closed his eyes and began to whisper the words he remembered from going to Queensbury Chapel in his youth.

Fitz stepped forward and shot him in the back of the head.

The sound reverberated through the hills, echoing off the rocks. The stench of cordite filled the air. Up above, the lark continued trilling its song, beating its wings into the breeze, proclaiming its joy at this beautiful spring day.

Next to the rocks, on top of the hill, three men surrounded a body lying prone on the ground, blood flowing from the hole in the back of his head.

'But...he hadn't finished... he was...' stammered Michael.

'Always better to do it when they're least expecting anything. Avoids the drama.'

'But he was still praying...'

'Ach, he can continue when he's up there. Talk to the man direct.'

Michael stared down at the body. He had spent the last evening chatting with this man, learning about his life and telling him about his own. Now, his body lay stretched out on the bare Irish soil, the eyes still and unblinking. Already, the face had that paleness which is the mark of the dead. He immediately thought of his father lying in his coffin at the wake. Staring out at all those people that had come to visit and drink his health. Too late for his father to hear any of the words. It was a shame they hadn't visited him during his life.

'Get the 'oul shovel from the car. We'll dig a hole for him beneath the ferns over there.' Fitz pointed to a patch of bare ground surround by a miniature forest of ferns ten yards away.

Reluctantly, Michael staggered back towards the car, each step felt like he was walking through peat.

Behind him, he heard O'Kelly say, 'Will I check his pockets?'

There was no reply from Fitz.

After what seemed like an age, Michael reached the car and opened the boot.

'Himself doesn't waste any time, does he?' said Davy, the driver.

Michael took out an old shovel and walked slowly back to the rocks.

'The pockets are empty, except for this.' O'Kelly held up a silver lighter, the rays of the sun glinting off its shiny exterior.

'Keep it. He won't be needing it anymore,' said Fitz.

Michael walked past the two of them and began digging in the stony soil, a fierce determination on his face. Isn't that what we've always been good for? Digging in the earth like badgers, scraping away at the skin of the land.

The shovel bit into the ground, striking small pebbles, lumps of dirt and scraps of decayed vegetation. Michael heaved it to his left, building a small hill beside the long rectangle of the grave. The deeper he dug, and the longer he scraped at the ground, the faster his muscles worked. The smell of the fresh earth filled his nostrils, driving him on, driving him deeper.

Dig. Lift. Throw.

Dig. Lift. Throw.

It was as if his muscles had some memory of this work even though he had never done a day's digging in his life. 'No son of mine is working the fields,' his father had repeated again and again. 'Study. Study hard. And then study

7

harder.'

Dig. Lift. Throw.

Dig Lift. Throw.

'That's enough,' shouted Fitz, 'we're not putting him in Glasnevin.'

Michael collapsed at the rim of the trench he had dug, his chest fighting for air.

'You grab his legs and I'll get him under the arms.'

O'Kelly took hold of both legs. 'Sure it's a terrible waste of a good pair of boots.'

'Leave them. We can't bury the man in his socks.'

They both lifted the British officer and scurried over to the grave that Michael had dug.

'Are you going to be getting out of there, or are you both going to share?'

Michael climbed out of the shallow grave. Fitz and O'Kelly swung the body and it landed like the proverbial sack of potatoes in the bottom but with one leg still sticking out at the side. Declan bent down and gently pushed the boot into the grave, adjusting the legs and the arms so that they were straight. It looked as if the officer was standing at attention.

'Will we say a few words?' asked O'Kelly.

'Aye, we better. You never know who's listening.'

Fitz clasped his hands in front of him, closed his eyes and lowered his head. O'Kelly followed suit, mimicking his pose.

'Lord, we commend to your grace, the body of this man. May he take his place by your side now and forever more. Amen.'

'Amen,' repeated O'Kelly.

'Now, let's get him covered up and we can go for a drink. I'm as parched as an owl.' He picked up the shovel and began to shift the earth back into the grave.

Michael watched as the dark soil slowly covered the officer's face and body, swallowing him up in the land and the stones and the moss.

Chapter 2

The rain came down like the day before the launch of Noah's Ark. The Catholic priest, hidden beneath a large blue and white golf umbrella, intoned the final words trying to prevent the water soaking into his Bible.

A small group surrounded the open grave. Black suits, black dresses, black umbrellas, all huddled together. As the priest mumbled his words, the gravediggers in their orange high-vis jackets, lowered the coffin into the ground.

Jayne Sinclair was the third person to step forward, picking up a sodden clump of earth and throwing it into the grave. It landed with a loud thump on the lid of the coffin. She said a quiet prayer and edged to the right to allow other mourners to throw their lumps of earth.

She wouldn't miss the bitch. Her husband's sister had been a pain throughout her marriage. Needy, spiteful, bitter, and those were just her good points.

She looked across at her husband, Paul. His eyes were red-rimmed. Despite herself, she felt sorry for him. She knew he would miss his sister. They had both bonded in their early years and remained close right to the end. Her cancer bringing them even more together in that strange way that a pain shared is a pain doubled.

There weren't many people at the funeral. Two of her ex-husbands had stayed away, while the last in a sorry bunch was throwing his earth into the grave now, showing no signs of emotion. Luckily, or unluckily, she had never given birth. Perhaps if any of her marriages had been blessed with children, it may have softened her edges, made her less self-absorbed.

But Jayne knew she could hardly talk, not having children herself. She had blamed the job, her old job. A detective has little time for children: the odd hours, the unpredictable schedule, the shifts, the all-consuming work. But she knew that was just an excuse. The truth was she never felt comfortable bringing children into a world where there was so much suffering and hate. And now she had left the job, she didn't know if she loved her husband enough to make a child with him.

He was still standing there in the rain, with his head bowed. She took his arm and led him away from the grave. They were followed by the other mourners, all nine of them.

Her phone rang. Without thinking, she reached into her bag and pulled it out. She didn't recognise the number. Spots of rain were already splashing on the screen. Her husband was looking at her as if to say how could you answer the phone at a time like this?

'Hello.'

'Is that Ms Jayne Sinclair?'

The voice was American and the amount of static on the line sounded like he was shouting across the Atlantic through a storm.

'Speaking.' She spoke as quietly as she could into the mobile.

'Good morning, Ms Sinclair, My name is Richard Hughes, you don't know me, but—'

Her husband let go of her arm and walked away in the direction of the cemetery gates.

'I'm afraid, I can't talk right now.'

'No problem,' the voice drawled, 'we saw your advert in

Family Tree magazine and would like to arrange a meeting. Tonight, at six pm, the Midland Hotel?'

She began walking after her husband, trying to catch him up. 'I don't know if—'

'Good, that's arranged, see you in the lobby at six.'

'Mr Hughes...Mr Hughes?' The line was dead.

She ran after her husband, catching him up as he was getting into the car.

'Sorry, work,' she said feebly.

There was no answer.

Chapter 3

'How could you answer the phone at my sister's funeral?'

He hadn't said a word in the car on the drive back from Southern Cemetery. She knew he would wait until they had stepped across the threshold into their house before he would begin. And right on cue, he had started. She was determined that she wouldn't rise to the bait. After all, he had just buried his sister. Now was not a time to argue.

'It was work,' she said, hanging her coat on the hook in the hall.

'It's always work. I thought when you left the police, our lives would be easier. But your hobby seems to have taken over where work left off.'

'It's not a hobby. It's my job. My new job.'

'Looking into people's pasts? That's not a job. It's just nosiness.'

She ignored him, walking into the open plan kitchen. They had remodelled the house twelve years ago when they first got married. Instead of taking a honeymoon, they had built a new space. It was his idea but she loved it. Sitting here in the morning drinking her coffee was the time she was most at ease, when he had gone to work, the house was quiet and she was alone, waiting to start up her computer and plunge into the past.

She specialised in genealogical research. Not the usual stuff, but more difficult cases; lost relatives, broken timelines, adoptions, hidden secrets. People with a past that they couldn't discover for themselves. She was good at her job, she knew that. Years of police training had given her the ability to dig deep into whatever had happened, even though it was often a long time ago. Her personal life might be a mess but her work never suffered. Not with the police and not with her new job.

'Even the vicar noticed that you were speaking on your phone. I saw him shaking his head as he left the cemetery.'

Sometimes, he was like a dog with a bone, unable to leave it alone.

She put the kettle on. 'Would you like some tea?'

'No, I don't want any bloody tea.'

'Well, I'm making some. It'll calm you down.' She realised as soon as the words were out of her mouth that it was the wrong thing to say. Never in the history of human discourse had telling somebody to calm down ever calmed them down.

'What did you say? I've just buried my sister for God's sake and you're telling me to calm down.'

'I just thought—'

'You know I asked people to come back here after the funeral. I thought it might be nice to talk about her and what she meant to them, but nobody wanted to come.'

'I'm not surprised.' As soon as she said the words, she knew now was not the time for honesty. But she was never good at placating people. Even in the Force, she was never the one sent to tell people their loved ones had been injured or killed. In fact, it was the opposite. She was the last person ever chosen to give bad news. Somehow, she lacked the ability to empathise with people. She tried, but always ended up saying the wrong thing.

'What do you mean by that?'

Her husband finally had his argument. The electric kettle started to bubble and steam poured from the spout. With a loud click, it switched itself off.

'What do you mean by that?' he repeated, louder this time.

Oh God, she thought, here we go. 'Well, I just meant, she wasn't the easiest person to like. She was an unhappy person who made the lives of others difficult.'

Her husband stayed silent. 'Did she make your life difficult?' he eventually said.

Jayne thought for a moment. 'No, I refused to let her.'

'Your work came first?'

She poured some hot water into the pot and emptied it into the sink. Taking the caddy, she placed two teaspoons of Darjeeling into the pot. She hated tea bags and all the convenience that went with them. It was the taste of tea she wanted not the ease of a paper bag.

'Are you sure you won't have any tea?'

'No. I'm going to bed.'

'But it's only four in the afternoon.'

'I just want to lie down.'

His anger was spent now. He slumped over with his head held between his knees. She knew she should have comforted him then, but she couldn't do it. She would have made a terrible mother.

He stood up slowly and shakily, taking a second to find his balance, before heading towards the door.

'Do you want me to bring you anything?'

'No, I'll be fine. Just need to sleep.'

The room was silent when he was gone. Above her head, she heard the creaking floorboards as he walked across their bedroom to hang up his jacket, followed by a soft thump as he threw himself on the bed.

She sipped her tea, enjoying the soft, warm smokiness

as it swam past the back of her tongue. The laptop was sitting on the counter. She flipped the Mac open and clicked Safari. Her emails came up immediately.

The first two she deleted. She had no need for life insurance or penis enhancement at the moment. The third caught her attention, it was from Richard Hughes.

Dear Ms Sinclair,

Apologies for disturbing you this afternoon. And additional apologies for requesting a meeting at such short notice. But once you meet my uncle, you will understand the need for speed. In this email, you will find two attachments. My uncle's adoption file and his original birth certificate. We began the process of searching for his antecedents two months ago and have now reached an impasse.

I look forward to meeting you at six this evening at the Midland Hotel.

Richard Hughes

The language was quite formal and educated. Nobody used words like antecedent or impasse any more. But the job looked too straightforward for her skills. And besides, she should stay with Paul in case he needed her. Schlepping across Manchester in the rain held no attraction. She picked up her tea and sipped it, glancing at the address. An ordinary private Gmail, nothing too special about it.

She glanced at the message again, seeing the two attachments sitting at the top.

'Bugger it,' she said out loud, opening the first attachment. It was a notice of adoption stating that the child, John Michael Trichot, an orphan aged four years old, was being adopted by an American couple, Thomas and Glenda Hughes. It was dated October 4, 1929, and signed at the bottom by the Matron of the Ilkley Children's Home, a Mrs Glendower, and the Resident Magistrate of the town, James Whittaker.

A fairly standard adoption certificate, nothing out of the ordinary. She glanced through it one more time. It looked straightforward to her, with all the formalities required by the Adoption of Children Act 1926 fulfilled to the letter. What nobody realised was that from the 1920s to the 1960s over 150,000 English children were sent abroad as orphans, mainly to Canada and Australasia. It seems this man was one of those transported at this time. She checked through the adoption papers, no additional information. Under the Act, there should have been reasons for the adoption and statements from the Children's Home, but there was nothing.

Strange. She made a note for herself to check out the Ilkley Children's Home.

She clicked on the second attachment, the birth certificate. The baby's name was repeated: John Michael Trichot, born July 16, 1925. She immediately smiled. Not a common name, probably of French origin. The birth certificate was English, so it should make searching for ancestors relatively easy.

'Thank God, he isn't a John Smith,' she said out loud. She often talked to herself as she investigated. She had done the same in the police, earning the nickname 'The Whisperer'. It wasn't a bad nickname for the force, better than most. One of her bosses went by the name of 'Lurch'.

Not for his resemblance to the television character but for his ability to accidentally bump into the breasts of junior female officers when he was drunk. A quick sharp squeeze of his bollocks had made certain he never attempted another lurch with her.

She scanned across the certificate. The father's name came next. Charles Allen Fitzmaurice Trichot. Even better, three Christian names. She hoped he had used all three of them in the census or in the army as it would make him easy to find.

His profession was listed as Gentleman. Funny, I wonder how you got that job? Apply with a CV in triplicate or simply be born with a silver spoon in your mouth? Probably the latter.

The mother was simpler; Emily Clavell. Fairly straightforward and to the point. Her profession was Spinster. She loved the old descriptions that cropped up on birth certificates. So much better than Housewife.

Her favourite was a Night Soil Collector, the ancestor of a millionaire football client with a famous temper. She had told him his grandfather was a water dispersal operative. He was as pleased as punch.

She decided to start with the father as, with his rare name, he was probably going to be the easiest to find. Unlike women, men very rarely changed the names they were born with. She logged on to Findmypast.com and typed in Charles Allen Fitzmaurice Trichot.

Nothing.

She restricted the search to the UK and eliminated the Allen and the Fitzmaurice, pressing return once more.

Nine results.

She clicked on the 1911 census. There he was, living with his parents in Hertfordshire. 21 years old. The only son of a father who was a vicar. A quick check of the 1891 and 1901 censuses revealed he had grown up at the same address. Not surprising, people moved around a lot less than they do today.

Then she clicked on the next section in the results headlined, *Soldiers, died in the Great War.*

First names: Charles Edward Fitzmaurice
Last name: Trichot
Service Number: 4267
Rank: Captain
Regiment: Princess of Kent's Own
Battalion: 1/5th Battalion
Birthplace: Sheppey, Hertfordshire.
Enlistment Place: London
Death Year: 1918
Death Day: 7
Death Month: 11
Cause of Death: Killed in Action
Place: Sambre Canal

It was the same man. The name and place of birth were exactly the same.

But if he were dead, how did he manage to father a child seven years later?

She sipped her tea, the warm smokiness of it slipped down her throat and warmed her stomach. Her eyes scanned all the way to the last result on the website search list. A newspaper report from The Times for November 30, 1918. The full page of the newspaper opened up with a small article outlined in yellow at the top right corner with a headline that immediately excited her.

MM Awarded to Captain Charles Trichot (Posthumous)

It is gazetted today that Captain Charles Trichot of the First Battalion Princess of Kent's Own has been awarded the Military Medal for Gallantry. During the crossing of the Sambre Canal, Captain Trichot led his men with valour gaining his objective despite losing most of his company to shellfire. With a small detachment of his men, he held off repeated attacks by the enemy, despite being wounded in the leg and chest. Captain Trichot died of his wounds at No.23 Casualty Clearing Station, Auberchicourt on the morning after the engagement. He is the only son of the Reverend Charles Trichot of Sheppey, Herts.

It was the same man, it had to be. But how does a man father a child when he's been dead for seven years?

She closed the laptop. Perhaps, she would keep this appointment after all.

Chapter 4

Midland Hotel, Manchester. November 14, 2015.

'I suppose you're here because you saw the same thing we did.'

Her client was old, very old. He sat in his wheelchair facing her, long arthritic fingers gripping an even older looking walking stick. To say the face had seen life was an understatement. It looked like a half-made bed in a doss house: a shock of white hair covered skin that had last been seen on a Shar Pei. Pendulous eye bags hung down over the cheeks. Inside the mouth, the teeth had a vaguely yellow tinge. But what stood out were the eyes. Deep blue pools of life that seemed to look into and through her at the same time.

'The man named as your father apparently died seven years before you were born,' said Jayne.

Her client nodded his head, but it was more like a slow, knowing bow.

Jayne looked at the printout she had made of The Times article. 'There must be an explanation. Perhaps, he was reported dead, then found alive as a POW?'

The old man sighed as if he was dealing with a difficult pupil. 'The newspaper report was explicit about him being shot leading a charge across the Sambre canal. They don't give posthumous medals to men who are still alive.'

The voice was deep, American, like a chocolate milkshake, only smoother and richer.

Jayne had finally decided to come to the meeting after checking in on Paul. He was sleeping like a baby. With a bit of luck, she would be home before he woke up. 'I don't know. There must be some explanation, otherwise...'

'Otherwise, how could I be here?'

'Precisely.'

'Could I get you anything to drink, Ms Sinclair?' The speaker was Richard Hughes. He had met her down in the lobby, approaching her as soon as she entered and guiding her up to a Midland suite on the seventh floor.

'Sit down, Richard,' the old man snapped. 'I'm sorry, Mrs Sinclair, my nephew sometimes acts like a love-sick puppy.'

She glanced at the man. He did have a sort of puppy dog expression, but one that was immaculately turned out in the latest Calvin Klein suit and Gucci loafers.

The old man twisted in his wheelchair towards his nephew. 'Go and make yourself useful. Get me my Scotch and a glass of something for the lady, here.'

Jayne caught the malevolent look that dissolved a moment later into a smile. 'The Macallan 18, Uncle?'

'What else?' snapped the old man.

'And for you, Ms Sinclair?'

'A glass of water will be fine.'

'Coming right up.' He walked over to the drinks trolley.

'I hate Ms, don't you? A sound like the after effects of a fart.'

'It's neutral. It doesn't define my status.'

'Nothing is neutral. And it defines you as much as any other word, Mrs Sinclair. You are married, aren't you?'

Again, the blue eyes stared at her. 'Yes, but you already know that. You also know my background, what I do, and probably what colour underwear I'm wearing.'

The old man chuckled. 'I don't know about the underwear, but everything else has been checked. Richard, give me the dossier.'

'Just a minute, Uncle.'

'Now, Richard, I can't wait for you all the time.'

Richard stopped pouring the whisky and handed him a folder from the top of the table. Jayne noticed there were other folders in a neat pile.

The old man took it without a word of thanks or acknowledging his nephew. He opened the cover and scanned down a typewritten page, reading aloud in his deep voice as he did so. 'You're married, no children. Husband's name is Paul, he works for a software company. You didn't take his surname when you married.' The blue eyes looked up at her. 'Why was that, Mrs Sinclair?'

'I liked my own name. It's the one I was born with.'

The old man harrumphed and returned to reading his dossier. 'One brother lives in London, you're not close. Mother dead, stepfather still alive. He has Alzheimer's. You don't know who your real father is.'

The last words caused a sharp stab of pain in her chest. The old man carried on without noticing.

'You're ex-police, twenty-one years in the Force. Resigned six months after your partner, Dave Gilmour, was shot dead in front of you.'

An image flashed across Jayne's mind. The loud bang of a shotgun, a hole in the door, Dave falling backwards, slowly, so slowly.

'Three years in genealogy, specialising in investigations. I checked with Lord Radley. He confirmed your credentials. You made sure his line didn't die out.'

'A relative, transported to Australia. Not a difficult investigation.'

'But done under difficult circumstances, wasn't it?'

'All investigations throw up obstacles.'

The old man scratched his nose with one long, wrinkled finger at the end of which hung a bruised nail. 'No doubt, you'll be wondering who I am?'

Richard Hughes arrived back with the drinks, giving Jayne her water and a crystal tumbler of whisky for his uncle. The old man held the glass with both hands and lifted it up to his mouth, sucking down a large gulp. 'The ice has melted, don't drown the Scotch. How many times have I told you?'

Richard reached over and took it off him. 'Sorry, Uncle, I'll make you another.'

'Useless as tits on a bull, that's what he is. And to think he's going to take over when I'm gone.' The old man stared at the back of his nephew before turning around to face Jayne once more. 'Where was I? That's right, I was about to tell you who I am.'

'No need. You are John Hughes, Chairman and founder of probably the world's largest distribution company, Hughes Transport. You're here to open Europe's biggest distribution facility in Warrington.'

'Not a pleasant place, Warrington. Reminds me of Pittsburgh without the excitement. And you are wrong, Mrs Sinclair, Hughes Transport is *definitely* the world's biggest distribution company. You've been busy.'

'Fairly easy to check out, Mr Hughes. A call to the hotel to get your name and the rest can be Googled. I don't like to meet new clients without knowing something about them.'

'So you'll take the case?'

'I haven't decided yet.'

'I will pay your usual fee plus a $50,000 dollar bonus if you give me a successful report before the end of the month.'

'That's just eight days away. Why the rush?'

'Two reasons. I will be in England till then so you can deliver the report to me in person.'

'And the second?'

'I have leukaemia, Mrs Sinclair. Two months the doctors give me.' The old man chuckled, the skin on his neck waving like flags in a breeze. 'After 90 years on this earth, they decide I only have a couple of months left. I think it's God's way of telling me to slow down.'

'What exactly do you want to know, Mr Hughes?'

'Oh, that's easy, Mrs Sinclair. Before I die, I want to know who I am and who my father was.'

'Do you have anything else for me to work with besides the birth certificate and your adoption papers?'

'Not really. I was brought to the States in October 1929. I always say I caused the Great Crash.' He chuckled once more. Richard Hughes passed him another glass of whisky. 'I was adopted by Tom and Glenda Hughes and given my new name. John Hughes.'

'I've seen it around.'

'It amused me to put it on the side of sixty-foot long trailers. I always made sure the letters were immense.' He chuckled once again. 'There's a certain irony since it's not even my real name.'

'Do you remember anything at all from that time?'

The old man stared into mid-air, forcing his mind to go back in time, a long way back in time. 'Nothing, I'm afraid. I've tried to remember but nothing comes. It's as if there was a wall there, no matter how I high I jump, I still can't see over.' He paused again.

Jayne could see him, staring into space, trying to jump harder to see over the wall.

'It's almost as if I didn't exist before I came to America. The earliest memory I have is of standing on the deck of the ship, holding somebody's hand, looking at the Statue of Liberty.' He chuckled. 'The classic immigrant's dream. But even then, I'm not sure if it actually happened, I was told it happened, or I saw it in a movie.' He lapsed into silence.

'Do you have anything from that time?'

'There's an old photograph. I think it was taken a couple of days after my arrival.' He gestured impatiently for his nephew to pass over the clear plastic sleeve.

Jayne looked at the photograph. It had serrated edges and was in black and white. A young boy was looking straight at the camera, a stern, composed expression on his face. He was wearing an overcoat that looked too small for him. In his left hand, he carried a book. His right hand was being held by a man but his face was out of the shot.

'I was four years old when this was taken. Strange to see an image of myself from so long ago. It could be a different person.' He gestured impatiently to his nephew again.

Richard took a small black book out of another folder and handed it to Jayne.

'This was the book I was carrying when I arrived, *The Lives of the United Irishmen*.'

'Not normal reading for a four-year-old.'

'I was advanced for my age even then.'

Jayne opened the book. On the inside front cover was an inscription, the ink faded with time.

To MD,
Our cause is true,
The fight is right,
We will be free,
To see the light.

From DF

'You have no idea who wrote this?'

'No idea at all.' He leant from his wheelchair to put his drink on the side table. Richard Hughes jumped up but was waved away dismissively by his uncle. 'Listen, Mrs Sinclair, Tom and Glenda Hughes were good people. They made sure I had a proper education, looked after me, treated me well. I loved them both, particularly Tom. Glenda was the harder woman. She was the one who pushed me all the time. I guess you could say she was the one who made me what I am today. Tom was softer, warmer than her. Even when they finally had their own child...' He pointed disdainfully at Richard, '...his father. Tom still treated me just like his own son. But they never told me anything about my real parents. Tom and Glenda were both killed in a plane crash in 1949.' He chuckled again. It was the noise of a baby being strangled at birth. 'Ironically, they were on their way to see me. I had just graduated from Stanford on the GI Bill.' The laugh stopped and the man stared into mid-air again.

For a small moment, Jayne could see the immense sadness at the heart of this incredibly wealthy man.

'I often thought my adopted parents were going to tell me something the day I graduated. Glenda had said she would. But they were both killed before they could say anything.' The deep blue eyes lost their watery sadness and focussed on Jayne. 'In some cases, they treated me better than their own son. But now I'm rich and old, and I'm going to die in the next two months. I just want to know who I am before I go.'

'I understand, Mr Hughes.'

The old man held out his wrinkled hands towards her. 'Tell me who I am, Mrs Sinclair. Just tell me who I am.'

Chapter 5

Lobby, Midland Hotel. November 14, 2015.

'I'm sorry about my uncle's behaviour, Ms Sinclair. He's old and he can get a little cranky at times.'

Richard Hughes had escorted Jayne down to the lobby of the Midland Hotel. 'I understand, Mr Hughes.'

'Call me Richard.'

She held up a plastic folder with the book and the photograph inside. 'Is this really all there is, Richard?'

'I'm afraid that's all, there is nothing else. We searched through my grandfather and grandmother's papers but there's nothing about the adoption.'

'It's not much to go on.'

'Can I be honest with you, Ms Sinclair?'

'Call me Jayne.'

'My uncle has become obsessed with this over the last couple of months. It consumes him to the point of ignoring everything else. Despite his age, he's still very much involved in running the company. Without him, decisions don't get made.'

'Was it you who made the initial investigation?'

He nodded. 'I found his adoption papers through a BIBA form. The bureaucrats in your country even wanted my uncle to go through counselling before they would let him access the birth certificate, but a sharp letter from our solicitors soon ended that crap. When we received the original certificate, I thought it would be simple enough to trace any living relatives or ancestors.'

'But then you hit a brick wall.'

He nodded again. 'I didn't get very far. His father had died seven years before he was born. How could that be?'

'I don't know, Richard, but somehow we will find out. Did you look into the mother's side?'

'She died in 1929. I could find no living relatives, another dead end.'

'Perhaps, these can help us.' She held up the plastic folder.

Richard looked down at his feet. 'My uncle is dying, Jayne. What you saw tonight was sheer willpower keeping him going. When I go back to the suite, he will be asleep in the wheelchair.'

'I could see he was ill.'

'I've looked for answers to this riddle and found nothing. It all happened nearly 100 years ago, for Christ's sake. It's dead and buried.'

'The past has a habit of giving up its secrets, Richard. You only have to look in the right places.'

'Honestly, what are the chances of finding out the truth?'

'I don't know until I've looked. One never knows. That's the beauty of genealogy, secrets reveal themselves over time in the most unlikely places.'

'Can I lay my cards on the table, Jayne, as we say in America?'

'Go ahead.'

'He's old, he's dying. I don't want to get his hopes up that you can discover his past in just eight days. Why don't you tell him you can't find anything. We'll still pay you. Then he can die in peace.'

Jayne stepped back. 'I can't do that, Mr Hughes. Your uncle has paid me to look for his ancestors. I will try my best to find them.'

'What is this Ms Sinclair, some sort of Genealogist Boy

Scouts Honour shit? Give me a break, will ya.' As he became flustered, Richard's accent became more American.

'It's not 'shit' as you so graciously put it, Mr Hughes. Your uncle, my client, has commissioned me to perform the research to the best of my ability. I am going to do that and report my findings to him in eight days. Is that clear?'

Richard Hughes' face had changed again, a smile dancing across his lips. 'I'm sorry, Jayne. Please forgive me. But you must understand I'm dealing with a man who has less than two months to live. In that time, he needs to sort out the company affairs. Otherwise, when he's gone, the world's largest transportation company is going to be going down the tubes along with the jobs of 88,000 men and women. Instead of sorting out the company business, he is obsessing about who he is and where he came from.'

'I understand Mr Hughes, but your uncle is my client, not you. I will report back to him in eight days with my findings. In the meantime, I will say good night to you.'

He put his hand gently on her arm. 'One last favour, Jayne. Can this conversation stay private between the two of us? You saw how my uncle treats me. I don't want him to know how concerned I am.'

Jayne took his hand off her arm. 'Of course, Richard. I'll be in touch.'

She turned and walked through the doors into the Manchester rain. This case was getting more complicated by the second.

Chapter 6

When she returned home to Didsbury that evening, Paul was still asleep. She pulled the duvet over his sleeping body and crept quietly downstairs.

The room was quiet, only the Ikea clock ticking on one wall. The cat mewed a welcome, padding over to rub his body against her leg and remind her that he hadn't been fed yet. She grabbed a tin of cat food from the shelf. Liver and bacon, sounds yummy, could eat that myself, filling his bowl in the corner with the food. He went straight over and began to eat. The poor little sod must be starving she thought. Then, she realised that she hadn't eaten herself since this morning. Good for the waistline, bad for the health.

She opened the fridge. There was a selection of food from the deli. Cheeses, hams, slices of saucisson, even pickled Polish gherkins which she hated but he loved. A tray of what were fancifully called crudités, but looked like a few raw carrots and a couple of dips to her. Paul had insisted on stocking up just in case people had come back from the funeral to their house. Fat chance of that.

She knew exactly what she wanted, though. From the side door of the fridge, she took a bottle of St Hallett Faith Shiraz. Not the best drop on earth but a good buy for ten quid. A good, jammy Aussie Shiraz would go down well. From an airtight container in the fresh section of the fridge, she selected a Valrhona Estate Grown chocolate from the Palmira Plantation. The honey and nuts of these Criolla

31

Cacao beans would go well with the wine.

Her idea of heaven. Chocolate and red wine. And God she needed it. The client was a bit of a nightmare, an unpleasant old man who made Richard Hughes' life a nightmare. 'I wonder why he puts up with it,' she said out loud. Why does anybody put up with anything?

She opened the wine, enjoying the satisfying pull of the cork. Always a good sign when it's nice and tight. A quick whiff to check for taint and she poured the rich, ruby liquid into a glass, adding an extra glug because she thought she needed it. She snapped the block of chocolate in half. What a lovely sound, the breaking of chocolate, putting one half back in the airtight box and taking the other, still wrapped in its silver foil over to the counter.

She flipped open the lid of her computer and logged on. Where to start? Well, Jayne, my love, you could try the beginning, it's usually the best place. But in this case, she knew her client's beginning was just the end of one life.

She sipped the first mouthful of Shiraz, holding it in her mouth, letting the cold liquid gradually warm as it played across her tongue. Good fruit, a pleasant drop. But it could do with a longer time to get a little warmer. She snapped off two squares of chocolate and popped them in her mouth. The initial hardness of the chocolate gradually softened, releasing its sweet bitterness across her tongue and teeth, where it blended with the aftermath of the red wine.

Better than sex, she thought. Well, at least, it was better than sex with her husband. An image of a snoring Paul lying fully dressed beneath the covers of the duvet elbowed its way into her mind, followed by a sense of guilt. God, he's lost his sister today and you can think about him like this.

She resolved to make it up to him in the morning. Be

nice, she thought, it's the least you can do.

Time to work. The one time she felt fully in control. It had been the same in the police. The soft stuff, dealing with people, holding their hands, massaging egos, she hated all that. What she loved was the nitty gritty of investigations and later, as computers began to take over their world, the power she felt as she delved into someone's life and world as she investigated them. It always amazed her how much people revealed of themselves online. Too much, far too much.

And now, the past reveals itself too. So many records had been digitised, the painstaking work of diving through dusty tomes full of indecipherable handwriting was less necessary these days. Sometimes, it was the only way to go, but the first step was always online.

She pulled across the adoption certificate John Hughes had given to her. The old man had been resident at The Ilkley Children's Home before he was adopted. She quickly typed the name into Google. 2043189 results in 0.38 seconds. Useless information, but she was sure Google were keen to tell everybody how quick their algorithms were. She bypassed the first two sites. Ads for adoption agencies, providing services. The third was more interesting. A Wikipedia article:

Ilkley Children's Home was situated at 23, Ireton Drive, Ilkley in an old Georgian house that had previously been a rectory. It was founded By Alderman George Dukinfield in 1901 to take in children whose fathers had been killed in the Boer War. It continued to take in orphans and unwanted children after the end of the war, eventually reaching its peak of occupation in 1920. The children in residence stayed there from two years old to 11 years old and, by this time, many were the offspring of single mothers from the mills of Bradford and surrounding areas. In 1920, the staff comprised a Matron, three sisters, two handymen and a gardener. The home burned down in mysterious circumstances in 1932. Fortunately, nobody was killed in the fire but the building was left a ruin. It was pulled down in 1946 and the new Drayfield Estate was built on the land.

That's all. A brief summary of thirty years in the lives of so many children. John Hughes had spent some time in this home before being sent to America. But how was the adoption achieved? The article said nothing about adoptions from the home. She wondered if the records still existed in some government archive in West Yorkshire. But the chances were remote. In those days, people didn't move paper records unless a home was closed or moved building. Most were probably destroyed in the fire. Nevertheless, she would have to check. She wrote a note to herself in the small book she always carried with her. Another legacy of her work in the police. Always write everything down. It had been drilled into her by her first desk sergeant. A traditional Lancashire copper who remembered the days before panda cars, when a beat was something you did on foot. 'Write it all down. Paper's t'only way to wipe your arse, and t'only way to cover it too.'

As she was writing the note to herself, she noticed the dark cover of the book through the plastic film of the file. Why a book? Why was the only thing a young child took with him when he left the Children's home a book?

She opened the folder and took it out. Pretty standard cover, *The Lives of the United Irishmen by James Cameron, Esq*. She opened it. The inscription stood out against the white of the inside page. The ink had faded slightly now,

34

turning a greyish blue from its original black. She turned over the leaf to the wonderfully ornate title page. Inside an elaborate, decorative Celtic border was the title and author. At the bottom, the name of the publisher, James Duffy and Co. Ltd. 30 Westmoreland Street, with a date of MCMXIV.

She quickly returned to school to work out what the Roman numerals meant. 1914. The book must have been published in that year, just before the outbreak of the First World War.

She didn't know why but she was certain this book was key to understanding what happened. Perhaps, it was the way the young boy clutched it in the photograph. Hanging on to the one piece of security he trusted when all about him was changing.

She flicked through the pages hoping to find a letter or another photograph.

Nothing.

The paper was of good quality though and the line illustrations seemed to have been done by a fine engraver. There was a craftsmanship here one didn't see anymore. The love of producing something well and which had a beauty all of its own. So different from the throwaway paperbacks of today, printed on cheap paper with even cheaper covers.

She turned it over. The book was as well finished at the back as it was crafted at the front. She opened the back cover and flicked through the pages of the index, moving forward towards the front.

Nothing inside.

She looked at the inside back cover again. Something was different here, the paper felt thicker. She held it up to the light.

The last white page of the book was stuck to the inside

of the back cover. She reached for the scalpel in the pen box next to her laptop. Deftly, she prised open the last page, cutting away the old glue where it had stuck the two pages together.

An ex libris mark was stuck inside, the glue having seeped out to stick the last two pages together. The piece was engraved and beautifully decorated in orange and green. On it, were the words:

EX LIBRIS COLLEGIUM UNIVERSITAE DUBLI-NENSIS.

Chapter 7

Dublin. March 24, 1915.

'Are you coming, Fitz?'

An old man sitting at the next table looked up at him spitefully, hissing between his teeth.

Michael Dowling held up his hand in apology, realising that the old man was the Emeritus Professor of History, the man who would be deciding his fate during the exams.

The old man tut-tutted loudly beneath his breath and returned to his book, adjusting his wire-rimmed glasses as he did

Michael leant in closer to Fitz. 'If you don't come now, we'll be late for parade,' he whispered.

'The old bastard will have my guts for garters if I don't get this essay finished for tomorrow.'

'Ach, there's time enough, you've got all night.'

Another loud shush from the Emeritus Professor followed by another spiteful stare.

Michael took his friend's arm. 'Come on.'

Fitz looked up from his book.

The Professor had returned to his notes. The old witch who ran the library was busy putting some large books back on the shelf three tables away. Furtively, he glanced either side of him and put the book inside his tweed jacket.

Michael stared at his friend, grabbing hold of his arm. 'You can't do that.'

'I just did.'

'But what if...'

The Emeritus Professor coughed. 'Young man,' he

drawled in a very English accent, 'this is a library. A place of learning. A place of solitude and peace where scholars can imbibe the ancient wisdom of the past without interruption. There are rules here that need to be followed, the first of which is that one must remain silent.'

'I'm...I'm sorry, sir.'

'If you persist in disturbing the peace and solemnity of this place, I will be forced to call on the Head Librarian to eject you.'

'I apologise for my friend, Professor,' said Fitz packing up his things, 'we were just leaving.'

'Well, whatever you were doing, do it quietly,' sniffed the Professor, adjusting his wire-rimmed glasses once more and returning to his books.

Fitz pulled down his jacket, ensuring the book nestled snugly under his arm. 'Come on Michael, it's time we were off.'

They bustled out of the library past the old witch at the front. They were just about to exit the main doors when they heard feet running after them and a voice shouting, 'You two, hold there.'

They both stopped.

Michael felt a tap on his shoulder. He turned round and saw the old professor holding a fountain pen out to him. 'I believe this is yours. You should be more careful with your property young man.'

'Thank you, Mr Eddowes. You are so kind.'

They pushed their way through the swing doors, out through the lobby and down the steps of the building. At the bottom, they both burst out laughing.

'For feck's sake, I thought he had us there.'

'Jaysus, when he tapped you on the shoulder, I fair shit myself.'

'I think I did.'

They both collapsed laughing again.

'Why did you take the bloody thing?'

'I dunno. Because it was there and that old shite of a Professor was looking down his long English nose at us. Why do I do anything?'

Fitz took the book out from beneath his jacket. 'The Lives of the United Irishmen'. I could have stolen worse.'

'Or better.'

'At least, I can use it tonight. Get the essay done.'

Michael checked the watch that hung from a fob at his waist. 'Jaysus, is that the time, we'll be late for the parade.'

'Don't worry, we'll catch the tram at St Stephens. Himself will be late, he always is.

* * *

They burst through the door of the drill hall in the old mill at Rathfarnham, laughing and out of breath.

'You're late.' The voice rang out across the room.

Immediately, they stood up straight. 'Sorry, Mr Pearse.'

'It's Sir when we're on parade, Dowling.'

The rest of the company were lined up in two ranks facing their captain. All were still dressed in their civvies, having just come from work or from St Enda's. In this company, most were clerks or students from the university or the school.

'Hurry up, get a move on, we don't have all day,' Willie Pearse said testily.

Michael Dowling and Declan Fitzgerald ran to the end of one rank and placed themselves on the end.

'Now, lads, since we are all here, finally,' his eyes glanced across at Michael and Fitz, 'I have some good news. The uniforms have arrived.' He said this with the broadest smile on his face. 'You can purchase them from me at your earliest convenience.'

'What we need is guns, not uniforms,' a voice whispered in a tell-tale Cork accent from the second rank.

'What's that?' said Pearse cupping his right ear. He was slightly hard of hearing. Orders and responses often had to be repeated.

'Nothing, sir.'

'Nothing comes from nothing, private. Where's that from?'

Pearse was determined to continue their education even as they were drilling.

'King Lear, sir,' said the same Cork voice from the back.

'What's that?'

'King Lear, sir,' repeated the Cork man, louder this time.

'That it is. Well done that man. Act One Scene One, most of you will have read that far, but I would hazard that few have read further.' The English teacher in him just wouldn't let up.

'The uniforms, sir, you were talking about the uniforms,' said Michael Dowling.

'Yes, they are now available to order. Lalor, the tailor, will make them at a special rate for the company. Just six pounds without boots.'

'Where am I going to put my hands on six pounds?' This came from the first rank, a Dubliner with the traditional whine bred into him from birth.

This time, Pearse heard the question clearly. 'I don't know, Private, but find it you will. The fourth company of the Dublin Brigade will be the best turned out troops in the

40

Volunteers. Do I make myself clear?'

'As a glass of stout, sir.'

Pearse pretended not to hear. He strode up and down in front of them, the heels of his boots clicking on the wooden floor. He had one major eccentricity for a captain. He always wore cavalry boots on parade. Beautifully polished and shined brown leather that gripped his calves snugly and ended just below the knee. 'Two other messages from Command. There will be a full parade in Kilmainham Park on Sunday, the 7 May.'

'But I'm supposed to be going out with my girl that day,' whined the Dublin man.

Willie Pearse raised his voice. 'Attendance will be compulsory for all members of the company.' The voice softened again, 'Listen, lads, the command want to send a signal to the Brits. Despite the war and all that's going on, Ireland still hasn't given up the struggle. We will have our freedom.'

'The Brits only understand one thing and that's a bullet shoved in the end of a rifle.' The Mayo voice again.

'That's true, but we're not ready yet. Soon, boys, soon.' Pearse reached into his pocket and pulled out a large sheet of paper folded into four. He unfolded it. 'Most of you will have seen and read this manifesto and its six articles, issued by the Provisional Committee.'

There was an audible groan from the ranks.

'But I am going to read it again. Not all of it, though, you'll be pleased to hear. Just the last article that reminds us why we are here today.' He reached into his pocket and placed a small pair of pince-nez on the bridge of his nose. He began to read in his special teacher's voice. 'The sixth article. The Provisional Committee demands that the present system of governing Ireland through Dublin Castle and the British military power, a system responsible for the recent outrages in Dublin, be abolished without delay, and that a National Government be forthwith established in its place.'

He folded the sheet of paper into four and placed it back into his pocket. The pince-nez were removed from the bridge of his nose and put into the inside of his jacket. His eyes ranged over the assembled men in front of him. 'We are committed, gentleman, to securing and defending the rights and liberties of the Irish people. Many of you will be under pressure to join the British military in the fight against the Germans. I urge you, as I have done many times before, to ignore that appeal.' He stared directly at Fitz and Michael and his voice rose until he was almost shouting. 'That fight is not Ireland's fight. It has nothing to do with us or our freedom. The years when Irish men went to fight for the British are over. The only cause we have to fight for now is our own freedom.'

Michael noticed the veins on his neck above the military collar had gone bright blue.

'Our own freedom. To be a free nation, beholden to nobody but ourselves.'

'And the bosses...' the Cork voice whispered so the other men could hear.

Pearse carried on as if nothing had happened. 'The fight will be sooner than you think, gentlemen. You must all prepare for that glorious day. It will come soon, of that there can be no doubt. Be ready and be prepared.'

'Like bloody boy scouts...'

'And be willing to lay down your lives for the cause of Irish rights and Irish liberties. Any questions?' He looked around him like a beagle with the scent of a fox. 'Good. Parade, Atten-shun.' Twenty-four pairs of heels clicked together. Both ranks stood upright, chests pushed out, heads back, chins jutting forward.

'Parade, dis-missed.'

There was a release of breath along the line and it gradually collapsed as men placed their hats and caps back on their heads, and began chatting with their friends.

Michael Dowling stepped forward to talk with Pearse. 'I'm sorry, Captain Pearse, but I can't make the parade on Sunday.'

'Oh, and why is that?' He was in the process of re-balancing his pince-nez on the bridge of his nose.

Michael wondered if it was blindness, not deafness that caused his inability to hear the responses of his men. Not knowing where the sound came from rather than not hearing it. 'It's my da's birthday. My sister's gone to a lot of trouble...'

'So your father's birthday is more important than the freedom of Ireland?'

'It's just a parade, not the end of the world?' Fitz had come up beside him, lighting a Craven A and expelling smoke as he spoke.

Pearse waved his hand in front of his face in a futile attempt to create a pocket of clear air. 'It's more than a parade, don't you understand, Mr Fitzgerald? It's a demonstration that the people of Ireland won't be fobbed off with vague promises of Home Rule when the war is over. We must show the British Government we mean business.'

'It's 200 men marching up and down in a park on a Sunday.'

'Mr Fitzgerald, if you display that attitude, I wonder whether you have the commitment necessary to serve our cause.'

A red flush rose on Fitz's face. 'You're questioning my

commitment?'

'No, Mr Fitzgerald, I'm questioning your attitude.'

Michael tugged at Fitz's arm. 'Come on, let's go.'

'My attitude? And what sort of attitude am I supposed to have?'

Pearse adjusted his pince-nez back. 'For years, the Irish have played at fighting for freedom. It's not a game, Mr Fitzgerald.'

'A few men marching around a field for a couple of hours on a Sunday is not a game? Is that how we are going to gain our freedom?'

'No, it's not. But it is a start.'

'They'd be better off raiding a barracks for guns.'

'That will happen, Mr Fitzgerald...eventually.'

'When it does, count me in, but marching up and down a park is a waste of my time.'

The pince-nez were pushed back onto the bridge of the nose. 'I will say this once, Mr Fitzgerald, so let me make this clear. If I don't see you on Sunday, you will no longer be welcome as a member of this company. Do you understand?'

Fitz nodded.

'I asked you if you understood, Mr Fitzgerald?' The voice was commanding now, an officer giving orders.

'Yes,' said Fitz.

Pearse smiled. 'You, on the other hand, Mr Dowling are excused duties for the day. I hope your father has a pleasant birthday. How old is he?'

'Fifty.'

'A fine age for a man. And now, if you'll excuse me, I have other duties to attend to.'

With that, he turned and walked over to another group of men in the corner, the cavalry boots making a rat-a-tat-

tat on the wooden floor.

Michael pulled Fitz out of the door of the hall and onto the street. 'You shouldn't provoke him like that.'

'Ah, the pompous prick gets up my arse.'

'Like Oscar Wilde, you mean?'

The both began to laugh, 'Ah, you're an 'oul shite, Michael Dowling.'

Chapter 8

Jayne snapped another square of chocolate and popped it in her mouth, letting it slowly melt across her teeth. Her mind returned to the puzzle in front of her. So, the book had once belonged to the University of Dublin. But how had it come into the hands of John Hughes? It was hardly the reading matter of a four-year-old boy. Perhaps, he had been given it at the children's home?

She looked at the picture the old man had given her again. There was a determination in the face of the young boy as he clung onto the book. As if, whatever happened, he was never going to be separated from it, holding on like a drowning man clings to a life jacket.

And where did the inscriptions fit in. Who was M D and who was D F? Did they have anything to do with John Hughes?

Too many questions and too few answers.

A shadow loomed over her.

'Still working?'

It was Paul, hair mussed up and clothes wrinkled from lying in bed.

She smiled at him. 'A new client. An American, looking for his past.'

He walked over to the tap, running the water for a while before placing a glass in the clear stream. 'Trying to find his long-forgotten ancestors so he can claim links to a dead Duke or to being 767th in line to the throne? That would be a talking point amongst the good folks of Scottsdale.'

She hated the way he disparaged her work, constantly belittling what she did. 'No, actually, a man looking to find out who he is.'

'Aren't we all?' He poured the rest of the glass down the sink. 'Look, I'm sorry about before,' he said to the wall above the tap, 'I was upset.' He turned back to face her. 'I know you didn't like my sister, but she meant a lot to me. I feel I let her down in some way.'

'She let herself down.'

'There you go again. Sometimes, you're just so bloody judgemental. Like nobody can make mistakes except you.'

She didn't want another argument. Not now. Not tonight. 'I'm sorry, I shouldn't have said it like that.'

His body relaxed. 'I'm going back to bed, don't stay up too long.'

'I won't. I'm nearly done for this evening. I'll just finish this glass then I'll be up.'

'Don't forget the chocolate.'

'How could I ever forget chocolate?' She picked up another square and popped it in her mouth.

She heard the door close and the clomp of his feet as he climbed the stairs. What were they going to do? It couldn't go on like this, the endless bickering and fighting. She thought back to the days after Dave had been shot. Paul had been her rock, the one man who had comforted and consoled her, listening again and again as she monotonously recounted the moments leading up to the shooting, constantly reassuring her that it was not her fault.

But, whatever he said, she knew it was. She knew she could have done more. There had been a moment when she heard a noise from behind the door. A moment when she could have pushed Dave out of the way. Should have pushed him away. But she didn't.

She finished the last of the wine. No more chocolate left either.

What did Paul mean when he said 'nobody can make mistakes except you'?

Chapter 9

'Nice to see you, Jayne. It's been a couple of days.'

'How is he, Fiona?'

'It's a good day for Mr Tomlinson. Definitely a good day. He's in the day room if you want to sit with him.'

Jayne stood back as the receptionist pushed the button to release the doors. They swung open automatically towards her. As they did so, the smell of cleanliness drifted towards her. It was one of the reasons she chose this particular home instead of the others. At least here, there was no smell of disinfectant, cooked cabbage and old people oozing out from the walls.

She still couldn't understand why they locked the doors though? To stop the patients escaping? But most of the people inside were physically dependent on their Zimmer frames. She couldn't imagine that they would be difficult to chase down. Probably another nightmare from Health and Safety.

She walked down a long corridor, decorated on either side with watercolours of birds. The place depressed her and she had only been here for ten seconds. What effect was it having on her father?

The corridor led to a large double door at the end. She pushed through and was immediately in a large space flooded with light from large bay windows and a glass roof.

The day room was a new extension to the Edwardian main building. It was the main reason why she had brought her father to this care home. The windows looked over the old gardens; an extensive lawn with rhododendron bushes at the end and a large beech tree off to the right. This was the least depressing choice in a long list of depressing choices. But with his Alzheimer's, she knew that it was the best place for him. It didn't make it any easier for her though. The sense of imprisoning him for doing nothing wrong other than being old filled her with guilt. Could she have kept him with her a little longer?

But Paul didn't want him living in the house anymore after the incident in the kitchen. Her father had put a tin of soup on the stove to heat up and forgotten about it. An hour later, the smoke alarms were blaring, firemen were running through her house and her father was sat in the corner staring into space, ignoring all the noise and commotion around him.

It was just one more in a long line of accidents. The doctors said with his illness there would be more, it was just a question of time. They advised her that he needed constant care, constant observation, for his own safety. Paul had reinforced their recommendation. He wanted the old man out of the house. She was left with no choice but every day she felt his loss, missing his company and his advice.

She walked into the day room. A group of old women were playing bridge at a table in front. They made no sound as they placed their cards gently onto the green baize of the table. On the left, an old-fashioned TV was tuned to the Jeremy Kyle show, the audience braying with disbelief as a 15-year-old denied he was the father of a woman's baby. Two women and three men were set around the TV, not really watching nor listening but just aware of the sound.

Her father was in the far corner, alone, in front of the window facing the beech tree, holding a book in his hands.

She stood behind him. 'What are you reading?'

He looked back at her, his eyes taking ages to focus on her face. For a moment, she thought he hadn't recognised her, before he said, 'Oh, it's you. I thought it might have been the nurse with my meds.' He checked his watch, 'She's late this morning.' He closed the book. She saw the cover, Rubicon by Tom Holland. History, always history.

Her father had been obsessed with reading history books as long as she could remember. Biographies, political histories, economic histories, diaries, military history, the history of history. As long as it was set in the past he would read it.

It was her father who had first interested her in genealogy. Dragging her back from the dark days after Dave's shooting into the past. Their past. Researching his family and his antecedents.

She had always called him Father even though he was really her step-father. He had married her mother when she was three years old. She had never taken his surname, keeping her mother's name as her own. Her mother would never tell her who her real father was. Even when she lay dying, her body ravished with cancer, she had remained silent.

One day, Jayne would find out who he was. But not today. Today was a day to spend with the only man she had ever known as a father.

She sat down beside him. 'How are you today?'

'Good. Better than yesterday, worse than tomorrow.'

She loved him when he was like this. When the disease infesting his mind had cleared like a fog lifting to reveal a bright blue sky on a sunny day. Today was a good day.

'I've got a new case.'

'Interesting?'

'An American. Adopted when he was four from a home

51

in Ilkley. Wants to know who he is.'

'Don't we all. Should be easy. He's done the checks with one of the adoption referral services?'

She nodded.

'He's got his original birth certificate?'

She nodded again.

'So what's the problem? Piece of cake.'

She loved his old-fashioned idioms. Occasionally, he would surprise her with one she had never heard before. 'The problem is, the man named as the father on the birth certificate died in the war seven years earlier.'

Her father pursed his lips. 'That is a problem.'

She reached into her bag and pulled out the folder, opening it and removing the picture.

He took it from her, searching for his glasses at the same time. 'Where are they? I had them a minute ago. Always losing the bloody things.'

She reached across and lifted the glasses from his chest, where they hung from a cord around his neck.

'Here they are, Dad. They're always here.'

He looked down at them as if seeing them for the first time. 'I know. It's just that I forget.'

For a second the words hung between them. The unsaid words. They never talked about his illness, as if discussing it would bring it back, here and now. If they ever did, it was referred to as 'Mr Jones.' A way they both used of distancing themselves from the horrible Germanic hardness of the word Alzheimer's, making it a joke between them both, their shared secret.

Her father coughed slightly, putting the glasses back on. 'This is him?' He peered at the old photograph. 'Fierce little chap, isn't he?'

'You should meet him now. He could chew the back end

off a bus.'

'Nice kid but not a nice man, then. Parents screw them up you know.' He twisted his head and looked at her like a blackbird looking at the ground, searching for a tasty morsel. Then shook his head making a joke of it and returned to examining the picture. 'Well-dressed, the coat has an expensive look to it. Shoes are well made, not tat.'

'You're doing the investigation for me?'

'Just looking at the evidence. Anything else?'

'Just the book he's holding in the photo.' She passed the book over to him.

'The Lives of the United Irishmen. Sounds good. Wouldn't mind reading it.'

'I don't think I can leave it with you, Dad.'

He opened it up, read the inscription and flicked through the pages. 'That's it?'

'That's it.'

'Not much to go on. You've checked the records of the children's home?'

'Not yet. But I'm pretty sure they don't exist. The place burnt down in 1932.'

'Could've been transferred before then.'

'I'll check.'

He picked up the picture again, examining it closely. 'Good quality clothes. Not the sort of stuff working people would have been able to afford.'

'They could have been given to him by the orphanage.'

'How long was he there for?'

She picked up the adoption certificate. 'He was admitted to the orphanage in February 1929 and released for adoption in October of the same year.'

'Pretty quick. Bureaucrats don't usually work that quickly in my experience.'

She loved his mind when he was like this. So sharp, so precise. He would have made a great detective, a much better detective than her. Instead, he had spent his life selling insurance. 'That's a good point, Dad.'

'Have you seen the lapel?'

'What lapel?'

He jabbed the photograph with his finger. 'There, can you see it?' He brought the image up close to his eyes. 'Something's on the lapel.'

'What is it? Let me see.' He handed the picture over to her. She checked both lapels. On the left one, a small bronze mark stood out against the green wool of the overcoat. 'Looks like a badge or something like that. I'll get it blown up. Might be something.'

'Or might be nothing. The 1929 equivalent of the Tufty Club.'

'The Tufty Club?'

'Before your time, young 'un. He took off his glasses and rubbed his eyes. 'Not a lot to go on, but I'm sure you'll do your best, kiddo. Time I took a nap.'

'Isn't it time for your lunch?'

'We call it dinner, here, Jayne. Don't you be putting on airs and graces with me. And yes it is dinner time, but today it's suet pudding. I can't stand suet pudding.'

'Shall I tell the nurse you're feeling tired?'

'Do that, and help me back to my room.'

'You will eat this evening, Dad?'

'Course I will. Monday is pie and chips. Never miss my pie and chips.'

'You promise?'

'Cross my heart and hope to die.' For the second time that day, there was a moment of silence between the two of them.

'Help me up, Jayne, the old knees are not as good as they used to be.'

'You'll be dancing the waltz this afternoon.'

He looked at the old women sat in the chairs watching in front of the television. 'Not with these old biddies, I won't. Two left feet this lot.'

One of the old women looked up quickly from her knitting. Saw Ian Tomlinson staring at her and quickly looked down again.

'Be good, Dad.'

'And if you can't be good, be better. I know all about that. Remember it was me who told you.'

'Every day, Dad, every day.'

Chapter 10

Jayne Sinclair sat down in front of her Mac in the kitchen. The drive from her father's care home near Buxton had been tedious but she was used to it. It was a time when her mind could mull over the problems of the investigation, leaving her body to somehow drive the car. Often, she found herself parking in front of the house unable to remember how she had got there. As if the car, like some old donkey on a beach, knew exactly which route it should take to get home.

A quick brew of tea and she was ready to start. She pulled her pad towards her and wrote out a list of things to do. Without her lists she was lost. They were all dated and numbered and, as she finished one item, it was crossed off in red biro.

The first item was clear. Call the library. She logged on, found the correct website, checked the details and called the first number.

The phone rang three times, then a rich baritone voice answered. 'UCD...sorry, I'll get that right one day, NUI Dublin Library.'

'Hello, my name is Jayne, Jayne Sinclair.' She still stumbled over her name, constantly wanting to say DI Jayne Sinclair. 'I'm afraid I have a rather strange request.'

'We are a university library, madam, we often receive strange requests. How can I help you?'

The voice had that musicality that could only be Irish, like listening to Seamus Heaney reading his poetry.

'I've been given a book of yours...'

'Published by the faculty or belonging to the library?'

Precision, she liked that. She would have to be exact with this man.

'The second... the latter,' she corrected herself. 'I think it was borrowed from the Library before 1929.'

There was a small cough at the end of the line. 'If it wasn't returned within a month, I'm afraid the fines could be quite sizeable. If I were you, I would just drop the book in the returned box on campus. We promise we won't follow up.'

'I wonder, could you check it out for me?'

'Madam, after 86 years, I do think it's too late to extend the loan of the book.' She detected a hint of amusement in the voice.

'No, no, I don't mean that. Could you check your catalogue for it?'

'Give me a second.' She heard the rattle of computer keys. 'Title?'

'The Lives of the United Irishmen by James Cameron Esq.'

'Sounds like a bestseller.' Again the hint of humour. She was beginning to like this man. She heard the rattle of keys on an old computer. 'We have three editions in the catalogue, published in 1888, 1914 and a more modern edition, published in 1992.'

'I've got the 1914 edition.'

'Ah, it should have the old ex-libris sticker in the back.'

'It does.'

'Beautifully designed that one. My favourite.' More rattles of keys. 'According to my records, that copy is still here. In storage, but still here.'

'How could I have it then?'

'Two ways madam. It has been sold and we haven't deleted the records.'

'How would we know?'

'On the title page, there would be stamp in big, blue letters saying, 'Discarded by University College, Dublin.' We can be very subtle us librarians when we don't want a book anymore.'

She checked the title page once again. 'Nothing.'

'Then, it's the second option.'

'Which is?'

'Stolen. Probably by one of the students. Anti-theft technology has improved a wee bit since 1914, but students always seem one step ahead. I'm amazed we have any books left in the library.'

'Does the library allow people to write inscriptions in its books?'

The man thought for a moment. 'No...that would be most unusual, unless of course the book was donated to us.'

'Was this book donated?'

'I'll just check, hold the line.' Again, the distant rattle of computer keys. 'Hello, are you still there?'

'Still here.'

'Good, the line had gone as quiet as a priest in a brothel for a moment. You're not ringing from here so.'

'Actually, I'm calling from Manchester.'

'Sure, it's a long way to go for a library book. Anyway, we bought the book new, it wasn't a bequest. The only thing inside it should be the ex-libris sticker. Not forgetting the words, of course.'

'Thank you, Mr...?'

'O'Malley. Damien O'Malley.'

And then an idea struck her. 'One more question, if I could?'

'You've solved the mystery of the missing library book of 1914, madam, how could I refuse.'

'If I were looking for former students of the university, say someone who studied at UCD from 1914 to 1929, where would I start?'

There was silence from the end of the line. 'Well, you've got me there so. You could try the alumni office. They would keep the records there I think, but I don't know if they go back that far. The dean's office may also have graduate records from the period. Either of those, I suppose.'

'Nothing online?'

'Ah, that would be a rare chance now wouldn't it? But I doubt it. Microfilm possibly but not digitised.'

She loved the way he said Microfilm with an extra 'u' between the l and the m, so it came out filum. 'Thank you for your time, Mr O'Malley.'

'My pleasure, madam. Do drop the book off, won't you? It would be nice to say hello to it again after all these years. And I promise there won't be any late charges. We'll let you off for good behaviour. You can't say fairer than that now, can you?'

Jayne was beginning to feel guilty. 'I will talk to the owner, Mr O'Malley. Thank you once again.' She disconnected the call quickly before he could ask her again.

The phone call had been useful. She had confirmed that the book came from the library and hadn't been sold. The inscription suggested it was given to MD by DF. Possibly, it was stolen from the library by one of the students, but why? And were MD and DF both studying at UCD at the time? Perhaps, the register of graduates would be able to tell her.

And how did it come to end up in the possession of a

young boy in an orphanage? That was more important. That was what she had to find out.

She added another item to her list. Find out about graduates from UCD for the period.

Now for the next phone call. Something closer to home. She didn't need to look up the number.

'Hello...' The voice was irritated, interrupted in the middle of something.

'Good afternoon, Rob. I can hear that you are in a fine mood on this beautiful day.'

'DI Sinclair, good to hear from you again.'

'Not a DI anymore Rob, just plain Jayne Sinclair.'

He laughed. 'You were never a plain Jayne, nobody could ever say that.'

'Less of the sexism, DC Tanner. You'll have the PC Police breathing down your neck.'

'It's DI Tanner now, get it right. But you already knew that, didn't you Jayne?'

'A little bird whispered in my ear down the pub. Well done, my old mate, you deserve it.'

'What can I do for you, Jayne, I'm sure all this buttering up is going to lead somewhere, sometime.'

'You can read me almost as well as you can fiddle a timesheet, Rob. There is something you can help me with...'

'Here it comes.'

'Does the lab still have the photo enhancement software?'

'It's been upgraded, cheaper than replacing all the CCTV cameras around the city. We can spot a burglar on the end of a ladybird's nose.'

'I was wondering, if I sent you across on old photograph, could you put it through the lab?'

'One of your investigations?'

'An American looking to find out who he is.'

'Aren't we all?'

'Why does everybody say that?'

'Maybe because it's true. It'll cost you.'

'The usual?'

'Valrhona, will do.'

Jayne had infected Rob Tanner with her love of chocolate when they worked together during the Madchester days. 'No problem, but Rob...'

'Yes?'

'Could you put a rocket up their arse? This one is urgent.' Jayne felt a presence behind her. She wished Paul wouldn't creep up on her like that, he had been doing it more and more often.

'One rocket, armed and ready.'

'Thanks, Rob, you're a star.'

There was a moment of silence down the phone. Jayne thought he had already hung up. 'When are you coming back, Jayne? The lads miss you.'

'Never, Rob. My days are done. Time to let the next generation of coppers fuck it all up.'

'Thanks to your training, we're making a fine job of it.'

Jayne could hear Paul putting the kettle on behind her. 'I'm glad to hear it, Rob, wouldn't have expected any more...or any less.'

She heard a laugh down the phone. A laugh that suggested Rob didn't do very much laughing anymore. 'I'll get back to you later, Jayne. The lab will try and fob me off but I know one of the girls...'

'She's fallen for your charms?'

'Don't they all...except you.'

Again, an awkward moment of silence. 'Thanks for your help, Rob, I owe you one.'

'One packet of Valrhona, as I recall.'

'Have a good day, and watch out, there's a lot of bad people about.' A stab of pain went through Jayne's chest as she repeated the words they always used before going out on the streets.

'And if you can't watch out, don't leave no marks. Bye, Jayne.' Rob repeated the usual answer but after Dave Gilmore's death, it always sounded hollow, as if the words didn't ring true anymore.

'Bye, Rob,' Jayne whispered. The only reply was that plaintive buzz to show the line was dead. God, she hated that sound.

'Want a cuppa?'

'Lovely. You're back early.'

'Thought we'd go out to dinner together. How about the Albert?'

'I can't Paul.' She pointed to her laptop.

There was an audible sigh. Here it comes, she thought.

'The plan was to spend more time together when you retired from the police. Seems I see you less now than when you were a full-time copper.'

'It's work, Paul. A client. I only have eight days...seven days now,' she corrected herself.

'So no time to take an evening off.'

She shook her head. 'Sorry, if I don't do the basics now, I'll never know the right direction to go in. It's a rush job.'

'You're always in a hurry. No time for anything. No time for me.'

'That's not true, Paul.'

'It is and you know it.' He put on his jacket. 'I'm going down the pub. I fancy some company.' He walked towards the door, turning just before he went out. 'Oh, I forgot to tell you. Jack Davies and his wife are coming for dinner on

Friday.'

'That awful man and his pretentious wife?'

'The one and same. Unfortunately, he also happens to be my boss.'

'You invited him?'

'Yes. And don't roll your eyes like that. Can you handle it or shall we take him out?'

She thought for a moment. Today was Monday, plenty of time to prepare. By then she should have cracked this case...or not. 'I can handle it,' she answered him finally.

'Your beef bourguignon and gooey chocolate cake would be perfect.'

'Beef and chocolate, a bit heavy don't you think?'

'He's not a light person.'

'Neither is the wife.'

'I'm off down the Swan. Sure you won't join me?'

'Give me an hour or so, and I'll come down.'

'See you later.'

She listened as he banged his way out of the door. Why did he always make her feel so guilty about her work? When he was on a project, working all the hours under the sun, nothing was said.

She turned back to her Mac. I haven't even started on the woman yet, his mother. She logged onto findmypast.com again and typed the name in the search field. Emily Clavell, clicking the name variants box just in case. She checked the birth certificate. 29 years old at the birth of her child in 1925, so that would give her a date of birth of 1896. Better try plus or minus five years just in case. Women were notoriously inaccurate about such things, particularly if the husband were younger than them. Not much has changed, she thought.

144 results.

Perhaps if she restricted the search to Yorkshire as the birth certificate showed a Bradford address? The edit came back with 27 records. Clavell must have been a popular Yorkshire name. Slowly, painstakingly she went through each of the results, looking for a possible link to her client.

On the thirteenth search, she shouted 'Got you' out loud. It was definitely her. Same name, same address. Parents Martin and Anne Clavell. Two brothers, the eldest also called Martin, and the youngest with the name, John. It was a start.

Now for births, marriages and deaths. After the third search, she came up trumps again. Emily Clavell, born in Queensbury, West Yorkshire in 1894. She checked the names of the parents: Martin and Anne. It was the same woman. So she had told a little white lie about her date of birth, shaving a couple of years off her age. Vanity, vanity, thy name is woman. Who wrote that? Probably a man.

Finally, she clicked the link to the register of marriages. Here it was. Emily Clavell married Charles Trichot between October to December 1924. She would have to request the actual marriage certificate to find out the date and the witnesses. She pulled out her pad and added another item to her lengthening list of things to do.

She was making progress, good progress. But still the central question remained: how could Emily Clavell marry a man who had been dead for seven years?

She closed her computer. Time to join her husband down the pub and drink the shocking Ribena-like liquid they called wine. Pity they didn't stock good bars of chocolate. Any pub that sold good chocolate would have her as a customer for life.

She heard the wind and rain beating against the window. A typical November day in Manchester. Wet and wild with the murky grey skies that sucked the colour and life out of everything. Despite that, there would be a few hardy souls hunkering down in the shelter of the doorway of the pub, sucking the life out of their cigarettes. Thank God she had never indulged in that vice. Plenty of others, but never that one.

She put on her coat. The wind and rain redoubled its efforts to break into the house. She didn't really want to go, but she would never hear the end of it if she didn't. Paul would nag remorselessly for the next week, playing the victim with all the nuance of Bette Davis.

God, why was marriage so difficult?

Chapter 11

Wicklow. October 25, 1915.

'Happy Birthday, Father.' The cake was covered in white frosting and on it sat a single candle. His sister had carried it into the study, followed by Michael, their mother, his younger brother, Martin and the cocker spaniel called Davy, who ruled the house.

Their father looked up from his newspaper, The Freeman's Chronicle. The headline trumpeted a significant advance by the British forces in some place in Turkey called Gallipoli.

Michael could see his father's mouth frown at the interruption, but his eyes gleamed. Secretly, he was happy his family had remembered. 'How old are you now, Da?'

'Too old to remember and too young to forget.'

'Ach, you're not that old,' said his mother.

'Brian Boru was still king of Ireland when I was born.' He coughed, a slow wracking cough.

'Don't be telling your fibs, now John Dowling. I remember you saying it was Niall of the Nine Hostages who was being the king when you were born.' His mother sat down on the arm of his father's chair. 'Now will you be having a slice of cake or shall I give it to the tinkers?'

'The tinkers will not be having my cake, not today,' his father said as forcefully as he could.

These days, the old man didn't move much from his chair and, if he did, it was just to stumble into his bedroom for a lie down. Michael was shocked at his appearance. He had only been away in Dublin for a couple of months but in that time the tall, strong man he had known as he was growing up had shrunk to this feeble creature, swallowed up by the cushions of an armchair. The will was still there, Michael could see that, but the flesh was weak, the cancer having eaten away all the strength his father had once had. A will that had frightened Michael as a boy, remorselessly pushing him to live a better life than his father had enjoyed.

His sister placed the cake on the table, lighting the single candle.

'Only the one?'

'Sure, if I put more, I'd never hear the last of it.'

'Make a wish,' Michael said.

His father closed his eyes, then leant forward and tried to blow a stream of air through his grey moustache onto the candle. But all that came out was a shallow puff. The candle wavered in the breeze before recovering its strength and continuing to burn brightly. Michael leant forward and blew it out.

There was silence for a moment before his mother began to clap and they all joined in. Even the dog wagged his tail and barked.

His mother took a knife and sliced into the moist dark sponge, glistening with currants and dried fruit.

'You've done me proud, Norah, there's enough to feed all Ireland here.'

'Away with ye, John, flattery will get you nowhere.' His mother had never lost the soft sounds of the Central counties, Abbeyleix was still there in every sentence.

His mother cut the cake quickly, giving Michael an extra large slice. 'He's a growing lad. Needs more to help him fill out.'

'What about me?'

'You too, Martin.' His mother passed another large slice

to his younger brother before finally taking a much smaller piece for herself.

They sat in silence for a while, the only sound that of fork against the best bone china. Finally, their father spoke. 'War's going well. Looks like they've made some sort of breakthrough.' He pointed to the paper. Their father followed the news every day, knowing where and when each battle was fought. He had even marched in the streets of Dublin protesting the rape of the Belgian nuns before the cancer had left him unable to leave the house.

'Ach, more claptrap from the press. It's the same as it ever was.'

'Michael Dowling, I will not have such language in my house.' His mother made the sign of the cross, bowing her head towards the picture of Jesus on the wall.

His father sighed. 'It's not the same as it ever was. The Hun is a stalwart soldier. It will be a long and challenging fight but the British Empire will prevail in the end.'

'You sound like Churchill, Father. And what's it to us, Ireland will still be Ireland whether they win their war or not.'

'When the war is won, Ireland will be free. You know what they promised Redmond and Dillon. If Ireland does her bit, then, at the end of the war, in the fullness of time, she will get her Home Rule.'

'Just words, father. Promises they have made for generations, and never delivered. The only way Ireland will ever be free is if the Irish people fight for their freedom. Freedom can't be given, it must be seized.'

Michael could see his mother trying to calm him down with her eyes.

'You've been listening to that madman, Eoin O'Neill again. One of your professors, isn't he?'

'He does teach history at UCD.'

'Him and the rest of the fools who signed that damned proclamation...' His father collapsed in a fit of coughing as if the mere mention of the man's name made him ill. 'Him and the rest of those fools...' he eventually said through clenched teeth.

'The Provisional Committee.'

'The Provisional Committee.' His father mimicked his words 'Pearce, Cannt, Clarke, Connolly, and the rest. All of them fools and traitors. How could they stab Redmond in the back like that?'

Michael sighed, it was like explaining to a five-year-old. 'The Brits promised us Home Rule and went back on the promise.'

'There's a war on, don't you know that?' His father slammed the plate with its cake down on the desk, and followed the noise with another bout of coughing.

'Calm yourself, Patrick. We all know there's a war. No need to shout.' His mother patted his father's back, helping ease the cough.

Michael couldn't help but notice a crumb of cake lodged in his father's moustache. He was tempted to lean over and wipe it off, but he knew now was not the right time.

'I've got some news.' It was his brother who had spoken for the first time. They all turned toward him. 'I've spoken to UCD and they've agreed to defer my enrolment.'

'You're not coming up? But I've arranged digs for you.'

Martin placed his hand on his brother's arm. 'I've joined the Leinsters. I start training in Birr next week.'

His mother's hand went to her mouth. His sister stood still. Even the dog seemed to know that something had happened.

'You've joined up?' Michael could barely get the words

out.

His brother nodded. 'Off to fight. After training, of course. It's a good regiment. Myself and three others from school joined together.'

Michael didn't say a word.

His father was smiling. 'It's the right thing to do, Martin. I'm proud of you.'

Chapter 12

Holiday Inn, Northampton. November 15, 2015.

David Turner hated waiting.

He knew it was his biggest weakness. He tried all sorts of techniques to control it. Deep breathing, chewing gum, counting down from 100. Anything and everything to take his mind off the one thing he couldn't stop thinking about.

Waiting.

Even out in the Iraqi desert, covered by a tarpaulin, huddled next to his mate and oppo, Charlie Tennant, he'd hated the waiting. They were in one of the SAS squads tasked to keep a lookout for weapons for the Shiite militias smuggled in from Iran, calling in airstrikes if anything moved. Or even if it didn't. They had huddled beneath that tarpaulin for days on end, only coming out at night to take a leak and grab a quick bite of what the Army laughingly called rations, perhaps because they gave them so little of it.

He preferred a 30K yomp over the Brecon Beacons in the middle of winter to waiting.

The phone rang. Its noise seemed extra loud in the small room he had taken in a Holiday Inn off the M1. A boring, bland hotel where nobody would remember him, not even the bored front desk staff.

He let it ring two more times before picking it up. 'Turner.'

'Mr Turner, I believe you are expecting my call.'

'I was contacted in the normal way. You have a job for me?'

'That is correct. A woman. I want you to follow her and report back.'

'Not on the phone, sir.' Turner always liked to call his clients 'sir'. It gave them a false sense of superiority. It was the same way he handled the officers in the Regiment. Public schoolboys full of derring-do, but not a lot else. Call them sir and they felt you had given them respect. Then just do what you were going to do anyway, whatever they said.

'How?'

'Here's a one-off email address, write it down then destroy the paper, you won't need it again. Tyrion47@gmail.com. Got it?'

'Yes, but that's from Game of Thrones, isn't it?'

He was getting sloppy in his old age. Have to tighten up. 'Well spotted, sir. Makes it easy to remember.' Again, the bland flattery he used with the officers. Always praise them for their intelligence, even though they didn't have a functioning brain cell to share amongst them.

'Ok, I'll send the details. But be careful with this one, she's an ex-police woman.'

'Thank you for the information, sir. Please head the email 'Office move'.'

'How do I contact you again?'

'You don't, sir. From now on, I contact you.'

'I've just sent the information to that address.'

'Thank you, sir. I'll be in touch.' He put down the phone. No need to meet this client. No need to meet any client. Meetings were dangerous. Turner prided himself on his ability to keep a low profile, to blend in with the crowd. Nobody noticed the innocent looking man in the everyday clothes until it was too late.

This was his strength and his calling card. Blandness. If

he could only rein in his lack of patience, he would be the perfect operative.

He would work on it but he wasn't hopeful. Now to open his laptop and access the information, after it had been bounced around the world on his VPN. Can't leave a trace, any trace, virtual or physical. That was the whole point of being a professional; being invisible. Go in, do the job, and get out, without being seen. He was good at his job. One of the best, with a track record second to none.

His speciality was terminations. He hoped this would eventually lead to a termination. He liked the cleanliness of termination, the finality of it. One minute a person was alive, thoughts and feelings running around in their head, the next they were dead, no thoughts, no feelings, nothing. There was something very satisfying when nobody knew a termination had been performed. An invisible job. No leads. No investigations. No questions asked. Just another unfortunate accidental death.

He had started to film his terminations a year ago. His own private snuff movies. Sometimes, he watched them again and again, a never-ending loop of death. If it was a hit and run, he switched on the dash cam. For everything else, he used a Go Pro Black Hero 4 attached to his jacket. It gave the best pictures, stunning clarity of his handiwork. Scorcese would be proud of him. Shame the director would never get to see his work.

The films showed he was good at accidents. Creative in his planning and execution of them. He laughed to himself. 'What an unfortunate choice of words,' he said out loud.

The beige walls of the Holiday Inn Northampton didn't answer back.

Chapter 13

Didsbury, Manchester. November 16, 2015.

The phone beside the bed rattled its displeasure. She caught it as it fell over the edge. 'Hello,' she answered.

'Good morning, Jayne. And how are we on this dull and dirty Manchester day?'

She checked herself. That vague wasted feeling from having drunk too much bad pub wine last night infested her body. She shook her head trying to rid it of the cotton wool that was stuffed in her brain. 'I'm all right, what do you want, Rob?' she croaked.

'You don't sound well at all, Jayne. And it's not what I want but what I can give you.'

She sat up in bed. 'That's quick.'

'They're on overtime at the moment. I slipped it into the night shift, asking for a quick turnaround.'

'In my day, it would have taken a week.'

'You don't have my charm, Jayne, never did.'

'Yeah, yeah, yeah...'

'You're in luck. Looks like some sort of badge he's wearing. I'll email over what I've got and send the printout round by courier. You still living in the same place?'

'I haven't moved, Rob. Still here.'

'Sounds like a heavy night last night?'

'Actually, a light night, it was the company that was heavy.' Jayne thought about last evening in the pub. Another argument. This time, because she was late. She reached over to the other side of the bed. Cold and empty. He had gone to work without saying goodbye. What was she going to do? She had to do something, it couldn't continue on like this.

'Three raw eggs in milk. Clears the head like molasses my dad always used to say.'

'Sounds disgusting.'

'It is and was. He died of a brain tumour by the way.'

'Thanks for the recommendation. I'll file it under UIT-BI.'

'A new file for us?'

'Useless Information to be Ignored.'

'Gotcha. YOMC.'

'Another file name?'

'Nah, you owe me chocolate.'

She put the phone down and jumped out of bed, immediately swaying on her feet as a wave of nausea hit her like the back end of a Manchester bus. 'Take it slowly, Jayne.'

She slipped into her normal working outfit; sweatshirt and training pants, put on some slippers and went downstairs. She caught sight of herself in the hall mirror. Ugh! She raced past without looking again. She needed coffee and quickly.

Into the kitchen, booting up the Mac and the Nespresso machine at the same time. She selected the dark blue capsule, the book said it was the strongest and slipped it into the hole in the top. Out poured a thick dark espresso that smelt divine. Shame it never tasted as good as it smelt, but never mind, she needed the caffeine at the moment.

She logged onto Gmail. There was Rob's message. She opened it up and saw a blow up of a round bronze badge against a green fibre background, almost as if it were lying on a carpet rather than against a coat. The badge was obviously already old when the picture was taken, with bits of the bronze already showing a few flecks of green patination. The overall shape was like a sunburst but interspersed were star points. She counted them. Eight points. Was it like a compass?

In the middle, she could just make out words but the script was strange, not like any typeface she had ever seen before. Cyrillic? Something from Russia. She squinted at the words. A circle with a line over it, followed by RONG. Then a space with a triangle, a T and then another triangle. What was next? She moved her head closer to the screen. The letters CLIA followed by something else but she couldn't make it out.

Strange. She'd never seen anything like it before. Was it Eastern European? Why would a young boy born in Bradford have a badge from Eastern Europe? Maybe, it wasn't from there at all.

In the centre was a stylised figure. Or was it an F?

She went back to the original photograph. The badge was small, perhaps just one inch around, Where would it have been worn? On the lapel as in the picture. But it looked vaguely military. As a button? On a belt? On a cap?

There was just too little to go on, but she knew where to go. Time to pay a visit to an old friend who made a living selling deactivated guns to criminals. Or at least, he had made a living until she put him away for three years.

Chapter 14

The bell rang as Jayne stepped through the door. The shop was on a terrace in Cheetham Hill, surrounded by a kosher butchers on one side and an Oxfam on the other.

An old man bustled through from the back. 'Hold your horses, I'm coming.' As soon as he saw Jayne, he stood still and held up his hands in mock surrender. 'DI Sinclair, I ain't done nothing wrong, clean as a whistle, me.'

'It's just plain Ms Sinclair, Herbert. I left the police a few years ago.' She could see Herbert Levy's shoulders relax visibly. He brought his arms down and stuffed them in a pair of voluminous trousers that had been made around 1945.

'This is a social visit then, Mrs Sinclair?'

'Oh Herbert, you know I don't do social.' She moved into the shop, dancing her way through the assorted uniforms, gas masks, ammo boxes, grenade launchers, trenching tools and other paraphernalia of the arms and militaria specialist.

'So you're a customer then?' he suggested tentatively, 'I can do you a very good price if you're looking for something for the man in your life.'

'How about cyanide?' suggested Jayne as she dodged a green rucksack hanging from the ceiling.

'You always did like a little joke, DI Sinclair.'

She ignored his use of her old title and didn't correct him. 'Not dealing anymore, Herbert?'

'I don't know what you mean. I'm strictly kosher these

days. A specialist in arms and militaria. Good business it is too. More money than fencing or thieving.' He moved behind the counter putting it between himself and Jayne.

She leant in to look closely at an old gas mask, touching the lens with the tip of her index finger. She held the finger up so Herbert could see.

'Cleaning was never my strong point, DI Sinclair, I've got better things to do with my time than play around with disinfectant and carbolic soap.'

'I'm surprised you even know the words, Herbert.' She wiped the dirt on her index finger on one of the uniforms, making sure he saw her. 'And how are you spending your time these days?'

'Oh, doing this and that...'

'This and that? Sounds very precise, Herbert. We'll try again, shall we? How have you been spending your time?'

Herbert appeared to think for a while. 'Most of the time, I've been studying. Picked up the habit in prison.'

'I hope that's all you picked up.'

'Like that gas mask you touched. That's a 1940 issue that one is. You know they issued over 38 million gas masks at the beginning of the war. Walt Disney even made a Mickey Mouse gas mask for the kiddies. Expected the Germans to bomb Manchester with phosgene gas they did. Only a few left now. 'Cos it's you, I'll let you have it for fifty quid. Can't say fairer.'

'Not interested, Herbert. I'm after information.'

'I told you, DI Sinclair, I'm not fencing anymore. Too many visits from your friends over at Cheetham Hill nick. Me, I sell this stuff all over the country now. I got a website,' he said proudly. He reached beneath the desk and handed her a card. 'Herbert Levy and Son, Arms and Militaria. Best cash prices for anything military. Beneath the heading there was a long list of items he bought and sold, each categorised under separate headings: Badges, insignia medals, citations. Uniforms, headware, equipment, webbing. Armour, swords, bayonettes, grenades, inert shells and cases. ARP, Home Gruad and utility clothes. Trench-art, flags, manuals, log books, letters, diaries, leaflets, postcards.

'You seem to have covered it all, Herbert, even if the spelling and punctuation leave a lot to be desired.'

Levy smiled proudly. 'I covers it all except I don't do German stuff. I've got my principles.'

'I'm sure you have, Herbert.' She pointed to the and Son part of the card. 'I didn't know you were married.'

He smiled again this time more sheepishly, 'I'm not, DI Sinclair, but the name gives the shop more gravitas. The punters want to buy from a settled business.'

'Not a fly-by-night shyster?'

The sheepishness changed to indignation. 'I made a mistake, DI Sinclair. I paid my debt to society and now I'm an honest merchant dealing in a very desirable product.'

'So, Mr Honest Merchant, you can deal in information for me.' She took out the picture the bike courier had brought round to her house and removed the note from Rob, before passing it over to Herbert Levy. 'What do you make of this?'

Levy studied it, sucking in breath through the gap in his teeth. 'Don't see many of these.'

'What is it?'

Levy looked up at her, cunning etched into every line on his unshaven face. 'What's innit for me, Mrs Sinclair? You did say you'd left the force, didn't you?'

'My personal thanks and gratitude, Mr Levy.'

The smile remained on his face. 'And?'

'And a promise I won't ring my old mates at Cheetham Hill nick, asking them to pay a visit to your shop to check every single piece of your merchandise.' She picked up the gas mask and blew the dust off it. 'I do presume you have proofs of purchase for everything here.'

Levy held up his hands again. 'Now, now, Mrs Sinclair, just a joke between friends, a little light-hearted banter.' He picked up the picture again. 'It's a cap badge, I think. Could be a belt buckle but it looks a bit small for one of those.' He bent down beneath the counter and began searching for something.

'Is it Russian? Or Eastern European?'

He came up with an old catalogue with an auctioneer's name and the date 1997 stamped boldly on the cover. 'What was that? Russian? You are a card, DI Sinclair. It's Irish. See the letters there...' He pointed to the middle of the badge. '...Gaelic that is. Just a minute and I'll find it for you. I know it's in here somewhere.' He flicked through the catalogue, occasionally lifting his head and comparing the picture with an image on one of the pages. Finally, there was another intake of breath through the gap in his front teeth. 'Here it is. Nice bit of kit. If you want to sell it, I'll make you a good offer.' He turned the catalogue round to face her.

She leant over. It was the same image as the badge on the picture of John Hughes as a young boy. She read the caption out loud. 'The Dublin Brigade badge was issued in the lead up to the 1916 rising. It consists of an eight point-ed star intertwined with a sunburst (the traditional Fianna symbol for battle) The words "Drong Áta Cliath" are writ-ten on a belt inside the star sunburst. This would translate as "Dublin Brigade". The letters "FF" also intertwine in the centre stand for "Fianna Fáil", not the political party, but

80

rather Fianna as in the old Celtic army and Fáil, the Irish for destiny. Officers would have worn a whiter metal version while lower ranks would have a bronze example.'

'Beautifully read, Di Sinclair. Just like you were giving evidence in court.'

'It's Irish?'

'As gefilte fish. Quite rare, these days. The Micks will pay well for one of these. In fact, they'll pay well for anything to do with the Easter Rising.'

She stared at him, not understanding.

'Police education these days...' He shook his head. 'Dublin 1916. Easter. The Irish took over the city...'

Chapter 15

He felt a little awkward standing on the step of the tram with his bandolier, his knapsack and his rifle. He could see by the way the others were staring out into the street and avoiding the eyes of the other passengers, they felt the same. Even Fitz had gone quiet as they trundled towards Liberty Hall.

The mobilisation had been an on-off-on affair. They received a notice on Good Friday, telling them to assemble at Liberty Hall at 11 o'clock on Easter Sunday morning. Fitz had been the first to complain.

'Not another bloody march.' He waved the paper with his orders on it in the air. 'And for the love of Jaysus, they're telling us to bring rations for three days as well as all our kit. Where are we marching to this time? Timbuktu?'

'Probably just another parade like St Pat's day. Show the colours to Dublin.'

'Dublin couldn't give a flying feck about the colours. They'll all be at the races in Fairyhouse. Which is exactly where I should be too. I've got my eyes on a lovely wee filly.'

'And how many legs does this one have, Mr Declan Fitzgerald?'

'Ach, Michael you have an awful tongue on you. Racing is the sport of Kings and myself.'

'Looks like you're going to be racing through the streets of Dublin yourself this time.'

When they had read the notice of cancellation of the

parade on Easter Sunday morning, Fitz had been ecstatic. 'Finally, somebody has knocked a bit of sense in their heads. For feck's sake, nobody wants to be traipsing around the country during Easter when they can be relaxing with a few jars and enjoying themselves. Talking of that, me throat's as dry as a weasel's jockstrap, fancy a pint or three in Rathfarnham?'

Michael thought about it. They had been living at St Enda's for six months now. It was cheaper than living in the city but being miles out and stuck on the school campus had meant little or no excitement.

'I've my essay for Tranter. You know what a stickler he is for timing.'

'Ah, have a day off. The essay and Tranter won't be back until after Easter. You've your whole life in front of you to write essays but there's only today for sinking a few jars.'

Who could resist Fitz? So they went out into town, returning only when the street lights were lit and the jars had been drunk.

Slightly the worse for wear, Michael had been woken by Oscar Tully on Easter Monday morning.

'Will you get yourself up?'

'Wha? Wha's up?' He tried to shake the beer from his head only succeeding in stirring it up once more.

'The parade's on again. I got a note this morning. We're to be at Liberty Hall by eleven with full kit and rifle.'

'What? Away with ye, it's been cancelled. Didn't you see the paper yesterday?'

'Aye, well it's on again. I'm off to wake the others.'

Michael struggled out of his warm, welcoming bed, dressed quickly and put all his kit together. Luckily, he hadn't unpacked it since yesterday. The sandwiches were looking worse for wear but what the hell, they would only be gone a couple of hours. A quick march up and down the streets of Dublin to show the people who they were, followed by a few speeches and he would be home this evening in time for lights out. He left the sandwiches beside his bed. There was bound to be food provided by the Cumann na MBan.

He looked at his watch. Nine o'clock already. He would have to get a move on.

Well, get a move on he did, and here he was standing on the deck of a tram on his way to the city centre with Fitz beside him. His friend had taken an age to wake too, moaning constantly about missing the races at Fairyhouse for some damn march through the suburbs of Dublin. But eventually, he had got him up and dressed and down to the drill hall. There they had been met by Eamon Bulfin and half the company that had bothered to come.

The tram was moving as slowly as ever, stopping every 100 yards or so to let passengers alight and pick up new ones. There were only eight of them on board, the other members of their company either not getting the message or already doing something else that day.

The ones that had managed to make it on time, looked smartly turned out. Two were wearing the green uniforms made by Lalor the tailor, with the two lieutenants, Eamon Bulfin and Harry Boland, in full uniform. The rest, himself included, were in mufti but with the accoutrements of the military: a bandolier across his chest with 20 rounds of ammo stuffed in it, a Howth rifle that he still hadn't finished paying for, a long-barrelled Smith and Wesson his brother had given him on his last leave from the army, and green puttees wrapped around his legs. In his case, they were all he could afford from Lalor's.

Bulfin had given each of them a cap badge as they assembled that morning. A small bronze badge with the emblem of the Fianna and their brigade designation proudly stamped on it. Michael, Fitz and the others had pinned it in the centre of their assorted hats. It was the one piece of kit they all shared.

The tram trundled on. Outside, Dublin was going about its business on Easter Monday. Well, as much business as ever got done when there was racing on at Fairyhouse. The streets were quiet with only a few brewers' drays delivering beer to the pubs to slake the thirst of the racegoers when they returned that evening.

The tram itself was half empty, or at least, it would have been had it not also carried the kit of the eight men from the Dublin Brigade.

They swung into St Stephen's Green.

'That's it. That's as far as I'm going,' announced the driver.

'Will you not take us on to Liberty Hall?'

'Not me. This tram's for the Green. It stops here and I takes my rest and my dinner.'

Michael looked at his watch. 12.30 already. By the time they had assembled at Rathfarnham Chapel, waited for the latecomers and then walked to Terenure to get the tram, it was past eleven o'clock. They would be late. E Company, 4th Battalion late again. Willie Pearse would be writing it down in his little book, shaking his head and tutting as only he could tut.

The other passengers were pushing past them to disembark from the tram.

'I'm ordering you to take this tram to Liberty Hall,' shouted Bulfin.

The driver turned off the engine and the tram went

silent. 'It's staying here and so am I.'

Bulfin took his revolver from its holster at his hip. The dark metal of the barrel still shiny and new.

'I'm ordering you to take this tram to Liberty Hall.'

The driver stared at him. 'This tram stops at St Stephen's and won't go an inch further. Now then if you gentlemen would get off my tram, perhaps you could start marching to Liberty Hall.'

A large woman with a poor, mousy husband in tow pushed past Michael. 'Will you not go home to your mammies, and leave the poor man alone.'

Her husband backed her up. 'You should be at church on your knees before God on this Easter Monday, not marching through the streets of Dublin.'

Fitz took a step towards the man and he retreated behind his wife.

Eamon Bulfin looked at his watch.

'Let's just get down and walk, Eamon, it's not more than ten minutes from here. We'll soon catch them up,' said Michael.

Eamon looked at his watch again, and then at the driver still sitting stubbornly in his seat.

'Right then men, get your kit and rifles, we're going to march to Liberty Hall,' he commanded as if this had been his intention all along.

'Get a move on, will ye? Me tea is getting cold and I've another tram to drive at one.'

They assembled as best they could on St Stephen's Green and then marched off with Eamon Bulfin in the lead and the rest of them following in his wake.

The people of the city, enjoying an early stroll with their families or simply breathing in the fresh air of the day, ignored them. The city itself was quiet as it always was on a public holiday with half the people at mass and the rest at the races.

It was only as they were approaching Liberty Hall that they began to realise this Easter Monday was different. A young boy, who couldn't have been more than thirteen was the first to greet them.

'You're late,' he said picking his teeth with a toothpick, 'they've all gone.'

'Where to?' asked Eamon.

'Dublin,' answered the small boy before running off into Liberty Hall.

A few seconds later, a man dressed in the bandoliers and wearing a badge of the Irish Citizen's Army stepped out to greet them. 'You're late,' he said.

'It's a long way from Rathfarnham,' mumbled Eamon.

'Aye, well you'll have to catch them up. You can take some bombs with you. They're on the handcart over there.' He pointed to an old cart with the legend, James Hewitt, Painters and Decorators, painted onto the side. Loaded on to the cart was a heap of wooden boxes.

'Where have they marched to?' asked Eamon using his best officer accent.

The man took his cap off and scratched his bald head. 'The GPO. Haven't you heard?'

'Heard what?' asked Fitz, receiving looks that could kill from Eamon.

'It's started.'

'What's started?'

'The Revolution. It's today.'

Eamon was getting exasperated with the man. 'What Revolution? We're here for the march.'

'There is no march, not today. We've taken over the GPO, and the Four Courts and the Union. We've taken over

87

the city. Ireland is rising.'

'What do you mean, man? What's going on?'

The man spoke slowly as if talking to a five-year-old. 'Don't you understand the English? We have taken over the city. The revolution has begun. We're going to throw the Brits out finally, after 700 years.'

Slowly, it dawned on Eamon, Michael, Fitz and the others what was happening. 'What shall we do?' asked Michael.

'Well, they all marched off to the GPO about an hour and a half ago. If I were you, I would go there. That's the HQ.'

Eamon took charge again. 'You heard the man, get your things together. We're marching to Sackville Street.'

There was a new spring in the men's step as they marched to the Post Office down Abbey Street, the cart trundling behind pushed by the young boy and two of the men.

There were more people on the streets. A few stopped and looked at the men as they strode past. Michael thought they might be excited at the idea of Ireland being free, but on their faces, he could only see indifference as if they didn't care. Or worse, as if it meant nothing to them.

But for Michael it meant everything. Finally, here was their chance to follow in the footsteps of Wolfe Tone and the United Irishman. He patted his left-hand jacket pocket. The book given to him last year by Fitz nestled there snugly. He always carried it with him, a reminder of why they were fighting. He looked across at Fitz. His perpetual smirk and air of insouciance were gone, replaced by an obvious pride in what they were doing.

The marched up Sackville Street, arms swinging and rifles held tightly against their shoulders. Up ahead of them on the left, the GPO stood solidly against the skyline, its replica Grecian facade dominating the buildings around it.

A shock of pride surged through Michael's body. This was what they were fighting for. This was why they had drilled and marched and polished all these months.

They turned left into Prince's Street and waited. They could see armed men at the windows, but the doors remained closed.

Eamon Bulfin banged on the door with his fist. A muffled shout came from inside. Michael couldn't hear what was being said, but Eamon suddenly became animated.

'Form a line across the street. The Lancers are coming,' he shouted.

They raced into position across Prince's Street as they had practised so many times at the old Mill in Rathfarnham. Fitz was on Michael's right and the rest of the men had spread out across the width of the road, their rifles all pointing menacingly forward.

The order came. 'Fix Bayonets.' This time it was shouted by Boland.

Neither Michael nor Fitz had bayonets so they just stood there. Around them, they could hear the rasp of steel as some of the men pulled the long knives from their scabbards, followed by the clicks and fumbling as they fixed them at the end of their rifles.

Finally, all was quiet again and the men just waited in the street.

Eamon Bulfin walked around behind them, shouting in his high-pitched voice. 'The Brits are sending in the Lancers, lads. Let's give them some Irish steel.'

Michael looked across at Fitz. His jaw was set tight and he had planted his feet firmly on the ground, one in front of the other, rifle pointing forward ready to open fire.

Was this it? Was this what they had been practising and marching and drilling for all these years?

Fitz raised his rifle to his shoulder. Michael followed him, the Mauser heavy in his arms. Would he be able to fire it? To see another human being in the sights and pull the trigger? Well, in the next few minutes he would find out.

Michael looked out past the end of the rifle into Sackville Street but couldn't see any Lancers. A group of men, women and children were watching from the side of the road, like spectators at a GAA match.

Then from above a rifle shot. The sharp crack of a Lee Enfield, followed by others, the deeper booms of the Howth Mausers and the taps of revolvers. A volley of shots from the roof of the GPO.

He heard the sound of hooves echoing on the hard tarmac of the road.

A riderless horse raced past, its eyes wild with fear. A young man ran out from the crowd of spectators to stop it. The horse, startled by the sudden movement, sheered away from him until he grabbed the bridle.

Michael noticed blood on the horse's flank, red against the white of the sheepskin blanket. He wondered if it was a man's blood or that of the horse. Another man joined the youth holding onto the reins, gentling the horse until it calmed down.

A cheer came from the roof of the GPO.

'Stand down men, the attack has been repulsed.' This was shouted by Boland.

Another cheer came from the Rathfarnham men. Then silence. The whole street quiet as if the Lancers and their charge had never existed. An eerie silence. Michael waited for someone to say something. Nobody did. It was as if they had all realised at the same time, that this was real. It wasn't an exercise any more. This was a fight for Ireland.

'Smash the windows. We're going in.'

Michael wondered why the men inside didn't simply open the doors facing Prince's Street to let them in, but it didn't matter. Two men stepped forward and smashed the windows with the butt of their rifles. The noise shattered the quiet on the street. Suddenly the crowd was shouting. Michael tried to hear what they were saying. It seemed to be two women who were shouting loudest.

'Go home to your mammies.'

'Shame on you with our men fighting in France.'

The shouts were taken up by others in the crowd.

'Why aren't you lot in France?'

'Join up.'

'You feckers should be fighting in feckin' France, not on the streets of Dublin.'

The men ignored them. Boland and Bulfin climbed through the broken window into the ground floor of the GPO where they were greeted by Padraig Pearse and James Connelly. Willie Pearse, the commander of their company and Padraig's brother, stood off to one side.

'Good to have you with us, Bulfin,' said Connelly.

'Sorry we're late, sir.'

'E company is always late,' sniffed Willie.

'It's a long way from Rathfarnham, sir.'

'Well, better late than never,' smiled Connolly through his moustache, 'we're glad you're here.'

'Can you open the doors to let the rest of the men in?'

Willie Pearse coughed. 'We can't find the key. Just climb in, will you?'

The rest of the men lined up to climb through the windows. One or two cut themselves on the edges of the broken glass. The man in front of Michael was being extra careful to avoid touching the sharp edges. He levered himself up onto the ledge but, as he did so, his rifle fell off his shoulder and the butt struck the ground. A loud shot echoed through the street and into the GPO.

Some men ducked. A few threw themselves down to the ground. Others simply stood there.

The man in front of Michael turned back towards him. 'I've been shot,' he whispered, before falling forwards into the GPO.

Immediately, men rushed forward.

Connolly shouted. 'Get the doctor for this man.'

Michael stood there, looking through the broken window into the GPO. The man lay on the ground with a dark river of blood seeping through his trousers and running out onto the wooden floor. Men surrounded him. A doctor, dressed in a British Army uniform rushed forward, pushing his way through the onlookers.

'Take him down to the clinic in the sorting office,' he commanded.

Three men rushed forward. Two took his legs and the other took his head, following the doctor.

Throughout all this the man remained quiet, the wild look in his eyes reminding Michael of the horse running through the street just minutes before.

He felt a shove in his back, Fitz was standing right behind him.

'Well, are you going to be standing there for the rest of your life, Michael Dowling, or are we going to join this Revolution?'

Chapter 16

David Turner had followed her to a small shop in Cheetham Hill, Herbert Levy and Sons. What could she want with arms and militaria? No matter. It was not his place to ask such questions. He had instructions and would carry them out to the letter until he received new ones. A good soldier he was. Or he should say, a good ex-soldier. And, like many others in his line of business, he came out of the Army with a degree in killing and not much else. Working for some poxy security firm with a bunch of trigger-happy Americans didn't appeal, neither did swapping one uniform for another by going into the police.

He decided to work for himself and loved it immediately, quickly gaining a reputation for being able to sort out problems with the minimum of fuss.

A bad debt? The money has been sent, thank you.

A cheating husband? Warning delivered with just a hint of the violence the man could expect unless he reformed his ways and withdraw his wayward willy. Coitus Interruptus, he always liked to joke.

A business partner with his hand in the till?

How many fingers would you like him to lose?

His reputation had grown and now he could be more choosy about the sort of clients he worked with, only accepting those who would pay his inflated fees. No more discounts. No more favours. No more mate's rates.

He checked his computer. The information on this assignment had arrived in his mailbox as instructed, with

'Office Move' as the title. An address and a photo of the target with precise instructions for a watching brief through the day, followed by a sharp warning in the evening. The time and form of the warning to be decided by him.

He had already scoped out the home of the target. An easy place to find in the suburbs of Manchester. An even easier place to watch sitting in his van marked A&E Electrical.

Anybody walking past would see him filling in a few forms on the front seat, having just completed a job. Or eating his lunch on his break. Or simply waiting for a homeowner to return so that he could start a job. Either way, he was covered. He even had a business card to give out in case anybody wanted one. Unfortunately, if they rang the 1-800 number, the phone would be answered by the madam of one of his favourite brothels. So it goes. You had to have a little fun on this job.

People tended to accept the presence of minor tradespeople. Plumbers, electricians, nothing too official, and nothing with the word contractor on it. He'd made that mistake once. Within half an hour, five people had come up to him in his car complaining about the noise from his building work. Work that had never started and was never going to start. So it goes.

She was coming out of the shop now. Nothing in her hands and looking the same as before. But moving quickly, as if she were in a hurry. He followed her as she accelerated down Cheetham Hill Road. She was driving fast, he would have to speed up to make sure he didn't lose her. He didn't like breaking the speed limit on jobs. Some keen copper in a car, out to make a point, could pull him over and he would lose the target.

She was putting her foot down. I wonder what happened in the shop to make her so agitated. Looks like she was heading home, though, back to Didsbury, just following the same route she took coming here, but in reverse.

He loved how predictable most people were. Always using the same password on multiple accounts made getting into their online life so easy. And don't talk to him about how easy it was to get into an answering machine. Hadn't the News of the World and the other papers been blagging phones for years. Not that he could do all that stuff himself, of course. But there were people who could and they could be bought as easily as shopping at Tesco.

Numpties. That's what he called the great unwashed, law-abiding, Daily Mail-reading, wife-swapping, wine-soaked, once-a-week-on-a-Sunday-shagging, doll's-house-living lot of them.

You've got to love their stupidity. They kept him in work and money and fast cars. But, above all, they kept him happy, every last single stupid one of them.

This one was no different, even if she was an ex-copper. He would carry on following her. And the warning would come this evening. Nothing too subtle. Warnings needed to be in your face. No matter if she went to the police. It just meant she understood she was being threatened.

And there was nobody better at delivering a threat than him.

Chapter 17

She put the key in the door, opened it slightly and listened for any sound.

Silence. Paul wasn't at home.

A few letters were lying on the floor in the hall; bills, bills and a few more bills for good measure. Nothing important, they could all wait until hell froze over.

She hurried to the kitchen and switched on the Mac. After the visit to the newly studious Herbert Levy, she had a hunch and was desperate to see if it would lead her to the mysterious MD. He had said the badges were given to members of the Irish Volunteers before the Rising.

Her homepage flashed on the screen and she typed in the words 'Participants in the 1916 Easter Rising' into Google.

Lots of hits. Good. She scanned the list. Wikipedia was at the top, followed by a genealogical site. She checked that. It gave 1599 participants in the Rising.

Good. Very good. The odds were narrowing considerably.

She scanned the rest of the results. Lots of information about the participants, particularly the leaders. Halfway down a link to a Military Archives site. The Irish Army had digitised its archives and had a whole section on the Easter Rising. They gave the number of participants in the rising as 2577. Even better.

She clicked on the alphabetic list at that site, reading the names of all those who had taken part in an uprising nearly

100 years before. This was a genealogist's gold mine. A sense of excitement rose in her. She knew she was finally getting somewhere.

Four people with the initials MD. She was sure her man was one of the four. But how to know which one he was? She checked the website. It had interviews with many of the participants. Apparently, the Irish government had decided to record oral histories of the Rising and the War of Independence that followed it, for their records in the 1950s.

Why? Nobody else was doing anything like that at that time. The British government certainly weren't, preferring to bury the errors and mass murder of places like Ypres, the Somme and Passchendaele in the mud of Flanders.

All her training and her years as a genealogist, told her she was close. Inside one of these testimonies was the identity of MD, she knew it, but it would take time. She would have to go through them one by one, looking for clues to help her. Did she know enough to work it out?

Time to call her client and let him know her progress. She forced herself to breathe deeply three or four times. Compose yourself. Do not communicate your excitement to him. We mustn't get his hopes up, not yet. Remember you have nothing concrete yet, just a few possibilities.

She picked up the phone and dialled the number she had been given. Richard Hughes answered after the first two rings.

'I'd like to speak to your uncle, Richard.'

'You have good news to report, Ms Sinclair?'

'Not yet. But there are a couple of good leads. This is more of an update.' She kept her voice level and calm.

'I'll get him.'

After a few seconds a deep, melodious voice came

through her phone. 'Mrs Sinclair, good to hear from you. I hope you've found the identity of my father.'

Manage his expectations. Don't get his hopes up. 'Nothing concrete so far, Mr Hughes, but I have uncovered a few leads that will benefit from further exploration.'

'For instance?' The voice was flat, deflated. She sensed a disappointment in the tone.

'Well, the book you carried with you across the Atlantic was published in 1914 in Dublin...'

'I could have told you that, Mrs Sinclair, it's on the inside cover.'

She carried on. 'It was purchased by the library of the University College Dublin in that year. I believe it could have been stolen from there in 1915. Stolen by DF and given to MD.' She was making a huge leap now, but all her instincts told her she was right.

'Better, but it still takes us no nearer to finding out who MD or DF were.'

'True. I intend to check the graduate and alumni records of UCD. They may help us solve the puzzle.'

'Or they may not.'

'Also true. I discovered one other thing of use. In your picture, you are a wearing a bronze badge on your lapel.'

'You noticed that? I wondered what it was.'

'Do you still have it?'

'I don't think so. I'm sure it's of no importance. Probably some Christmas gift I'd been given. Or something from the church or orphanage.'

'Actually, it wasn't anything like that, Mr Hughes. It was a cap badge from the Dublin Brigade of the Irish Volunteers. These badges were only given out to members just before the Easter Rising of 1916.' Despite her best efforts, excitement was creeping into her voice.

'The Easter Rising, you say? I was wearing a badge from the Easter Rising?'

'That's correct, Mr Hughes. Or at least you were wearing an Irish Volunteers' badge of the period. We can't be certain the man who owned it took part in the Rising.' Manage his expectations, she told herself. 'Who gave the badge to you, Mr Hughes?'

There was silence on the other end of the phone. Eventually, the old man answered. 'I don't know, Mrs Sinclair, I just don't know. As I told you, I don't remember anything from this period, it's a complete blank.'

She could hear the old voice becoming more and more exasperated.

'Why would I have something like that, Mrs Sinclair?'

'That's what I don't know, Mr Hughes. But I'm certain it is significant. What's more, I checked with the military archives. There were four men with the initials MD who took part in the Rising.'

'My father could be one of those men?'

She hadn't managed this well. She could feel his anticipation and expectation rising. 'I don't know, Mr Hughes. I don't want to get your hopes up...'

'You must go to Dublin, Mrs Sinclair. Find out the truth.'

'I don't know if that is necessary, Mr Hughes, most of the military archive records have been digitised...'

'Most but not all, am I correct?'

'Yes, there are always records that they haven't got round to scanning yet or ones they've missed.'

'Plus you need to check at UCD as well?'

'True. They haven't put any graduate records online.'

'So what are you waiting for? I don't have to remind you that you have just six days left to make your report. And I will pick up all the costs. Money is no object, Mrs Sinclair.'

'I'll book a flight to Dublin tomorrow.'

'Good. I was sure you'd see it my way, Mrs Sinclair.'

Jayne felt resentful at the prodding of this man, it was time to bring him down to earth. 'I may find nothing, Mr Hughes.'

'Oh, I have confidence in you, even if you don't trust yourself. You've made more progress in two days than my worthless nephew made in six months. Report back when you get to Dublin, Mrs Sinclair.'

'Mr Hughes, I...' With that final order, the line went dead and she was left speaking to a buzzing noise.

'You're going to Dublin?'

She jumped at the sound of the voice. Paul had crept into the kitchen while she was on the phone. He was standing beside her, staring straight at her.

'Just for a couple of days, the job...'

'Have you forgotten we have a dinner with my boss on Friday?'

'It's Tuesday, I'll be back by Thursday evening. Don't worry, there will be plenty of time.'

She leant forward to kiss him. He stepped back.

'This is important to me, Jayne. He's been pushing me for this dinner. I think he wants to tell me something. A promotion, maybe.'

'That's wonderful, Paul...'

'Don't screw it up, Jayne. I've been waiting for this for a long time. I deserve it.'

'I won't. I'll be back in time. Just two nights in Dublin so I can crack this case.'

The window in the kitchen shattered with a sharp crash. Something hard thudded against the far wall and rolled on to the floor.

Instinctively, they both ducked down beneath the counter.

Jayne moved first, her training taking over. She ran at a crouch to the wall next to the shattered window, crunching glass as she did.

She stood up and peered out through the broken window.

Nothing.

She looked back into the kitchen. Paul was just popping his head above the counter. Glass lay everywhere, covering the wooden floor. In the middle of the room, a half-brick lay all on its own. Around it, a rubber band and a folded sheet of paper.

Crunching more glass beneath her feet, she picked up the brick. Probably came from the skip at the end of the road, she thought. She pulled off the rubber band and opened the sheet of paper.

The words were written in stark black, block capitals.

LEAVE IT ALONE.

Chapter 18

From the roof of the GPO, Michael could see most of Dublin laid out at his feet. A small parapet ran round the outside where he and the rest of the company could hunker down, leaning their backs against it and talk about life, their families, and what would happen after the revolution.

There wasn't much sniping on those first few days. A few shots occasionally came their way from the direction of Trinity College.

After the first encounter with the Lancers, there was no sign of any British troops for a long time. Michael was certain they would come but not sure when. The lads would be ready when they did, and the Brits would find a warm welcome from the roof of the GPO if they ever stepped out on to the street below them.

In those early days, they didn't have much to do. Michael and Fitz had helped out equipping a first aid centre in an old sorting office. They used beds requisitioned from Clery's, the department store across the street.

'Well, at least if I die, it's going to be the most comfortable death I'll ever have,' said Fitz as he plumped up one of the pillows. 'A man could die happy on one of these beds.'

'Less talk about dying, Fitzgerald,' said Bulfin quietly.

'Could I take one of these home with me after the revolution?' This was from a Dubliner who lived in the slums, one of Connolly's men.

'You will not,' ordered Bulfin, 'these are to be returned to Clery's once we've finished with them. A free Ireland doesn't steal other people's property.'

'More's the pity. You could make a fair few wee ones with the help of these springs.' The Dubliner jerked his hips backwards and forwards lustily. Bulfin marched out of the first aid station without answering.

The rest of the time they spent up on the roof looking over Dublin. They were fed from time to time. A canteen had been set up in the basement and the Cumann na mBan girls came round with warm, milky tea in big steel pots.

About seven o'clock on the first evening, they had their first meal.

'Would any of youse boys like a bit of stew?'

Fitz woke up from his position against the parapet and stared at the young woman who had asked the question. She was tall, wearing a green hat that made her appear even taller. Two long tendrils of curly hair drifted past either side of her face, framing the liveliest blue eyes.

'I said, would any of youse men like a bit of stew?'

'We heard you the first time. And you might want to keep your head down, there's a sniper over there on the roof of Trinity.'

Instinctively, the woman ducked her head.

'Will you stop it, Fitz,' Michael said, 'he hasn't fired in over an hour and he couldn't hit a barn door from five yards away. Don't go scaring the young woman.'

She coughed and stood up straight smoothing down her clothes. 'I'll ask youse for the last time, would anybody like stew?'

Fitz grabbed his mess tin and stood up. 'From a fair Colleen such as yourself, it would taste like the elixir of the gods.'

'Three things, Mr...?'

'Fitzgerald. Declan Fitzgerald.'

'Well, Mr Fitzgerald. Firstly, I'm not a 'fair Colleen'. My name is Bridget and I'm a tram driver from Ballsbridge. Second, I didn't make it so I'm not sure how good it tastes, but all the other men are having a plate and nobody has died so far. And thirdly, if you want an elixir of the gods, I suggest you take a wander over to Guinness's. It's just over there, not far.' She pointed over to the famous brewery with her free arm. 'Now, will you be wanting the stew or not?'

Fitz held out his mess tin and she began to ladle some of the thick brown stew into it.

'Will you be wanting more?'

'Not yet a while, this will do me fine for now.'

'Good, for a moment there I thought youse was going to eat me out of house and home. Anybody else?'

Michael stood up and held out his mess tin. As he did so, there was a shout of 'Will you look at that?' from one of the lads.

They leant over the parapet and looked down into O'-Connell Street. The smallest man they had ever seen was carrying a naked mannequin over one shoulder and pushing a dog cart with his other hand. Inside, the dog cart was piled high with assorted clothes, pots and pans and a large aspidistra.

'What's he doing?' asked Bridget.

'They've been looting the stores since this afternoon. We're supposed to stop them but I don't have the heart,' said Fitz.

The small man was joined by two children, both no older than seven and neither wearing shoes. One of them carried a giant rocking horse in his arms, and the other a collection of feathered hats. The small family struggled on down the street with their load, watched by the men high up on the roof of the parapet.

'I hope they make it home,' said Bridget.

'So do I.' Fitz stared at her and she looked down at her stew.

'Well, I'm off to see if others want feeding. Can't stand here gassing with youse all day.' She walked away towards the exit.

'Will you bring me more, later?' shouted Fitz.

'I will if there's any left. And I'll see if I can find some elixir of the gods, just for you,' she shouted back over her shoulder without looking at him.

When she was gone, Fitz carried on looking at the space where she had vanished from view. 'I'm going to marry that woman.'

'Oh, Fitz, the only man I know who brings romance to the middle of a revolution. Can't you stop thinking of women for just once in your life.' Michael poked him in the shoulder.

'I'm serious, I'm going to marry that woman.'

'Away and eat your stew. There'll be plenty of time for romance later, we've the Brits to get rid of first.'

Fitz ladled a large spoonful of stew into his mouth. 'Not bad. Now, if you don't want yours...'

*　*　*

The rest of the evening passed peacefully, broken only by the occasional sniper's bullet and the explosions of fireworks looted from a store further up the street. When the first Catherine Wheel went off, they had all reached for their guns, expecting an attack at any minute.

One of the men pointed towards where a crowd had

gathered. Suddenly, the centre of the crowd erupted with an explosion of light: greens, reds, whites and blues, all vivid colours, followed at the end by a loud screech.

'Will you look at that? We're in the middle of a revolution and they're setting off fireworks.'

There was the crackle of a string of bangers, men jumped out of the way as the small explosions landed in the middle of them. Michael stood up and watched the crowd. Small circles of sparklers were being held by children, brightening in one place, only to fizzle out after thirty seconds, followed by another bright light in another section of the crowd.

The men on top of the roof watched this display for about twenty minutes, until the fireworks were exhausted and the crowd began to drift away.

'That was a fine show. The noise would wake Boru himself. Scared the death out of me.'

'Wait till you hear the sound of bullets whistling past your ears. Then you'll know the meaning of being scared.' Bulfin had appeared silently on the roof. 'Better get your heads down, lads. You'll be needing the sleep later.' He detailed a few men to keep watch whilst the rest hunkered down against the parapet.

Michael couldn't sleep that first night though. How could he? Finally, they had risen against the Brits just as Wolfe Tone and the United Irishmen had done over one hundred years ago.

He listened to the sounds of the Dublin night from the roof. The crack of breaking glass as the people looted the shops. There was an echo of firing from the South but he couldn't be sure where it had come from. The stream of curses and swearing as somebody was robbed of a treasure he had just looted.

A quiet Dublin night, like many others before it. But this time they were in charge. They held the GPO, they controlled the city.

The following morning a rumour went round the men on the roof like pox in a brothel.

'The Germans have landed.'

'Where?'

'Kerry,' said one.

'No, I heard it was Ballina in Mayo,' said another.

'It's neither,' said a third man, 'they've landed in Tralee. I have it from the man himself.'

They all nodded their heads. Tralee it was then. When would the Germans get to Dublin and what would the Brits do?

All speculation was ended by Willie Pearse later that morning. 'No German landings have been reported,' he stated.

'And what about the risings in the rest of the country?'

'We haven't heard anything yet. There seems to be confusion. O'Neil's advertisement in the paper stopped people from mobilising. We're trying to communicate with the West at the moment.'

'Aye, it nearly stopped me. I would have spent the day at Fairyhouse, except for Michael here,' said Fitz.

'What about the arms? Have they landed yet?'

'There's been no news. We'll know when we know.'

'Is there anything you can tell us?' This from the man with the Dublin accent.

Willie Pearse smiled. 'There is. We control the centre of Dublin and we've got men over at the Four Courts, The South Dublin Union, Jacob's Factory, Mount Street Bridge and Boland's Mill. If the Brits come across, they'll get a roasting.'

All the men gave a cheer. 'Now, I want you to meet Jimmy Black. We're expecting an attack from the Brits any moment, so he's going to show you how to use the grenades.'

A tall man with bandy legs and a rolling gait stepped forward, obviously a man who knew the back of a horse from the front.

He held up a round tin with a small metal nipple sticking out of the top. It was the size and shape of a cocoa tin. 'This 'ere is a fuckin' grenade. It ain't a very good fuckin' grenade. I'd much prefer a fuckin' Mills Bomb or one of the German's fuckin' stick grenades.' He spoke with an educated British accent, but an accent interspersed with swearing as if using the foulest words somehow made him one of the people. 'But it will do at a fuckin' pinch.'

One of the men, I think it was Colm Murphy, put his hand up. 'What's it for?'

'What's it for?' repeated Jimmy Black. 'It's for blowing the fuckin' bastards up, that's what it's for. And believe you fuckin' me, when those bastards attack this fuckin' place, you're gonna be glad you 'ave a few of these fuckers to lob down on them. Now, you may have guessed I spent most of my life in the fuckin' Army.'

Fitz stuck his hand up. 'And which Army is that, would you be telling us?'

'The British Army mate. Jesus, when you were suckin' on your mother's tit, I was blowing up stuff all over the world. The Boers didn't know what fuckin' hit them.'

One of the Maynooth men who had come in that morning put up his hand. 'Would you be careful of your language? There's no need to swear or take the Lord's name in vain.'

Jimmy Black stared at him. 'Don't fuckin' swear? Are

my ears hearin' right? You have half the British Army waiting to throw a ton of trouble your way, and you're worried
about my fuckin' language. Jesus H. Christ. You want to
live through this or do you want to die like another fuckin'
martyr?'

The man from Maynooth who two days ago had probably been living in the seminary kept his mouth shut.

'Good.' Jimmy Black shifted his weight from one foot to
the other as if he were still up on a horse and was trying to
change direction. 'Well, staying alive is easy.' He scratched
his long patrician nose with a claw-like finger, pausing for
dramatic effect before speaking again. 'You have to kill the
fuckers before they fuckin' kill you. Clear?'

The men nodded their heads.

'This is how you do it. You see this here metal bit. It's
called a percussion cap for the clever bastards among you.'
Here, he stared pointedly at the man from Maynooth. 'Now
after you've hit it, you've got three seconds before this little
fucker goes off.' He swung his arm above his head to strike
the percussion cap on top of the parapet. 'Do be careful,
ladies. If this goes off while you're still holding it, you can
say goodbye to giving yourself the one-hand shuffle or
dancing the doodle.' He brought the head of the grenade
down on top of the parapet. A metallic crack rang across
the roof of the GPO. 'Now, you have to count to three.
One...two...three...and then you throw it away. Preferably
towards a crowd of British soldiers.'

He held out the tin can at arms' length.

Everybody stared at the can for a second and, seeing
that Jimmy Black wasn't going to throw it away, ducked
down or turned their heads away, desperately looking for
cover from the nails and assorted bits of metal when it exploded.

'Oh, I forgot to tell you, I removed the explosive from this one,' said Jimmy with a smirk. 'Any questions?'

Fitz put up his hand once more. 'Could you show us again, to be sure? But, take us through it a bit more slowly this time.'

* * *

The rest of the day passed quietly, like that dull time as the clouds began to form on the horizon before an immense storm.

They had helped a couple of men from Liverpool set up a radio transmitter on the roof.

'See, said Fitz, 'Even the Brits are here fighting with us.'

'I ain't no Brit,' growled the man from Liverpool.

Fitz didn't answer, instead he turned to stare at the two flags that waved in the Easter breeze at the corner of the roof. On the left over towards Henry Street, the Tricolour with its stripes of white, orange and green fluttered wildly. While on the right, the green flag of the Irish Republic clung to the flagstaff, its heavier fabric unstirred.

'No, there ain't no Brits anymore, not in Ireland at least.'

The man from Liverpool nodded, tucked the spool of wire under his arm and slowly played it out down the stairs.

As he did, a shot rang out from across the street. Michael heard the whine of a bullet, followed by the spark as it ricocheted off the stone of the parapet. Everybody jumped to their posts.

Down below, the looters ignored the shots, carrying on down Sackville Street with their new possessions.

'There's smoke over towards Cathedral Street. I think

Lawrence's is on fire.' Michael pointed out over the parapet. A column of black smoke was reaching up towards the sky, getting thicker with every passing second.

'It's started,' said Fitz pulling back the bolt of his rifle.

For the rest of the evening they stayed alert, nobody slept.

The sounds of looting still drifted up from the streets below, but less now, as if all the good stuff had already been stolen. There were fewer people on the streets now, the excitement of the first day having died down.

Occasionally, people did approach the front door and shout at the men guarding the windows. Most of the time, it was curses but Michael heard one old lady very clearly as she shouted up at them.

'I've come to post a letter.'

'The GPO is closed. Haven't you heard there's a revolution going on, missus?'

'And what's that got to do with me? I'm only after wanting to send some money to me sister in Limerick.'

'Away with you now, the Post Office is closed.' A different voice, an officer's voice this time.

'But how's my sister going to get the money?'

This time no answer.

Michael looked over the parapet. The old woman was still standing there, an old black shawl covering her head. He couldn't see her face but he could hear her voice, the voice of Ireland.

'Well, the least youse fellas could do...' she eventually said, '...is throw me out a few stamps.'

A few seconds later a stone flew out of the window with an envelope wrapped around it. 'Now be off home with you.'

She bent down to pick it up. 'Thank you lads, and may

the blessings of God be on ye.'

She ambled off down Sackville Street in the direction of the river. Michael watched her slow progress till she vanished around a corner. He couldn't help but think of his mother. What would she think of him now? She probably wouldn't approve.

'How could you fight in Dublin with your brother suffering in France?'

He had no answer except there never was a good time to rebel against any government. The only right time was now.

He turned to Fitz. 'What the hell are we doing, Fitz?'

'Making history, Michael.'

He touched the book nestling in his pocket. Would the United Irishmen be proud of them? He hoped so.

He hoped so.

* * *

Occasionally, during the night, shots came from across the other side of the Liffey, just enough to keep them awake and at their posts. Around four there was a fresh volley of rifle fore, this time from the North, near the hospital.

'The Brits are closing in,' he said to Fitz beside him.

'We'll be ready when they come.' Fitz sighted down the barrel of his rifle. He seemed to come alive during their time in the GPO, becoming stronger, more focussed. Gone was the devil-may-care lad that Michael loved. In its place was a man he didn't know anymore.

The world had changed around him and he didn't know when it would stop.

Around seven o'clock in the morning, Willie Pearse leant down and tapped him on the shoulder. 'I've a job for you, Michael.'

'I'm your man.'

'Do you know Dublin well?'

'Like the back of my hand.'

He looked at his watch. 'It's seven, now. At nine, I want you to come down to the lobby. General Connolly has a message he wants you to take to the Mendicity.'

'Can Fitz come with me?'

'No, just you, we can't spare any more men from the GPO.' He stood up straight and addressed the men on the roof. 'Well, it's the third day lads, and we've heard the Brits are coming.'

'About bloody time. That lot would be late for their own funeral.'

'Get yourself ready, make sure your weapons are clean and you all have enough grenades.'

'Will there be any food?' This was from Fitz. He may have changed but his stomach was just the same.

'There may be, but if you feel hungry I'll send up some cans of sardines we found. But don't throw away the oil, we'll need it to cool the guns later.'

'Aye, there you go. I'm to die stinking of fish.'

'Less of the talk of dying, Fitzgerald. Get yourself ready, lads.'

With that he nodded at Michael. 'Don't forget, Dowling.'

Fitz watched him go down the stairs to the next floor. 'What was all that about?'

'Nothing. He has a job for me.'

* * *

113

Michael went down to see General Connolly on the ground floor of the GPO without telling Fitz. There was no point. He would have wanted to come as well, but Willie Pearse had made it clear that he was to go out alone.

The windows of the main hall were all smashed now, with sandbags protecting the gaps and men posted at each one. The door was barricaded too. Inside, the air was dark and thick.

Connolly was in the middle just by the main counter, leaning over a map of Dublin, surrounded by Padraig and Willie Pearse, and Tom Clarke. He had just returned from a tour of inspection of the area around the GPO and was sporting a slight arm wound. As Michael approached, he looked up.

Willie Pearse stepped forward. 'This is Michael Dowling. He's to take the message to Heuston at the Mendicity.'

'You know Dublin well, Mr Dowling?'

He saluted as smartly as he could, 'As well as anybody, General. And a student at UCD.'

'Good man. Here's what I want you to do. Take this way to the Mendicity and give this message to Heuston.' He pointed to the map and followed a route that took in O'-Connell's Bridge and Merchants Quay. 'Let me know what you see and how he is. Have the British attacked him yet? We thought he wouldn't last long, but maybe the Brits don't have as many men as we thought. Come back as quickly as you can.'

He handed me a note written on paper headed with the words The Irish Republic.

'And take him a copy of War News.' It was Clarke who spoke, handing a single sheet of the newspaper. 'We've got to get the news out to our people.'

'Yes, sir.'

Connolly put his good arm around Michael's shoulder. 'Take care, soldier, look after yourself.'

He just nodded his head like a man used to carrying out orders.

'Good man, good man.' Then Connolly turned back to his map and his discussions, he was forgotten. Willie Pearse walked him to the Henry Street exit.

'Tell us what you see, Michael. It would be better if you didn't wear these.' He pointed to the bandolier and belt. 'You should leave the rifle behind as well. I'll take good care of it.'

He patted the pocket of his jacket. 'I'll put the Smith and Wesson in my pocket.'

'But no stupidity now. You're to report back as soon as you can, not try to take on the British Army on your own. Is that understood?'

'Yes, sir.'

'Good man, on your way then. And may God go with you.'

He opened the door and Michael slid out into the street. For a moment, he stopped to gather his thoughts and his bearings. He adjusted his jacket and pulled up his trousers, taking one last look at one of the men standing guard at the window. The man nodded. Michael nodded back, pulling his cap down over his eyes and walking towards Sackville Street.

The street itself was almost empty with most pedestrians keeping to the pavements and the shop doorways. Some were carrying the spoils of their forays into the shops and department stores of Dublin: a woman's dress over the arm of one man, a porcelain sink in another's. A child with a violin and a banjo slung casually over his shoulder. An old woman, ragged shawl over her shoulders, with four top hats perched precariously on her head and, in her hand, a silver mounted cane.

Other people were just standing around and staring, watching the spectacle that was the Rising and waiting for something to happen. A dead horse, left by the Lancers, lay in the street, its eyes glassy and unseeing.

Michael edged his way past a makeshift barricade and pushed his way through the crowd, unchallenged by anybody. As he did, he caught snatches of conversation.

'It's not right, sure it's not. Them fellas in there when our men are in France.'

'When will the trams start running again?'

'They ought to be shot, the lot of them.'

'I haven't had a bite of bread for two days since those buggers started their shenanigans.'

Michael drifted past these conversations, down Sackville Street and across the bridge.

Occasionally, he heard shots coming over from Trinity and St Stephen's Green but that was all. It was as if the whole city was on holiday not in the middle of a revolution. There was even an old man, with his gaily-painted organ grinding out a tune, his monkey, cap in hand, running through the crowd looking for pennies.

Then, as he was about to walk through the crowds of people at the end of the bridge, he heard a loud cheer and the revving of an engine. A truck, filled with British soldiers, drove down the street, followed by another pulling a caisson of ammunition. Soldiers poured out from the back of the truck like khaki ants in search of sugar. The caisson was quickly unlimbered and the truck reversed back up the street.

The crowds of people stood around, their hands in their

pockets, like country farmers admiring the livestock at a fair. Instead, they were admiring the arrival of the British soldiers.

Michael hurried down Merchants Quay towards the Mendicity before the soldiers could set up a cordon. The music of the organ grinder mixing with the sound of more revving engines and the sharp rap of military boots on cobbled pavement.

As he rushed down the Quay, keeping close to the Wall, he began to see fewer and fewer people. The air became denser, more febrile. There was the scent of gunpowder all around, infesting the walls of the houses and the shops, hanging like a mist of the Liffey.

Up ahead he could see the dark shape of the old poorhouse. A hastily built barricade was thrown across Usher's Quay in front of it. He walked up to two young men who were guarding the barricade. 'A message from General Connolly for Sean Heuston.'

'What's the password?' asked one of them. The other lowered his rifle towards Michael, the bayonet inches away from his chest.

'Password? Nobody told me about any bloody password.'

The young man who had asked the question couldn't have been more than eighteen. He took off his cap and scratched his head. 'I'm not supposed to let anybody in without the password.'

The bayonet wavered in front of Michael's eyes, the man holding it said nothing.

'Listen, my name is Michael Dowling, I'm from E company, 4th Battalion. My Captain is Willie Pearse and my Lieutenant is Eamon Bulfin. I've an urgent message for Heuston.'

A light seemed to go off in the young man's eyes. 'Oh, you'll know Fitz then. Declan Fitzgerald? Mad for the horses is himself.'

Thank God for Fitz, thought Michael. 'Aye, I know Fitz. He's in my company.'

'You'd better pass then, friend.'

Michael edged past the sharp point of the bayonet and the silent man on the other end of it. 'By the way, what's the password in case I need it again?'

'The one for here is Saoirse. And for over there,' he pointed to the dome of the Four Courts across the river, 'it's Freedom. Not many of the fellas over there have the speaking of the Irish. Sean is up the steps on the right.'

Michael hurried into the old institution, for so long the only place where the poor of the streets of Dublin could get a bowl of soup or a hunk of bread. He climbed up some old stone stairs, past three bundles of dishevelled rags clutching Lee Enfields, to the first floor and found an exhausted Sean Heuston sitting in the middle of a room staring into space.

Michael coughed.

'Who are you?' barked Heuston suddenly alive and bristling with anger.

'Begging your pardon, sir. I have a message from General Connolly.' He reached into his pocket and passed the folded paper over to the man.

He stared at it for a few moments before opening it quickly and scanning the contents.

'What's your name?'

'Michael Dowling, sir.'

'Do you have your wits about you, Mr Dowling?'

Michael didn't know how to answer.

'Do you have your wits about you, Mr Dowling?'

118

Heuston repeated.

'I do, sir.'

'Well, remember this and tell it to General Connolly. I already sent one of my own men with the message but a reminder will do no harm. The Brits are massing in the Royal Hospital, I'm sure they will attack soon. I don't know how long we will last. We managed to push them back yesterday but it was a close run thing. If we are to hold, we need reinforcements. Have you got that?' The man's voice was old, far older than his years. It was as if his throat had aged since the Rising, becoming older, courser, hoarser.

Michael nodded.

'Now tell it back to me.'

Michael did as he was told, remembering Heuston's dispatch word for word.

'Good man, what did you see on your way here?'

'I think the Brits are bringing up artillery. I saw a caisson being unlimbered at the bottom of Westmoreland Street and troops forming a cordon.'

'They mean to bomb us out.' Once again, he stared into mid-air. Michael could see how tired the man was. A tiredness that seemed to seep out from his eyes.

'Have you had anything to eat?'

Michael shook his head.

'Well, we have a few scraps of stale bread and a couple of tins of bully beef left. You're welcome to feast on that.'

A bullet struck the wall outside. Immediately, Heuston was on his feet. 'Here they are, lads. At your posts...'

There were muffled shouts from the floor above and the three bundles of rags rushed into the room, taking positions behind sandbags at the windows.

More shots thudded into the walls on the outside of the Mendicity, sending shards of granite shooting into the air.

One bullet struck the far wall above Michael's head. He threw himself down on to the ground.

'There's himself on the roof of the Royal,' said one of the bundles of rags, before firing in the direction of the hospital. 'One day I'll get the wee shite.'

Another bullet thudded into the wall, showering Michael with lumps of plaster.

'I suggest you stay here a while, Dowling,' said Heuston. 'The Brits will keep firing now, but if it's like yesterday, they'll knock off at lunchtime.'

'If it's all the same to you, sir. I'll be getting back to the GPO.'

Michael stood up. As he did, a bullet whistled past his head and embedded itself in the wooden cabinet behind him.

'You will stay here until one. That's an order, Dowling.'

'Yes, sir.'

On the floor above, Michael heard a volley of shots ring out and a voice shouting, 'Got the bastard.'

The men at the windows began firing too, working their Howth rifles and Mausers with a concentrated ferocity.

From his position behind one of the window casements, Heuston shouted, 'Make yourself useful, Dowling, bring up more ammunition from the basement.'

Michael did as he was told and, for the next two hours, ferried boxes of ammo up to the men at the windows of the Mendicity.

As Heuston had predicted, the rifle fire slackened off to nothing at the dot of one pm.

'I'd take the time to make my way back to the GPO if I were you, Mr Dowling.'

'You don't want me to stay, sir?'

'My messenger hasn't returned so you need to go back

120

and let them know what's going on. The Brits are working their way around us. We'll hang on for as long as we can.' The voice, so animated just a few moments ago during the fighting, was now like that of an old man tired of waking up each morning.

'Yes, sir.'

'Good. I wouldn't go down the Quay if I were you. Too many Brits coming out of the woodwork. I'd go across Church St bridge and past the Four Courts. Our men still control the area, according to my reports.'

Michael saluted and it was returned by Heuston with a touch of his finger to the side of his head.

'Good luck, sir.'

'I'm going to need it, Dowling. By God, I'm going to need it.'

Michael turned to go, taking one last look at Sean Heuston. The man was staring into mid-air again, unaware of Michael's presence. The late April light shone lazily through the window, throwing the man's face into sharp relief. Like a statue, thought Michael, just like a statue.

He hurried down the stairs and out onto the Quay. The same two men were still guarding the barricade, their feet surrounded by spent bullet cases. He hurried past them and shouted 'Saoirse.'

'Say hello to Fitz for me,' the young one shouted back. 'Tell him Loch Allen won at Fairyhouse. The bookmaker has his money for him.'

'I will. Take care.'

'Aye, take care yourself, watch out for the English. You can't miss them, they're the ones with the guns and the tin hats.'

Michael smiled and hurried over the Quay towards the Bridge. The sun was high over Dublin, a few clouds lazily chasing each other over the sky. A blackbird sat on his perch next to the river, claiming the world and the patch of grass as his and his alone.

He turned onto Church Street bridge going towards the Four Courts. The end of the bridge was barricaded and he could see armed men standing behind it.

When he was halfway across, there was a soft whoosh like somebody expelling air from his cheeks, and then seconds later, an explosion in a building facing the river.

Michael ducked down behind the parapet of the bridge, covering his head with his arms. He looked around him. Others were doing exactly the same, surprised by the noise of the explosion.

Another thump from over towards Trinity, a whine in the air and another explosion, closer now. He peered over the parapet. One whole side of a building on the Quay towards Sackville Street had collapsed revealing a mass of wood, slates and red bricks. Michael could see into one of the rooms. Purple wallpaper. Who would choose purple wallpaper for a house?

Another soft pop on the far side of the river and a cloud of off-white smoke rising to heaven. He stuck his head back down beneath the balustrade of the bridge. But no explosion this time. Or at least, none that he could see.

The men at the barricade were standing up, shouting and waving at the people on the bridge. He got up and ran doubled up towards them, moving as fast as he could. Others were doing the same. A woman pushing two children in front of her, shouting in a high-pitched voice, 'Run and don't stop', over and over again as if the more she shouted it, the faster her children would run. The children were confused, not knowing what to do. The youngest was crying, upset by the shouting of his mother.

He ran to the tallest of the children and picked him up, tucking him under his arm. Then shouted at the woman to follow. The woman seeing what he had done picked up the crying child and ran after him.

Behind them, another soft crump as the shell left the barrel of the gun.

Michael ran past the outside edge of the barricade and ducked down beneath it, putting the child back on his feet. The mother pushed through after him and grabbed hold of her child without saying a word to him.

'The Brits have started the shelling. It won't be long now.' The voice came from a man with a ginger beard and field glasses pinned to his eyes. 'They've got eighteen pounders over at Trinity and a gunship on the river.' He pointed his glasses down the Liffey. 'I hope to God nobody is left inside Liberty Hall.'

Michael wasn't sure to whom the man was talking but it wasn't him. He stood up and dusted down his trousers. The woman and her children were rushing away down Church Street.

He sat back down again behind the barricade. From across the river, in the direction of the Mendacity, he could hear the sound of firing. The rat-a-tat of machine guns now had joined the sharp crack of the Lee Enfields. He thought about going back to rejoin Heuston and his men in the old poorhouse. To make one last stand in that old institution, surrounded by the memories of all the Dublin poor that infested the walls.

As he sat behind the barricade, the shelling ceased and the noise of firing at the Mendacity increased. More volleys, more machine guns, the explosions of grenades, and more smoke over the dark, satanic buildings.

And then it too suddenly went quiet.

The man with the field glasses took them away from his eyes. 'The Mendacity's gone.'

That was all, nothing more. A statement of fact.

The shelling began again down the river. The dull boom of cannon from a riverboat directed at the Liberty Hall.

Michael made up his mind. 'What's the safest way to the GPO?'

'Ah, now the shelling's started it's all much of a muchness. You takes your chances whichever way you goes. My advice to you is go home.'

With that, the man with the ginger beard walked away towards the Four Courts. As he did so, there was an explosion over at the south-east corner of the building. Smoke drifted lazily up to the sky and flames darted out from the windows.

'But if I were you, I wouldn't go that way.' The man pointed at the fire. 'The Brits have the range.'

Michael looked down Church Street. It was now empty of civilians, the woman and her children had vanished. In the distance, he could see another barricade up at the corner of Mary Street, next to the old church.

Michael began to walk that way, keeping in to the side of the Four Courts, opposite to the direction from which the shells were being fired. He wondered if he could take the man's advice and go back to St Enda's and Rathfarnham, but dismissed the idea as soon as it occurred to him. He had a job to do. Go back to the GPO and report to Connolly what Heuston had told him. Nothing else mattered now. Nothing else could matter.

He turned right and went down behind the back of the Four Courts, passing the men mounting the barricade. None of them paid him any notice, staring out down the road down towards Smithfield.

The streets were eerily quiet now, the people having rushed to the safety of their homes as soon as the shelling had started. He could still hear the crump of the shells and the occasional explosion as they found their targets. There seemed to be more guns firing now, or, at least, he could hear the sound of more guns.

The sky had darkened but was not completely dark. Instead, a red glow burned and brightened in front of him. In the air, he could smell burning and the sharp tang of cordite, like the days after Bonfire Night. Guy Fawkes should have blown up Parliament and the lot of them in it. Now, that would be a day worth celebrating.

He crossed Greek Street, keeping close to the shops and houses on the right. Here and there, windows had been broken to enable people to get to the treasures inside. His feet crunched on the broken glass that lay strewn across the pavement.

The dark form of a man stepped out in front of him. Michael reached for the revolver in his jacket, gripping its handle and wrapping his finger around the trigger.

The man just stood there in front of him, not moving an inch.

Michael called out to him. 'Who are you? What do you want?' Desperately, he tried to keep the nervousness from his voice.

At the sound of his question, the man melted back into the darkness from which he had come. Michael shook his head. Had anyone been there or had he imagined it all? He stared into the space where the shape had been. Nothing. Get a grip on yourself, Michael Dowling.

He walked on down Mary Street, past the market on his right, its usual hustle and bustle replaced by the stillness of a morgue. Up ahead he could see flames shooting out from the top floors of a house. The upper corner was missing where a shell has struck it. Three men were trying to fight the flames with nothing more than buckets of water. As Michael edged past, he glanced across at a pile of bricks and plaster and wood that had fallen from the house. In the middle of the debris, something small and limp hung between two wooden laths.

He stepped closer to it, tripping over the edge of the pavement as he did. In the flickering light of the flames, the shape became clearer, more obvious. Four little fingers pointed upwards towards the sky.

He took one more step closer and followed the fingers down past a palm and across the dust-covered skin of a child's arm lying against a lump of white plaster. The arm seemed to appear and disappear, one minute illuminated and the next blending in with all the debris from the building.

Michael looked up to where the face should have been.

There was nothing.

Up above his head, a shock of red and orange flame roared like a dragon, shooting up to the sky.

In the fierce light, he saw it.

A young girl's face, no more than three years old, staring out from beneath the pile of plaster, eyes dead to the world, dead to life.

One of the firemen shouted across at him, 'Oy, you, get away from there. Do you not hear me? The whole lot is going to come down.'

He backed away from the pile of rubble, but his eyes were drawn back to the small hand. It was holding a ribbon. A pink silk ribbon. He could see the tiny nails against the fabric, half-formed, ungrown, unbitten.

The flames shot up towards the sky once more, accompanied by the sound of roaring, like a monster unleashed from the earth.

Michael backed away from the fire, his eyes fixed on the little girl. Her dead body forming and unforming in front of his eyes as the flames burned fiercely with an orange glow. The flames of hell here on earth.

His back hit a brick wall on the far side of the street. He tried to move further backwards, trying to get away from the horror, but the wall wouldn't let him.

The child was still there, though, her hand still clutching the pink ribbon.

The firemen had unrolled a hose from their truck and began to pump water onto the flames, but it just seemed to enrage them as they burned brighter, shooting higher into the sky.

A fireman pushed him down the road, away from the burning house. 'Get away, why don't you? This lot'll come down any second.'

He stumbled away towards the GPO, not looking behind him. Up ahead and to his right, more fires were turning the sky red and orange.

Red sky at night, shepherd's delight. The words from his youth came into his head. But there were no shepherds in Dublin, not anymore.

The image of the child's hand clutching the pink ribbon stayed with Michael Dowling for the following days. And, the more he thought about it, the less he could remember. Was the ribbon really pink? Or were the reds of the flames colouring the image. Was the child really dead? If he had dug beneath the debris would the child be still alive? Could he have saved the child?

These questions haunted him as he staggered back into the GPO, and was welcomed back by his comrades. Somehow, he composed himself and reported what he had seen to General Connolly.

'The Brits have started shelling the city. We haven't heard anything from Sean Heuston since you saw him. I'm thinking the Mendicity has been captured.'

Michael thought about the two young men, guarding the barricade and wondered what had become of them.

The General coughed. 'Go and get yourself something to eat. You look like you've seen a ghost.'

He found Fitz down in the basement where the canteen had been set up. He was talking to Bridget.

'Welcome back, Michael Dowling. And how did you enjoy your little jaunt around the bright lights of our city?'

There was no answer from Michael.

Fitz saw the terrible tiredness in his eyes. 'You must be hungry. Get yourself some of Bridget's delicious stew and you can tell me what you saw.'

Bridget ladled out a large helping of brown sludge into a mess tin. They sat down at one of the tables that had been made from upturned crates.

'People are dying, Fitz.'

'What do you expect, Michael, we're at war.'

Michael took a spoonful of stew. As he put it in his mouth, he realised he hadn't eaten anything that day. 'Children are dying, Fitz,' he eventually mumbled.

Fitz rubbed his nose and looked at him with his ice blue eyes. His voice softened, gone was the playful tone, the smirk at life and the world. In its place was a new anger. An anger Michael had never seen or heard before from Fitz. 'Children have always died, Michael. Whether it was from lack of food or lack of shoes. From TB or measles. From poverty and injustice and cruelty. Remember the famine. A third of our people were dying of starvation and we were still exporting grain and cattle to England. At least now, they are dying for something.'

'A free Ireland?'

'Yes, a free Ireland. So we can decide our futures for ourselves, and not let any bastard Englishman dictate our lives.' Fitz put his large hand on Michael's arm. 'You need to sleep. Put your head down in the corner over there. Bridget will look after you.'

Michael stood up quickly, 'I've got duty on the roof...'

Fitz's heavy hand forced him down again. 'There's plenty of men up there. You take a rest. I'll wake you if you're needed.'

Michael nodded his head slowly. A terrible weariness had come over him. Tiredness that seeped into his bones infesting his heart and soul.

'You'll wake me up.'

'I will. And so will Bridget.' Fitz smiled across at the woman behind her table. 'Ah, but it breaks my heart that the first thing you will see when you wake up tomorrow morning is her lovely face. That pleasure should be mine and mine alone.'

For the first time in a long time, Michael smiled.

Chapter 19

Dublin. November 17, 2015.

The flight on Aer Lingus was uneventful. Only the pilot's lovely brogue as they prepared to take off reminded her that she was on her way to Ireland.

Manchester Airport had been a scrum. Despite making vast profits over the years. She had taken a cab to the terminal and the fun had begun. There were long queues to check in and even longer queues to go through the security checks. Young children, tattooed men, old wives in peasant blouses off to seek some winter sun, crowded in long lines, waiting to go through the scanners.

The security people were friendly enough in that bluff Northern manner. 'This way, love. Take off your shoes and belt, please.' But the whole process reminded her of the film she had once seen of the old Chicago stockyards, with long lines of cows waiting to be slaughtered. She knew it had to be done, modern life and modern terrorists made it indispensable, but there had to be a better way of going about it.

The stewardess offered her tea or coffee. She chose the latter as the least worse of two evils. Paul had been shocked when the brick came through the window. He had insisted on calling the police at Didsbury Station. After half an hour a young uniform came round with a PCSO. The detectives were either too stretched or too lazy to bother. She could have given somebody a call but she knew there was no point.

The young uniform, he can't have been more than a year

on the job, asked a few questions;

Any rows with the neighbours?

Any disagreements at work?

Anything stolen?

He directed most of his questions at Paul as the man of the house. Sexism was still alive and well and living in Manchester. She didn't bother to tell him she was an ex-copper. Somebody might twig it later, but better to leave this young one in a state of ignorance.

Why had somebody put a brick through her window? She thought back to her cases. Had anybody just come out of prison and wanted to level the scores. She had nicked a few tearaways in her time, but most were confirmed thieves who thought a stretch inside just a cost of doing business. She couldn't remember anybody with a grudge against her. And why now? Why would someone throw a brick through her window right now?

What did the message say? Leave it alone. What was 'it'? Her investigation into the family of John Hughes? But she had barely started, only making a few phone calls and visiting Herbert Levy. Ever since she had started on the case, she couldn't shake the feeling that she was being watched. An annoying sensation. That morning she had looked over her shoulder a few times as she walked through the airport, but saw nobody. Perhaps, she was jumpier than usual after the events at her home but the feeling was there. Was somebody watching her?

She sipped her coffee. It tasted bitter and sour at the same time. How airlines managed to screw up the easiest drink on earth to make was beyond her. She placed the plastic coffee cup on the tray in front of her. She couldn't drink any more of that dish water.

The brick must have been aimed at her, Paul had no enemies she knew of. He wasn't the type to make enemies or friends. It was a warning and not a very subtle one. Why did somebody not want her to investigate this case? Was it the Irish angle? Or the fact that it concerned the IRA or, at least, a forerunner of the IRA? How had anybody known?

Then she thought back to the phone calls to Ireland. Had the librarian talked to someone? Or was it Herbert Levy? Had the old fence been pissed off with her visit?

The more she dwelt on it, the clearer the message became and the angrier it made her. How dare somebody throw a brick through her window. When she found him, and it was a him, she would break both his arms and shove the brick down his throat. How dare he invade her home?

But who was he? That was the question. And why did he do it?

Despite herself, she drank another mouthful of coffee and immediately wished she hadn't. She put the cup down and breathed out. 'Calm yourself, Jayne. Calm yourself,' she said out loud.

The young man sitting next to her looked across. 'Don't worry, I sometimes get nervous during flights too.'

She smiled back at him as sweetly as she could. 'Thank you,' she managed to mumble, when she really wanted to shout out, 'I've just had a brick put through my kitchen window. I'm not nervous, I'm furious and I could kill someone right now!'

'I do this flight every week. It's as safe as the Bank of Ireland.'

Jayne was just about to remind him that a few years ago the Bank of Ireland had nearly gone bust, but she thought better of it and smiled instead. He went back to staring out of the window.

She wanted to drink some more of the dish water masquerading as coffee, but couldn't face it. It was lucky that Paul hadn't made the connection to her new case. Neither did the young uniform. He went off back to the station to file his report. Paul called in a glazier to do a temporary fix, muttering about the unnecessary cost and worried about what his boss would think.

She would have to handle both of them when she got back to Manchester. Eventually, the detectives would get off their fat arses and come to pay her a visit, particularly when her name flagged up on their computers. While, Paul would worry at it like a sheepdog until it eventually occurred to him to ask her what she was working on.

It took his mind off her trip to Dublin though, thank God for that. She couldn't face another row.

The pilot's soft lilt came over the loudspeaker again. 'Well, no sooner than we're in the air than we're on the way down. Dublin in twenty minutes. Cabin crew prepare for landing.'

A quick hop across the pond that was the Irish Sea. Funny that such a small separation between two small islands had produced such radically different cultures. She had noticed the Special Branch man was checking all the passengers on the flight. He didn't see her, but she knew he was one of the spooks, remembered him from a course they had both been on.

Funny, after nearly twenty years of peace in Northern Ireland, they were still checking the passengers. Somebody had to do it, she thought. Cushy number down at the airport. She would have hated it, though. She preferred the thrill of the chase, working the streets, having cases of your own. She hated these bureaucratic jobs; watching flights or ferries, making notes in a file, clocking in and out.

The plane bumped down on the runway in Dublin. The

pilot's voice came over the tannoy once again, 'We have just landed at the most beautiful city in the world. For those Irish returning home, we wish you a fond welcome. And for those visiting for the first time, have a great craic.'

She was here. Would she be able to find John Hughes' father?

Chapter 20

Dublin. November 17, 2015.

She checked into the Woodham Hotel. The room overlooked O'Connell Street and could probably do with a refurbishment but she didn't care. She wasn't here to relax and be pampered. She was here to work.

The Central Office of UCD, now called NUI, was located at 49, Merrion Square. She left her bag in her room, grabbed her laptop and briefcase and stepped out onto the bustling street.

A long line of taxis waited on the street in front of her. Should she take one? No, better to walk and get a feel for the city. According to her map, the address couldn't be more than a mile away across the river.

She turned left and walked down the broad street towards the river and the statue of O'Connell himself at the end. Pedestrians jostled for a right of way, buses blew their horns, car brakes squealed. It was like the centre of any other city on earth. The buildings on the opposite side of the road were a particularly ugly utilitarian mixture of brick and cheap concrete.

Just like the centre of Manchester before the IRA blew it up, she laughed to herself. There were till some people who thought the City Council had paid the IRA to put a van full of explosives next to the Arndale Centre to get government money for regeneration. It was Manchester's version of a conspiracy theory.

After three hundred yards of nondescript restaurants, tourist shops, emporia selling green costumes and t-shirts with leprechauns, she passed the statue of Daniel O'Connell lording it over the street that bore his name and crossed the dark green sludge that was the Liffey. The modern buildings disappeared and a new Dublin opened up. Or rather, a Georgian Dublin, altogether more elegant and refined. It was like one of those people with a broad Manchester accent whose voice changed when they answered the phone. Hyacinth Bucket becoming Hyacinth Boukay.

She turned left beneath a large portico and the world had changed yet again, another face of Dublin. Trinity College her map said, a place of beauty and quiet in the midst of the chaos. God, she hated the crap that copywriters and their clients insisted on spewing out. But the blurb was right in one respect. It was beautiful.

Her pace slowed and, for a moment she forgot her search and her client and her husband, just drinking in the November sun, feeling the bite of a cold breeze on her face, closing her eyes, imagining herself back here in 1915.

She smelt coal smoke in the air, heard the clang of the trams as they crossed over the points, traced the clop-clop of a Shire horse as it delivered a wagon load of beer, heard the calls of the newspaper boys as they shouted of battles and death and destruction far away in France.

What was that? She twisted her head to feel the whispers on the wind. Whispers of a rising, of freedom, of insurrection. She opened her eyes. They didn't often come, these 'moments' as she liked to call them. But ever since she had been a child, they had visited her at the strangest times, usually brought on by a place, smell or a person. It was like the past had come alive and she was surrounded by it. She was still herself of course, and still aware, but she was no longer in her own time but transported back to another, long dead.

Her father had always teased her about it, saying it was just the product of an overzealous imagination. But the moments had remained, still occurring, even when she was in the police.

She remembered going to the scene of one particularly grizzly killing in Moss Side. One minute she was standing at the entrance to the door, SOCO officers walking past her dressed in their white coveralls, the next she was watching and hearing the man attack his wife with a butcher's knife. The blood spurting across the wall, her cries for mercy, his snarls, the grating noise as the knife cut through the skull, snagging on some bone, and his breathless grunts as he tried to pull it out.

It was as if she were with him in the room at the same time as the crimes were committed. Even stranger, when the pathologist produced his report, all the details she had imagined when she had entered the house were written there in black and white, right down to the incisions into the bone of the skull.

She shook her head. Must concentrate, can't dwell in the past, not now, not here.

She looked at her watch, 3.15. She had to move quickly. Otherwise, the office might shut for the day.

She walked across the courtyard, striding more quickly now, not letting herself be sidetracked. Under another portico and she found herself walking beside a cricket pitch. The British had definitely been here. If there was one thing that defined a British presence, it was a cricket pitch. She never understood the attraction herself. Maybe, it was creating an area the old colonial administrators could call home in the centre of something utterly alien.

Across a quiet park, courting couples sitting on benches as they had sat for hundreds of years, and out through a metal gate onto a narrow lane.

Peace and quiet were behind her now, as she climbed some steps back onto the main road, clogged with waiting traffic, spewing its light blue exhaust into the air. Air that smelt and tasted so different from just a few moments ago in the centre of Trinity College.

She hurried down the road, crossed at the traffic lights and Dublin changed again. A Chameleon of a city, or a vaudeville artist changing its costumes to entice and entrance the audience. Merrion Square was perfectly Georgian, like many of the squares in the West End of London, but more elegant and infinitely more sophisticated. She turned right at the end of one of the corners and there it was, 49 Merrion Square. A large bronze plaque on the door announced the National University of Ireland's General Office. She pushed open the door and walked up to reception.

Nobody was there.

She tapped the top of a bell on the counter and a few seconds later a head popped round the corner. 'Can I be helping you?' The speaker was a large woman wearing horn-rimmed glasses and a twinset, complete with a string of pearls. The voice was efficient rather than friendly.

'I'm looking for a relative who I think went to the university.'

'Was it before or after 2000? We went online for people who graduated in the new millennia. Makes it terribly efficient, but a little cold, if you know what I mean.'

Thinking of the hours she spent in front of her laptop, Jayne nodded. 'I certainly do. I'm afraid he may have graduated during the war.'

'The 'Emergency', we call it. De Valera loved his euphemisms and his neutrality.'

'No, not that one. The First World War.'

'That's going back a fair bit. Was he your granddad?'

Jayne nodded, biting her lip at the blatant lie.

'There's a form for that, under here I am thinking.' She reached beneath the counter. 'Here it is. Just complete it with your name and address, email, and details, and we'll send you the search in ten days, plus a copy of any degrees he may have taken at the college.'

'There's another problem, I only know his initials. I think they were MD.'

'You don't know your own grandfather's name?'

'I was adopted,' Jayne invented quickly, 'I'm trying to find my past and who I am.'

'Aren't we all.' The woman thought for a moment. 'It will be more difficult with just initials. There could be a lot of fellas with the initials MD graduating at that time. Give me a second.' She went back behind the wall, returning a few moments later with a tall, older man with a shock of grey hair pulled back from his forehead, wearing an elegant green tweed jacket, tortoise shell spectacles and a cream cravat. A distinguished-looking man who seemed to have stepped out of a 1950s novel. 'I've explained your problem to Sean, he knows the archives far better than I ever could.'

'Madam,' he said formally, 'there are two sets of records that may be of use to you. A list of undergraduates attending the College exists for those years, as does a list of those who matriculated during that period.'

Jayne's brow furrowed at the strange word. She had never been to university herself and was unaware of the terms they used.

He noticed. 'Took exams in that period. Nobody matriculates anymore, a shame really. We could search through those years but we would probably turn up quite a few

139

MDs. How would you know which one he is if you don't have a surname?'

Jayne realised he was right. How could she know which was the right MD? And he may not have even gone to UCD or graduated from there, maybe he had just sneaked into the library and stolen the book. 'Thank you for your time. I realise it's a bit of a wild goose chase. Sorry to have bothered you.'

She turned away and walked towards the door. That was it, any possibility of finding the elusive MD of the inscription seemed to have vanished. This trip to Dublin was another in a long line of wild goose chases. Paul would be pleased. She could hear his voice now revelling in her disappointment, 'How you could think that you could discover the identity of a man from a book inscription is beyond me. You're a good detective, Jayne, but not that good.'

She wouldn't give him the pleasure of reminding her of the difficulties of her job. As she opened the door to leave the office, she turned round and gave it one last go. 'But there's one other piece of information I have.'

The man in the green tweed jacket was still stood behind the counter watching her leave. He smiled. A friendly smile. 'What is it?'

'I think he may have been in the Dublin Brigade of the Irish Volunteers during the Easter Rising.' She took out the picture of the cap badge. 'We know he wore this badge.'

It was a stab in the dark. She didn't know he wore that badge at all. She just knew it had been on John Hughes' lapel when he arrived in America.

The man looked at the image. 'The archives have many records from that time. Letters, posters, and diaries from the participants. I don't think there is a list of Volunteers from the university. They weren't terribly welcome at that

140

time, you see.'

She loved his old-fashioned formality, so like her own father. 'It's not much help, is it?'

'Not here. But you might want to have a chat with Captain Ellis at the military archives in Cathal Brugha barracks. I'll give him a call if you like?'

'Could you? That would be great.'

He picked up the phone and dialled a number. He explained her situation very quickly and then listened, nodding his head as people do. 'Can she book a time to see you?'

Jayne nodded her head, pleased at his proactivity on her behalf.

'Tomorrow, at 10.30 am?' He looked at Jayne. She nodded again. 'Ok, that's confirmed. The woman's name is...'

'Jayne Sinclair.'

He put down the phone. 'Captain Ellis will see you tomorrow, Mrs Sinclair. He knows more about the Easter Rising than anybody else. If he can't help you, nobody can.'

'Thank you, Sean, for all your help. You've been a Godsend.' She leant over the counter and planted a kiss on his cheek.

The old man blushed, wiping his face. 'Happy to help.' He stammered finally as Jayne was closing the door.

Chapter 21

Manchester. November 17, 2015.

He relaxed back on his bed in the Premier Inn. All these places were starting to look the same to him. They were even beginning to smell the same. That hint of slightly damp carpet in the air that seemed to get everywhere; in the closets, in the towels, between his sheets, on his skin.

The target had understood the subtle hint of a brick through her kitchen window. He had watched her this morning leave her house with a suitcase, head to the airport and board a flight to Dublin. She had obviously done a runner. His little message had worked.

It was noon. He would ring the client and tell him of his success. Another job well done with the minimum of effort and stress. He picked up his burner. Use the phone once and then throw it away. Luckily, these were cheap in the shops in Rusholme. Three for the price of two. Like everything else these days, they were on discount. Who paid full price for anything anymore? Except his clients, of course.

He dialled the number and waited for the client's voice to come on the line. It rang three times before it was answered.

'Turner here.' That was his nom de guerre. Nobody knew his real name. Even for him, it was lost in that age before he became a soldier and learnt his trade. 'The message has been delivered and the person involved has decided to leave town.' Keep everything vague, you never knew who was listening at GCHQ. One of his old mates, perhaps.

'She's gone to Dublin.'

'How did you know?' The client was smarter than he thought. Perhaps he wasn't the only operative working this case. The client was rich enough to afford his fee after all. If there were another watcher, he would have to be careful.

'She's gone to Dublin for work. Your message was too subtle. It needs to be clearer now. More precise. Do you understand?'

He thought for a moment. The job was escalating which meant more money for him. He was pleased, he enjoyed an escalation, it added some pleasure to the job satisfaction. 'Is this full-time or just half-time?' His notes to the client gave certain words to be used in case of an escalation. Full-time was a termination of the target. Half-time was a warning with bodily harm. He enjoyed using football terminology in his notes. Easy to deny the meaning if anyone was listening. We were just talking about football, governor, honest.

He heard the client flicking through the pages he had been sent. 'Neither for the moment. I want you to go to Dublin, find out what she's up to. Get her computer. I want to see what she's discovered so far. Don't screw it up.'

The bluntness of this client annoyed him. He wasn't using the code words but issuing orders in clear language.

'Do you understand? Report back to me when you are in the city.' The officer's voice again. He was losing control of this. But before he could respond the line went dead.

'Fuck you and your mother,' he shouted into the dead phone.

Turner was tempted to ignore the order and stay where he was. There were plenty of other clients who wanted his services, he didn't need any aggro from this one. But the fee was good and he'd already been paid up front. If he were to quit now, the client would put it around that he had lost his bottle, couldn't take the heat anymore.

'Fuck it.' Time to get on a flight to Dublin. A quick call to an old mate living in the city and he would be picked up at the airport, have a driver, a bit of extra muscle in case it was needed and some local knowledge. You could never underestimate the benefit of local knowledge. He had learnt that in Iraq and Afghanistan.

He dialled the number. 'Ronnie, it's Dave Turner. How you doing? Listen, are you up for a couple of days of free-lance? It's worth a monkey to you.'

He could hear that Ronnie was pleased about the dosh. Ex-soldiers always needed ready cash wherever they lived. And Ronnie needed money more than most. A little fond-ness for the ponies was his problem. For 500 quid, he would kill his mother and bury her too. 'I'll send you the flight details. And, one last thing, you need to find a woman for me. Not that sort of woman, fuckwit. Her name's Jayne Sinclair and she arrived in the city today. You'll get on it? Good. See you this evening.'

Great, that was sorted. Ronnie was one of the best men he'd ever known. An Irishman who somehow found himself serving in the British Army. Well, it takes all sorts to fight wars and the Army wasn't that choosy.

A quick check with Manchester Airport and he knew the next flight was at 5.30 pm. Time to pack his stuff and check out of the hotel. He wouldn't miss the smells.

He threw the burner in the bin after removing the sim card. He was overly careful but nobody ever got killed by being too cautious.

After ten years in this game, he wasn't going to take it easy now.

A smile crossed his face. It looked like this job was fi-nally getting interesting.

Chapter 22

Dublin. November 17, 2015.

'Hello, is that Jayne Sinclair?'

She had picked up her mobile while half-asleep and answered the call. The neon green numbers on the digital clock beside the bed read 23.30. 'Speaking,' she mumbled down the phone.

'It's Richard Hughes, Mrs Sinclair. I'm just ringing to let you know that my uncle has had a relapse. I'm at the hospital now.'

She was instantly awake. Years of being called late at night by the police had given her the ability to instantly click her brain into gear. 'What's happened? Is he okay?'

'It doesn't look like the end is far away.'

'But he told me he still had two months to live.'

'He's been pushing himself hard recently. I told him not to come to England but he insisted.'

'Can I talk to him?'

'He's sleeping now, sedated.'

'Do you want me to continue my investigations?'

There was silence on the end of the phone as if Richard Hughes was thinking of the correct answer. 'I suppose you should. He may get better but the doctors are not offering any hope. He drifts in and out of consciousness, becoming agitated when he is awake. That's why the doctor has sedated him.'

'Agitated?'

'Keeps asking about you, I'm afraid. 'Has she found him? Has she found him?' Over and over again.'

'I haven't discovered anything concrete yet. I've got a few leads I'm following up in Dublin, but there was so little to go on...'

'Don't worry, Mrs Sinclair, I understand.'

'I'll try to move faster, give him the closure he needs.'

'As you wish, Mrs Sinclair.'

'Where are you now?'

'Still in Manchester, at the Royal Infirmary.'

'I'll be back just as soon as I've found something concrete.'

'You'd better hurry, Mrs Sinclair.'

She put her phone down on the bedside table. The truth was she didn't have much at the moment. Perhaps, there were no links to the Easter Rising and Dublin? Perhaps, this was all just a wild goose chase with the real truth much closer to home? She hadn't even begun to look into the background of John Hughes' mother yet. She would do that when she went back to England, and do it quickly. She had so little time left, the truth about this case was getting further and further away, like a tide ebbing out into the distance.

She stayed awake for the rest of the night unable to sleep, listening to the sounds of Dublin below her window; the roar of the night buses, the crash of broken glass, the shouts of drunken men as they wended their way wearily home.

She thought about calling her husband but she didn't want to speak to him right now. He would just ask her when she was coming back. And the truth was she didn't have an answer. She didn't know if she was ever going back to him

Chapter 23

Cathal Brugha Barracks was just a short walk from her hotel in the cold November air of a Dublin day. She decided to leave her laptop and valuables in the safe in her room, taking just a notepad and John Hughes' book and certificates with her.

She approached the guard room of the barracks and a young soldier guided her to the archives section.

Behind a desk sat a tall man in army uniform. She coughed and he looked up. 'Captain Ellis?'

'And you must be Mrs Sinclair. Sean rang me yesterday.' He stood up and shook her hand. A firm handshake but not crushing. 'Just give me a sec, will you? The Army loves its forms even more than it loves its uniforms.' He sat down again, completing his requisition quickly before placing it carefully in his out tray. 'I only want a few pens. It's like the Spanish Inquisition.'

She stared at the hard, Swedish chairs in the archive room. 'There's no comfy chairs, though.'

'No, the Irish Army doesn't do comfort. Not in our DNA. How can I help you, Mrs Sinclair?' He gestured for her to sit in one of the uncomfortable chairs in front of him.

'My client is looking to find his father. He was adopted from England and taken to America when he was four years old in 1929.'

'He's not Irish then?'

'I don't know. But he was born in England and I'm trying to find his father for him. He had just two possessions

147

when he arrived in America, This book...' She passed over the copy of The Lives of the United Irishmen. 'If you look inside you'll see it was published in 1914 and was originally in the library of University College Dublin. You'll notice the handwriting on the inside leaf?'

'I didn't know library books came with inscriptions.'

'That's the point, they don't.'

'And the other possession?'

She passed over the picture of the badge. Captain Ellis smiled as soon as he saw it. 'The Dublin Brigade Cap Badge. This one was issued just before the date of the Rising on April 24, 1916.'

'Who would it have been issued to?'

'Volunteers who were mobilised at that time. Some had uniforms, others were dressed in mufti or whatever clothes they brought with them when they mobilised. The badges for the Dublin Volunteers were the one feature they had in common. They are quite valuable if you have one, Mrs Sinclair. Collectors, you know.' He sniffed disapprovingly, shrugging his shoulders.

'I was wondering if the book and the badge were somehow connected?'

'I see where you're going with this. That maybe the cap badge and either MD or DF are connected.'

She nodded her head.

'Well, there's an easy way to find out.' He tapped a few keys on the computer in front of him, then turned the screen round to face her. 'Here's the list of confirmed participants in the Rising. It's on our website.' He scrolled down. 'As you can see, there are four participants with the initials MD.'

He pulled out a piece of paper and started writing. 'Michael Daley.' He scrolled through the list. 'Martin Dillon, there's another.' He wrote once more. The pen didn't produce any ink. He threw it in the bin beneath his desk. 'Ach, you'd think a country that could produce a Yeats and Joyce and Beckett could produce a decent pen.' He pulled another from the mug on his desk and wrote down a name. Finally, he wrote one other.

'There you go.' He pushed the paper with its four names towards her.

She read them;

Michael Daley.

Martin Dillon.

Michael Dowling.

Maurice Duggan.

One of these men could be John Hughes' father but which one?

'Now, you said your man was four years old in 1929. Well, it won't be him then.' He stabbed Martin Dillon's name with his index finger. She noticed it was stained a deep mahogany brown at the end. A heavy smoker, not so common these days. 'He was killed in 1923, during the Civil War. Put in front of a firing squad.'

'Really?'

The archivist shrugged his shoulders again. 'They were difficult days, don't you know? Irishman fighting Irishman. Not a time we are particularly proud of. And it won't be him either.' He pointed a finger at the last name. 'Stayed in Ireland all his life, became a minister under De Valera and had ten children. His son was a minister too. Runs in the family, you know.'

'Politics.'

He nodded. 'Ireland's always been run by clans. True in the 1500s and true today.'

'So it could be either Michael Daley or Michael Dowl-

149

ing?'

'If he is the man you are seeking…?'

'Do you know anything about either of them?'

'Neither name rings a bell. But we do have over fifteen hundred witness statements from the time. In the fifties, the government decided, for some reason, to interview all the old fighters that had taken part in the War of Independence, as we called it. The testimonies were recorded. We put them online last year.'

'So Michael Dowling or Michael Daley could be mentioned in the statements?'

He nodded once again. 'But there are over 55000 pages to go through. There's a search engine but it's not up to much.'

'I don't have the time. I need to report back quickly to my client. He's dying...'

'I'm sorry to hear that.' The archivist looked at the pictures once more. 'We could try looking for DF?' He went back to his computer and scrolled down it. 'There's only one. Declan Fitzgerald. I remember him. One of the old IRA. Never gave up the struggle, even into his eighties. Dead now of course. But I remember we have his testimony. Would you like to see it?'

'It's a long shot but, right now, I'll try anything.'

He pointed to a microfilm reader in the corner. 'I'll get the correct film. You know how to load it up?'

'I learned it at my mother's breast, Captain Ellis.'

'Don't we all? Then, you won't be needing any help from me so. Do let me know how you get on, won't you?'

'Thanks for your help, Captain Ellis.'

'Call me Tom, unless you join the Army, then a simple sir will do.'

'Thank you, sir.'

He smiled and walked away. She checked the contents of the microfilm on the box. Declan Fitzgerald was the sixth testimony on the list. She put the reels on the reader, threading the film through the spools, before switching it on. The light shone out brightly. The image was slightly out of focus. She adjusted the dial and a page swam into view. A typed page against a slightly yellowed background, almost sepia. She whizzed through the film, stopping occasionally to check a name against the list on the box. Finally, she saw a printed front page, with typewritten insertions.

Roinn Cosanta.

BUREAU OF MILITARY HISTORY, 1913-21

STATEMENT BY WITNESS

Document No. W S 1693

Witness

Mr Declan Fitxgerald

#, Lugar Road, Ballsbridge, Dublin.

Identity

Member of Irish Volunteers

E Company, Dublin Brigade.

Subject

GPO,1916.

Conditions, if any, stipulated by Witness.

Nil

File No: S580

For a moment, she hesitated. Was this where she would finally find out the truth? Or would it lead her ever further into those dark corridors where the past lies hidden in shadows and alcoves.

There was only one way to find out.

She pressed the button to advance to the next page and began reading the story of Declan Fitzgerald.

Chapter 24

Dublin. April 24-28, 1916.

My recollections of that week nearly forty years ago, are they worth reading? I have my doubts. After all, a lot of water has passed under the bridge since then. My memories are clouded with what happened afterwards and hindsight is a wonderful thing, is it not? Especially for those who are still alive to tell their tales.

But you'll not get any tales from me, not after all these years, just the truth as I remember it, warts and knobbly bits and all.

I'd joined the Volunteers with my best friend, Michael Dowling. Well, we marched up and down here and there to keep the likes of Padraig Pearse and his brother, Willie happy. I would have missed the Rising completely had not Michael come into my room at St Enda's and dragged me out of my bed. I'd a few wagers on some of the fillies at Fairyhouse that day and after the parades were called off on Easter Sunday, I thought I'd be able to see the horses in action.

Michael, of course, had a different idea. He was always the more obedient of the two of us, there was none of the rebel in Michael even though he spent the next week on the roof of the GPO with the rest of us.

We went off to war in a tram, carrying our kit and our rifles. We must have looked a sight sitting there on the wooden seats, having paid our fares, with our rifles between our legs. I didn't know then that we were the rebels and we were going to take on the might of the British Army over the next six days. I just thought it was another one of Pearse's little marches through the streets of Dublin. It would create no more bother than blocking the beer from getting to the ale houses.

It was only after we got to Liberty Hall that I found out the truth. We did march that day but it was to take control of the GPO not to listen to speeches in a park.

The first couple of days were quiet with one exception; I met my wife. She was one of the members of the Cumann na mBan and I'm always happy to tell everyone we met over a bowl of stew. We were married in 1917 after I returned from Frongoch and we're still married to this day 38 years later. She's been my partner in the struggle for a United Ireland through all that time. In ups and downs, through thick and thin. And I don't mind saying the best thing that came out of the whole week was meeting her. Forget the rest of the stuff.

I'm sure the others will go on about how glorious the struggle was. If you don't mind me saying, I think that's a load of codswallop. Pearse and his blood sacrifice, all it got was us locked up for a year and him and fifteen others put up against a wall and shot. Now it was the big fella, Michael Collins, who understood that better than most. Later on, we didn't lock ourselves in old buildings waiting for the Brits to shell us out of our hideyholes. We went after them on the streets and shot them, giving no quarter. Shame Collins sold Ireland down the Liffey afterwards though. But you folks will not be wanting to hear about that, will you? Especially from an old Fenian like me.

Anyway, after the first days in the GPO, we were all alright. Sitting on the roof, watching the people go about their business as they had always done.

It was on the Wednesday morning that I noticed that

Michael had gone missing. I thought he might have been shot and wounded. I remember going up to Pearse, Willie it was, and asking him if he had seen Michael.

He looked down at me, squinting through his pince-nez. 'He's gone on a mission for General Connolly.' I don't like speaking ill of the dead, and he died bravely in front of that British firing squad, but he could be a pompous arse.

I waited all day on the roof for Michael to come back. The shelling had already started when he finally returned. But it wasn't the same man who had left that morning.

He kept talking about a dead child and a hand holding a pink ribbon. Wherever he had been to, something had happened to turn his mind.

Myself and Bridget did our best to calm him down but Michael was never the strongest of souls at the best of times. We put him in a corner of the sorting office and covered him with a blanket, watching over him as he tossed and turned all through the night.

I suppose it was at this time that myself and Bridget fell in love. It seems a strange thing to do in the middle of a revolution but there's no telling when the little fella is going to shoot his bloody arrow. The more we talked, the more we realised we shared the same ideas and goals in life. If anything, she was even more committed to the cause of a United Ireland than I was. One day, we'll see it happen. It's 1955 now and I hope to God it's going to happen in her and my lifetime.

Anyway, I was telling you about the final days in the GPO. Michael woke up on the Thursday morning and seemed to have recovered, back to his normal self he was.

The shelling had continued through the night in the City. Across the street, the Imperial Hotel above Clery's was already ablaze. Nothing had reached the GPO yet but the lower end of Sackville Street, close to the river, was a wreckage of collapsed buildings and smouldering ruins.

Up on the roof, the sniping from the Rotunda had increased and we were forced to lie flat behind the parapet to avoid the bullets as they thudded into the stone of the Post Office.

I had just gone down to the next floor to get some water when there was a loud explosion above my head. Dazed men came tumbling down from the roof, their faces scarred by shrapnel. One man, a tall blond lad with a mop of unruly hair, one of the Maynooth men, I think, had blood pouring from his head. He was helped down the stairs to the dispensary. I heard later that he lost his eye.

The firing increased in volume and was joined by the occasional woodpecker tappings of machine guns. The sounds came from all sides now. It was as if a steel rope was being tightened around our throats, strangling the life out of us.

Michael said we should move the bombs down from the roof in case they exploded. We rounded up a few of the men and some of the prisoners and began to move the grenades down to the basement. One RIC man, obviously not happy at handling live bombs, was visibly shaking as he walked down the stairs, his knees buckling with every step.

We had nearly finished this job when there was another loud explosion this time on the fabric of the roof itself. Fire and smoke began to filter into the telegraph room beneath the roof, extending its reach down the stairwell.

A group of men rushed up to get the hoses onto the fire, but, by then, the water pressure had given out and the job was hopeless.

We were ordered down to the lobby, abandoning our

post on the roof. I had loved being there, watching Dublin in the throes of revolution from my perch at the centre of it all.

Down in the main hall, we were kept awful busy. Myself and Michael helped out whenever and where we were needed; filling mail sacks with coal to form a barricade across the entrance, moving munitions out of the basement into Henry Street, blocking the windows with more mail sacks. All to prepare for the attack General Connolly knew was coming.

Through it all, the shellfire and the sniping had become heavier making movement in and out of the GPO increasingly difficult. General Connolly himself had been wounded in the legs by shrapnel as he had taken another one of his tours of inspection in the streets around the building. Michael had carried him down to the aid station, where he was treated by one of the prisoners who was a British Army doctor, caught when the GPO was taken over. Despite the pain, his spirit, his fortitude was undimmed, making time to joke with the women from the Cumann na mBan who took care of him.

'It's a grand thing to be wounded to get all this attention,' he joked.

He was still at the centre of things, though, directing people from his stretcher. Myself and Michael often had the job of carrying him around, so he could 'just take a look at the corner over there.'

When we were free, we joined in the long line of men throwing buckets of water over the spreading flames. But it was like pissing in an ocean of fire. The flames kept getting stronger, devouring the top floor.

The main lobby stank of smoke and sweat. The floor was awash with coal dust leaking from the barricades. Here and there, crates of ammunition were sitting unattended, waiting for an attack that never came.

By Friday evening, the decision was taken to evacuate. I was standing next to Michael when Eamon Bulfin passed on the news.

'We're to move into Henry Place. From there we're going to make our way to join the men in the Four Courts. Gather your things. Be ready to move in ten minutes.'

'Bout bloody time,' I said, 'this place is done for. Time to fight our way out.' I grabbed a long Lee-Enfield and made sure my pockets and bandolier were full of bullets.

'We never did throw those grenades,' said Michael.

'Thank fuck for that. You know they were made at Liberty Hall. I wouldn't trust those feckers to make my arse.' I apologise for the language but you have to realise we were under attack and I'm not going to sugar-coat the truth like a lot of the other witnesses have. I've told how it was all my life and I'm not going to change now.

Michael took his Howth Mauser from the counter. He still hadn't fired it yet despite everything. He was never to fire it, the Brits took it off him before he had the chance.

'Form a line, we're going one by one out of the Henry Street door. There's a Lewis gun covering the road, so we'll have to dash across to get to Henry Place.'

Bulfin led the way, his Smith and Wesson in his hand and his face set. I saw Michael take a last look at the GPO. The blackened walls, the coal dust-streaked floor strewn with broken glass and the scattered crates of ammunition stared back at him.

Did we ever have a chance or was this always supposed to be our Alamo? A place where we were to find a glorious death celebrated by failure.

I elbowed him in the side. 'Will you get a move on

there, Michael, sure the roof will be in on top of us by the time you've said your goodbyes.'

Reluctantly, Michael followed the man in front out of the door. It was almost as if he didn't want to leave the GPO. There had been arguments amongst us that it would be better to make a last stand here as the building collapsed around us. To fight on to the death, have the street singers celebrate our sacrifice in songs of our courage in the face of death. But the leaders had kiboshed that. We were ordered to leave and leave is what we would do.

The man in front of Michael stopped. Bulfin was at the corner, directing people to dash across the road one at a time. As each one ran across, the British machine gun behind the barricade at the end of the street would open up, peppering the narrow road with bullets.

All the men in front of him had made it across, but it was only a matter of time before the gunner found his range.

Bulfin tapped Michael on the shoulder, 'Your turn, Dowling.'

He jumped into the road and, running close to the ground, dashed across the street. The bullets whistling past his head but he kept running, only a few more yards to go before he reached the safety of the next alley. A hand reached out to pull him in. The bullets struck the bricks above his head. Chips of brick sliced down, one cutting his cheek just below the eye. I watched him touch the blood with his fingers, bringing them up to his mouth and tasting the red liquid on his hands.

I was the next one to run across the street. 'Are you ready to catch me, Michael?' I shouted before launching my body away from the shelter. I didn't bother to run low, just charged across like an Irish bull in a field of cows.

The British gunner was waiting for me.

A trail of bullets exploded on the street around my legs. The gunner was aiming lower now, using the sparks where the bullets hit the road to adjust his range.

The bullets followed me across the street like children following the Pied Piper. Just as they were about to strike home, my foot hit a cobblestone and my whole body jack-knifed launching me into the air and down into the road. I watched as the bullets struck above my head, sparks flaming, slamming into the wall.

Michael ran out from his shelter and grabbed my hand, hauling me to my feet and dragging me to the safety of the lane.

'That was a feckin' close-run thing,' I shouted.

'The fall saved your life.'

'It was a graceful sort of a fall, though, wasn't it?'

'No.'

'You've an awful mouth on you, Michael Dowling. Couldn't you leave a man with his dreams.'

Bulfin joined us having negotiated the run himself. 'Come on you two, we're to spend the night in a house on Moore Street.'

'I thought we were going to the Four Courts?'

'Orders have changed.'

We found a room to sleep in that night. Outside, the sniping and shelling grew louder like Banshees howling outside our window, desperate to get at us. But inside we slept the sleep of the gods. It's strange how we could sleep then. I wouldn't have thought it possible. But sleep we did, with the noise and the shelling and the flames dancing in our dreams.

The following morning we were sitting around waiting for orders when the news came in that we had surrendered.

'I thought we were supposed to fight.'

'Those are the orders from Plunkett,' said Willie Pearse.

'And does General Connolly agree?'

'He does. We are to surrender to the Brits this afternoon. The order has gone out to the other detachments in the Four Courts, Boland's Mill, the College of Surgeons and the South Dublin Union.'

'So that's it then?' I said.

Pearse didn't answer.

I went and sat down on the floor next to Michael. 'We're giving up,' I said.

He just sat there playing with his shoelace, wrapping and unwrapping it around his finger.

'Did you not hear what I said?'

There was a long sigh and, in a quiet voice, he said,'Was it worth it?'

'We've gave the Brits a good run for their britches.'

'Aye, but at what cost?'

'Nothing we can't afford, and twice as much again.'

'Paid in children and old people?'

'Paid in bullets and dead soldiers. Listen, Michael, do you ever think the Brits are going to give us our freedom out of the goodness of their hearts? One day, they'll just say to us, 'Here you are lads, a free Ireland, go and enjoy yourselves.' A pig's arse, they will. We'll have to fight for every inch of sod and every ha'penny brick. Do you mind me?'

And then I remember, he looked at me with his head cocked over to one side, 'I don't know, Fitz. I just don't know.'

Bulfin's head appeared in the hole in the wall. 'Get your kit together.'

We traipsed out to Moore Street and assembled out

there, a dirty, raggedy-arsed band of proud men lined up along the road.

Willie Pearse called us to order. 'Attenshun! Left turn. Quick march.' We strode down Moore Street and across Upper Sackville Street to the Gresham Hotel side.

I looked over my shoulder at the ruins of Dublin; the ragged teeth of demolished buildings, smoking fires, soot-stained walls and, here and there, piles of debris which children climbed on top of to play King of the Castle. And over it all, a thick pall of smoke smelling like it was something from Dante's Inferno.

We were halted by a group of British officers just below Gresham's. Willie Pearse went over to talk to them and came back to tell us to lay down our weapons. One by one, we walked to the tram track, placing our rifles, revolvers and bandoliers between the lines. Michael laid down his Howth gun with extra care. He had never fired it once during the revolution. He didn't even know if it would fire.

I followed him with my Lee Enfield and my Webley, adding them to the pile. Seeing them there, with the rest of the arms and ammunition, gave the fight a certain authenticity, a badge of courage for me. We had fought a good fight.

As soon as we had finished laying down our arms, British soldiers ran up to us and began to search our pockets.

'You'll find nothing there, you English bastard,' I shouted at one of the soldiers. I watched as Michael quickly removed his cap badge and hid it down the front of his trousers.

'Gotta search you anyway. And besides, I'm from Dublin myself, from over near Cabra way. Youse lot had them worried, you did.'

'Aye, had ourselves worried even more,' I replied.

The soldier from Cabra took out my cigarette lighter and clicked the wheel. 'That's a good flame, that is.'

'Me mammy gave me that.'

He flicked the lid closed and put the lighter in his own pocket. 'Thank her from me.'

While the search had been going on, a crowd had begun to gather on the side of the road. It wasn't long before the catcalls began.

'Ach, youse should be ashamed of yourselves.'

'Go and fight in France if you want to fight.'

'Look what you've done to our city.'

'Should be shot the lot of them.'

The crowd began to push forward, threatening us. The soldiers pushed them back with the butts of their rifles

'Go away back to your mammy, you shites.' An old woman, her head shrouded in a black shawl, shouted through broken teeth. She leant forward and spat at Michael. The spit arched upwards and landed between his feet.

'Next time, I'll get ye.'

The people would change their tune eventually. Shame it took the deaths of sixteen good men to help them see the truth.

The soldiers formed two lines on either side of us and marched us toward the Rotunda. I wasn't sure whether they were there for our protection or to prevent us from escaping. A bit of both probably.

We marched past the jeering crowds of women, men and children, some spitting, some shaking their fists, some just standing there shouting the foulest curses at the top of their voices.

The British ordered us to sit on the lawn in front of the

Rotunda. It was soon packed with men as other groups were crowded into the same area. Michael and I sat back to back on the wet grass.

'Well, we did ourselves proud,' I said.

'You think, do you?' he replied.

'Aye, I do. Another glorious failure. But for a week, we held back the might of the British Army and controlled our city.'

'They might not agree with you.' Michael nodded towards the crowds at the end of the street.

'Ach, they'll come round, they always do. But next time, we're not going to lose and we're not going to play like gentlemen.'

'There's going to be a next time?'

'Michael, haven't you realised?' I said, 'For a clever man, you can be a stupid ass. This is just the beginning, don't you realise? It's just the beginning.'

And it was. But for Michael I think it was the beginning of the end.

Chapter 25

Dublin. November 18, 2015.

She switched the machine off. So Declan Fitzgerald and Michael Dowling were good friends. Were they the DF and the MD in the inscription?

Don't jump to conclusions, Jayne, examine the evidence. Remember what happened in the Yorkshire Ripper case. Six months of wasted activity, even interviewing Peter Sutcliffe and letting him go, all because the copper in charge was convinced the Ripper was a Geordie.

She corrected herself. The man in the inscription was probably Michael Dowling. Now she had to find evidence that linked Michael Dowling, a man in the Irish Volunteers, with a British soldier killed in Flanders in 1918. But what could it be? She didn't have an answer to that question yet and wondered if it would ever come to her.

Captain Ellis was hovering behind her. 'Did you find what you were looking for Mrs Sinclair?'

'I think so. Or at least part of the answer. Declan Fitzgerald mentions Michael Dowling in his witness statement. They were obviously close.'

'From what I know and have researched, they were comrades in arms. Went to UCD together and fought in the Rising together. Dowling was slightly wounded and they both ended up being interned in Frongoch.'

'What's Frongoch?'

The Captain laughed. 'A place in Wales. You could say it was the University of Irish Freedom.'

'I don't understand.'

'After the Rising, most of the participants were sent

across to England and interned around the country. The more dangerous, or what the Brits believed were the more dangerous, were sent to an old German POW camp in North Wales at a place called Frongoch.'

'How can I find out more?'

'I don't know. We have a few bits and pieces here. But I guess any records that exist will be held in London at the National Archives.'

'Thank you for your help. Could I get a printout of these pages?'

'No problem. You know Declan Fitzgerald's daughter is still alive?'

Jayne sat up in her chair. 'How can I find her?'

'I remember her coming to the launch of the archives. She's an old lady but still active in the movement.'

'Active?'

Captain Ellis laughed again. 'Like her da, she's still fighting for a united Ireland. Even after the Accord, she was writing to the papers, denouncing the 'treachery'.'

'How could I get hold of her?'

'She's in the directory, I think. Lives out Ballsbridge way, never married as far as I know, except to the cause, of course. Hang on a minute, I'll find the address for you.'

He went back to his desk and pulled out a telephone directory. 'I still like these 'oul things. An archivist and his bits of paper.' He flicked through the thin pages, stopping at F and scanning his finger down the page. 'Here she is. Ellen Fitzgerald. There's the number. I'll print out the pages for you while you make the call.'

She dialled the number on the page. A home number. Maybe the woman was only the one that used landlines these days. She couldn't remember the last time she had used hers.

166

A querulous voice answered the phone. 'If you're one of those telemarketers, ye can feck off.'

Jayne held the phone away from her ear. 'Ms Fitzgerald? Ms Ellen Fitzgerald?'

'I'm not interested in life insurance, answering any ruddy survey or getting me windows fixed. They're not broken.'

'It's okay, Miss Fitzgerald, I'm not selling you anything or from a telemarketer.'

'What do ye want then?'

'I'd like to talk to you about your father, Declan Fitzgerald.'

The phone was quiet. 'What about me father?'

'Could I come round to see you?'

'What about me father?' Louder now, querulous again.

Jayne employed the voice she used when questioning nervous witnesses. Don't lead them. Ask open-ended questions. Use a neutral tone. Push for detail but don't suggest anything to them. 'I'm at Cathal Brugha Barracks, the Military Archives. I'm researching Michael Dowling. Did your father know him well?'

The voice changed again. It was more wistful now, almost sad. 'He knew Michael well. Said he was the best man that ever lived. I never met him of course. He was gone before I came into the world.'

'Gone? You mean dead?'

'I don't know, me da never said. Just gone. I've got some pictures if you want to see them. Me da kept them safe through everything.'

'I'd love to see them, Miss Fitzgerald. When could I come round to see you?'

'Well, I have the bingo this afternoon. And after that, I've promised Father Sylvian help with the Christmas decorations. But you could come and see me tomorrow morning.'

'About nine o'clock?'

'Make it nine thirty. After me tea and toast.'

'I'll see you tomorrow, Miss Fitzgerald.'

The voice became suspicious again. 'You're sure you're not after selling me something?'

'I promise. I just want to talk about your father.'

'See you tomorrow at nine thirty. Don't forget now.'

'I won't. Thank you, Miss Fitzgerald…'

The phone clicked off before Jayne could say anything more. She picked up the directory and copied the telephone number and address. It was better than ringing Miss Fitzgerald again and disturbing her.

Tom Ellis handed her the printouts. 'I should warn you, she's a bit abrupt is our Miss Fitzgerald. I've felt the lash of her tongue before now. Waspish, you might call her, if you were feeling uncharitable.'

'I've dealt with worse.'

'I'm sure you have. Me, I prefer the documents, they don't answer back.'

'How do I get to Ballsbridge?'

'Where are you staying?'

'The Woodham.'

'I would get a taxi if I were you. My bet is you don't have the time to navigate our public transport system. You need a degree in maths to work out the timetable.'

She held out her hand. 'Thank you for everything, Captain Ellis.' She felt the warmth of his grip again.

'Glad to be of help, Mrs Sinclair. I hope all the trouble you are going to is worth it.'

'So do I, Captain. So do I.'

She would have to stay in Dublin another night. Paul

would not be happy. More than that, he would be furious. But if she checked out of the hotel and interviewed Ellen Fitzgerald, she could get the 1.30 flight out of Dublin back to Manchester, and arrive with plenty of time to cook the bloody dinner for Paul's bloody obnoxious boss.

'God, I hate being a wife,' she said out loud and instantly a wave of guilt washed over her.

Captain Ellis raised his head. 'My wife says exactly the same thing. Is it something to do with us men, do you think?'

Chapter 26

Dublin, Woodham Hotel. November 18, 2015.

She opened the door to her room. As soon as she stepped into it, she knew something was wrong. It was as if the air was different, sullied. She could even smell that somebody had been there, somebody who was not the maid.

Cautiously, she advanced into the room. It looked exactly how she had left it, except tidier. The maid had been there. Perhaps, she was over-reacting. Her mind was playing tricks, the feeling of being followed had affected her.

She sat down on the edge of the bed. Not like her at all. Normally, she was calm and collected, the job had taught her that. Dispassion. The ability to look at even the most callous murder and not show or feel a drop of emotion. But this case was getting to her. The stone through the window. The feeling of being followed. The sense that something was happening she knew nothing about.

She shook her head. Pull yourself together, Jayne Sinclair. You were a copper for 21 years, act like one. She thought about getting a stiff drink from the mini-bar, but she hated the taste of whisky. Perhaps she would go out later and get a bottle of wine and some chocolate. That's what she needed, a good bar of chocolate before she went through the onerous task of calling her husband and the client.

The first was a difficult call, telling him she was staying an extra day. And then she remembered her client was lying in a hospital. Was he conscious? Would he be able to speak? Had he died already? If he had, all this work was in vain.

She stood up, took off her coat and threw it over the back of the chair. But before the wine and chocolate, she needed to check her emails. She went to the wardrobe and opened the door. Inside was one of those small, box-like safes always found in hotels. She tapped in the numbers 0403, the date of her wedding to Paul. The number she always used when she needed four digits for a password. Each time she thought of that day. Her happiness, his smiles, the laughter of friends, the line of bobbies as she left the registry office, truncheons extended to form an arch. It always made her happy.

But where had it all gone wrong? Her and Paul constantly bickering, never having time to actually listen to each other. Perhaps, if they had children, it would have been better. But then she thought of her friends who had divorced despite the children. The sad women left behind with a couple of kids while the men went off to find a new field to plough.

The funny thing was, being police was supposed to be deadly for marriage. The long hours, shift work, the constant threat of danger. Her and Paul had survived all that intact. It was when she stopped being police the trouble started. As if Paul now wanted her to be the dutiful, old-fashioned wife, staying at home parked in front of the stove. She couldn't do that any more than she could iron a shirt. Why was he expecting it from her?

She pressed the open button on the safe, the date 0403 still illuminated in green in a small window.

Strange, why was the number still displayed. It should have gone off when she closed the door this morning.

She reached in.

171

Nothing.

It must be at the back.

Her hand explored the interior.

Empty.

She bent down and stared inside. A grey metal wall and a fabric-lined base stared back at her but nothing was inside.

She had put her Mac in here this morning before she left, hadn't she?

She looked around the room. It wasn't on the desk or beside the bed. She thought back to this morning. Getting dressed, making the decision not to carry her Mac, putting it inside the safe, closing the door, pressing the keys with the number she always used. 0403.

She looked inside the safe again.

Empty.

Her Mac was gone. But, who would have stolen it? The maid? Doubtful, she would have had to know the combination.

Somebody else from the hotel? Of course not.

There was a noise outside her room. Somebody was there. She took an umbrella from the wardrobe, creeping quietly to the door and listening. Somebody was outside.

She wrenched open the door and raised the umbrella, ready to strike hard at whoever it was.

A maid stood there, her arms holding towels. 'Turn down service,' she said.

Jayne lowered the umbrella. She could feel her face reddening, the cheeks becoming hotter. This case was getting to her. She shook her head, 'No, thanks.' She turned away but as she did so a thought occurred to her. 'Did anybody go in my room today?'

The maid smiled. 'I let your husband in. He'd forgotten

his key. Guests are always doing that. Men particularly.' She watched Jayne's expression. 'I did do the right thing, didn't I?'

Jayne smiled. 'He's always losing the bloody keys. Typical man.'

The maid smiled back. 'Can't live with 'em, can't live without 'em. That's what my ma used to say, and she should know, her having six kids and all. Anything else I can get you. Some water?'

'No, I'm fine, thank you.' Jayne closed the door. A man had been in her room. Was it Paul? Had he come to Dublin without telling her?

She picked up her mobile from the desk and called him.

'Hello.'

'Where are you?'

'Good afternoon, good to hear your voice, Jayne. Good to hear yours, Paul.' He mimicked the conversation they should have had before saying, 'Where am I? Where I always am at this time of day. Sitting in my office, working on a stupid presentation that I have to deliver to the European sales team in exactly...ten minutes.'

'You're not in Dublin?'

'Noooo, why? Should I be?'

'No...it's nothing, just wanted to hear your voice,' she lied, 'sorry for disturbing you, finish your presentation.'

For the first time, concern crept into Paul's voice. 'Is everything ok, Jayne? You sound a little strange...anxious.'

She forced herself to laugh. 'It's nothing. The stress of the case, that's all.'

'Well, see you later, do you want me to pick you up at the airport?'

She thought for a moment. Now was not the time to tell him, but she was going to do it. 'Actually, Paul, that's why I called. I have to stay another night in Dublin.' She hurried on before he could say anything, 'I'll get the 1.30 flight back tomorrow, so I can still cook dinner, don't worry.'

She could hear a loud sigh on the end of the line. The voice when it spoke was eerily calm as if this were just one more in a long line of disappointments. 'This dinner is important to me, Jayne. It's what I've been working hard for.'

'I know, I know. Don't worry, I'll be back in time.'

'See you tomorrow.'

'Love you.' It was the first time she had said it in a long time. She realised it came out tentatively, not as a declaration of her feelings. She waited for the reply. It was a long time coming.

'Love you too.'

Then the line went dead.

She sat down on her bed, finally kicking off her shoes. Tomorrow, she would have to get the interview done as quickly as possible. She would turn up early, the old lady wouldn't mind. Then pre-arrange for a cab to take her to the airport. She could leave nothing to chance.

She glanced at the safe once more. Her Mac still hadn't materialised. Somebody had stolen it, masquerading as her husband. But who? And why? It must be to do with the case. But why would anybody want to steal her Mac?

A shiver shimmied down her spine. That feeling of being followed had been correct. She must learn to trust her instincts again. A brick thrown through a window and now the theft of her Mac. It was all connected to this case. It must be connected

She thanked all the Gods she knew, and a few she didn't, that everything had been backed up to the Cloud. All that was missing was last night's notes and those she could remember anyway.

Why would anybody bother stealing her computer? All she had to do was buy a new one and download all her files onto it. The theft just didn't make sense.

She stood up and opened a bottle of the Woodham's free water. She could report the theft to hotel security, but they would call the police. Some half-baked Irish copper would be questioning her for hours. They might be able to get a description of the man who had entered her room from the maid, even a few pictures from the hotel cameras. But what would that do, except delay her even longer in Dublin. She couldn't risk that.

There was no point. Whoever had stolen it, knew what they were doing and knew how to break into a hotel safe. She remembered the brick through her window in Manchester. Who was trying to stop her investigation? And, more importantly, why?

Chapter 27

Dublin, Ballsbridge. November 19, 2015.

The taxi stopped in the middle of a row of terraced houses, each one painted in a slightly different pastel colour.

'Here you are, missus. Number 18, like you said.'

She handed over the money on the meter, adding 10 Euros as a tip. 'Now you'll be here at 11 o'clock to take me to the airport?'

'Don't worry, missus, punctuality is my middle name. Actually, it's Patrick, but I'll be on time anyway.'

She stepped out of the cab. '11 o'clock.'

'On the dot, missus. Or my middle name isn't...'

'Patrick.'

She closed the door and the taxi moved off. She stood outside the light pink house. A curtain moved in the down-stairs window. She was early but she was certain the old lady wouldn't mind. Before she could knock on the door, it opened.

'You're early. I'm still after having me tea and toast.'

Tea was pronounced tay. The door opened wider.

'Well, come on in, the tea's getting older and the toast is getting colder.'

She stepped right into the front room of the house. It was like stepping back fifty years. Small and cosy, a flight of birds flew up the brown wallpaper, their wings desper-ately trying to escape. A two-seater settee, covered in quilt-ed throws and old cushions was pushed to one side. A fire burnt in the grate giving off a scent of the earth, grassy and rich. Next to the fire, an old chair, the cushion indented from years of use, perched like a cat in front of the warmth. And, in front of the chair, a basket full of balls of wool, needles and a half-finished piece of knitting in bright pink.

'It's for the bairn, two doors down. They don't have much. I help how I can.' She pointed to the open door. 'Let me finish me tea and toast.'

Jayne followed her into the small kitchen with its old stove, single tap over a white porcelain sink and small table nestling against one wall.

'There's a pot of tea brewed. I'll get you a cup.'

A slightly chipped cup was placed on the table. Jayne pulled out the chair and sat down. 'I'd like to thank you for taking the trouble...'

The old lady held up her hand. 'We'll talk in a minute. Let me finish me tea first.'

She sat down opposite Jayne, putting the fingers into her mouth and pulling out her dentures, dropping them into a glass of water on the table. 'The bits of toast get stuck to the palate. They'll scrape the life out of me if I let them.'

She picked up the toast, dunked it in the half-drunk cup of tea and chewed it with her gums.

Jayne poured a cup of tea from the pot. It was thick and stewed, more like porter than anything else. She added a gulp of milk from a bottle on the table. The tea hardly changed colour, remaining a shade of tanned leather normally seen on cheap sofas.

Miss Fitzgerald finished the last of the tea and toast. 'That's me settled now for the morning. Let's go into the room and sit by the fire. It'll be a mite more comfortable there.'

Jayne supped her tea from the cracked cup. The tannins hit the back of her throat giving her a jolt. She quickly put it down and followed Ellen Fitzgerald back into the living room. The old woman took her place by the fire, the knitting needles clicking away between her fingers before she had even finished sitting down.

'Now, what was it you were after asking me?'

Jayne decided to dispense with the speech she had planned. This woman was all business despite her age. 'It's about your father...'

'A grand man, he was. Never gave up on the cause, although it gave up on him more than a few times, let me tell you.' She stared into the fire. 'He died believing in a United Ireland. One day, it will come but not in his or my time, I am thinking.'

'He took part in the Easter Rising?'

'He did and gave him a pension for it. Took them a while but they eventually got round to giving him the money he deserved. Penny pinching heathens the lot of them.'

'I read his testimony in the Barracks...'

'Aye, I went to the opening. I was invited you know,' she said proudly. 'Didn't stop me telling them shites what I thought of them and their free sherry.'

'He was quite detailed about the events of 1916 and later.'

'He told them a few things, I'm sure.' She stared into the fire once again. 'I have a few pictures in an old album in the sideboard over there. Not many mind, but I'll let you see them. Go and get them for me, will ye?'

Jayne followed the bent, pointing finger to an old dresser in the corner. She hadn't noticed it when she came in as it was covered with a white lace cloth and a collection of china figurines.

She walked over and opened the top drawer. Inside was a row of medals and a few old pamphlets printed in the

1970s. 'Troops out now' stamped in thick block capitals on the cover with a name beneath. Declan Fitzgerald.

'Just move that stuff aside. It's at the back.'

She reached into the drawer and felt the plastic cover of an old album. She pulled it out. On the cover was a seaside picture and the words, 'Memories of Tralee'.

'That's the one. Give it over here and I'll show you.'

Jayne passed the album over and knelt down beside the old lady. She noticed a faint smell, a mixture of milk and age and damp that came from her. A wrinkled hand, with one old cut healing slowly, opened the book.

'He used to love these pictures. They were his pride and joy. Many a night he used to sit in this chair and look at them. When he wasn't reading or working, of course.'

'He went to UCD?'

'He did. Studying history he was. But as he told me, he left without ever getting the certificate. Preferred making history to studying it, he used to joke. Well, they all did, didn't they? A lot of them left early and never went back.'

She pointed to the first picture. A man smiling at a camera dressed in a uniform. He was a handsome man, with a bright smile, and a devil-may-care attitude. Behind his head was a painting of the countryside, a backdrop from the photographic studio. It gave him the air of a country squire, a man in uniform fighting for a country he loved.

'This was taken just before 1916, he told me. He borrowed the uniform from one of the other men. A bunch of them from their company in Rathfarnham went off to have their pictures taken one day. He said there was a group photo but the Brits took it off him in Frongoch.'

'The prison camp?'

'That's right. He was put there after the Rising. Said it was the best place to be for a revolutionary. He learnt more

179

there than anyone else. Michael Collins himself was one of his teachers. Of course, they fell out later over the treaty but that was only to be expected. There's a picture somewhere...' She flicked forward past some family shots on a beach. 'Here it is. Taken from and an English newspaper, it's a bit faded now. He often took it out and looked at this photo. I should get a copy made before it fades even more.'

The picture showed eight men, thin and shabbily dressed in clothes that had obviously seen better days. All were standing to attention, backs stiff and arms down by their sides. Nobody was smiling except one man. Behind them, Jayne could see the stone walls of their prison.

'Was this taken in Frongoch?'

'That's what my father said. Taken one day back in 1917, I think.'

Chapter 28

North Wales. Frongoch. March 19, 1917.

Michael would always remember the day the photographer came to Frongoch. Himself and Fitz had been listening to a lecture on guerrilla warfare by the adjutant, Dick Mulcahy.

Fitz elbowed him in the ribs. 'It's like being back at college, except here we're learning how to kill people.'

'Shush, your man is talking.'

'Always make sure the drivers are targeted in an ambush. If you stop the lorry, he can't go anywhere, can he? Kill the driver and you kill all the men in with him too.'

There was a sharp rap on the door. In walked Michael Collins as he often did, to check up on the men who were attending.

Mulcahy stopped what he was doing.

'Carry on, Richard. Don't mind me, I'm just here for a listen.'

Mulcahy returned to his blackboard sketch showing the best place to triangulate fire in an ambush. 'As I was saying, it's important to immobilise the driver. What's the best way to do that?'

'Shoot the bugger,' a voice with a thick Dublin accent answered from the back.

'Aye, that's the way to go. Shoot the driver and they won't be going anywhere quickly,' repeated Mulcahy.

Fitz turned to Michael and whispered, 'He's a bloodthirsty 'oul shite.'

Mulcahy stared at him. 'What was that Fitzgerald?'

'Nothing, sir, just clearing my throat, it's awful parched.'

'Well, clear it quietly.' Mulcahy looked down at his feet and then across at Collins standing by the window.

'There will be a lot of shooting by the time we're finished. Freedom will never come without revolution but I'm afraid the Irish people will be too soft-hearted for it. To bring a revolution to fruition you need ferocious, blood-thirsty men with no regard for death, or the spilling of blood.' Mulcahy's voice was rising as he warmed to his theme, his eyes becoming wilder the more he spoke. 'Revolution is no job for children, and it is no job for saints or sinners. During revolutions, any man, woman or child who is not for you is against you. Shoot them and be damned to them.'

The room was stunned by the vehemence of Mulcahy's speech.

A hand rose on the left.

'It's that Old Fenian, Rafferty. I wish he would shut up,' whispered Fitz under his breath.

Collins appeared to hear and glared at Fitz.

'You want to ask a question, Mr Rafferty?' said Mulcahy.

'Aye, I do. You're talking a lot about ambushes and guerrilla warfare and shooting and the like. But what about Dublin? Are we not going to rise again like we did at Easter?'

It was Collins this time who spoke. 'Answer me this, Mr Rafferty, how big is the British Army?'

Old Rafferty shrugged his shoulders. 'I don't know. Millions, I believe.'

'And how big are we?'

Rafferty looked around the room. Around twenty men were sitting behind desks facing Collins at the front. 'The

Volunteers?'

'Aye, us, the lads, the Volunteers.'

Rafferty rubbed the straggly beard on his chin. 'Again, I don't know. Maybe 1,000 in Dublin, more across Ireland.'

'So maybe 5,000 in total.'

'Aye, that would be a fair number.'

'And how many arms does the British Army have?'

He shrugged again. 'I don't know. Millions I am supposing.'

'And how many do we have?'

'There you have me, Mr Collins. I'm thinking you would know the figure far better than me.'

The rest of the class laughed, breaking the tension.

'I do, Mr Rafferty, I do. And I'll tell you it's not many. So answer me this, why would we take on the might of the world's largest and best-equipped army in an open fight with no arms and few men?'

Rafferty didn't answer.

'Look at us now, we did it once, our leaders were executed and we are here, locked up safe and sound beside some cold Welsh mountain.'

'But it was a glorious day for Ireland.'

Collins' face and his voice changed. He leant forward, his huge body dominating the tiny classroom. 'We've had enough of glorious failure in Ireland. We're the experts at 'glorious failure'. We sing songs about it, children learn it in their cribs, we celebrate the men who died gloriously as they failed.' He slammed his fist down on the table. 'Not anymore, gentlemen. Not anymore. Sixteen men died for our glorious failure, executed in Kilmainham Jail.' He took a deep breath. 'Next time, we will win and create a free Ireland. It's going to be bloody. It's going to be tough. And, by God, Mr Rafferty, there will be no fecking glory in it.

But we will win, gentlemen. And in winning, we will write the new songs of a free Ireland.'

He looked at every man in the room. Then, a broad smile flashed across his face. 'Until that time, let's eat more of this swill the Welsh call food. There will be more lessons tomorrow morning, gentlemen, when you will learn about the terrible beauty of the enfilade. Before then, I have a few announcements. There will be a parade this evening at six pm. Apparently, we are to have some British press here this afternoon, no doubt to check up on the terrible animals they have imprisoned in their zoo. You will all be smart and shaven for the parade. None of your Dublin slovenliness, Fitzgerald.'

'No, sir. I mean, yes sir.'

'Good morning to you all.'

All the class stood up. There was the noise repeated throughout classrooms all over the country; chairs being scraped back, books closed, gossip among friends, the plaintive cry of a blackboard being wiped.

'Will you explain the ambush to me once again, Michael. What was Mulcahy on about?'

'We'll do it back in the hut, Fitz. It's all about creating crossfire and anticipating the actions of men under stress.'

'Thucydides is easier.'

'The Greeks always are. And he's tomorrow. Old Rafferty is giving the lecture. Your man was a teacher in Maynooth before the Rising.'

'Aye, I can still smell the priests on him.'

They saluted Collins as they walked past him and out into the corridor. As they reached the open air, Fitz stood up and breathed in. 'How long are we going to be in here?'

'As long as they want us.'

Here was Frongoch Camp in Merionethshire, Wales.

They had been sent there after receiving a notice of Intern-
ment from a captain in Kilmainham Jail. There had been no
trial and no judge or jury. Simply a piece of paper inform-
ing them of their fate.

At first, they had been 1800 strong but then many of the
young lads had been released in June and then more in December. A gesture of Christmas goodwill the Brits called it.
Now, there were just 600 diehards, left still locked up in the
camp.

There were actually two camps. A North Camp with
rows of wooden Nissen huts built to house the German
POWs who had inhabited the area before them, and a South
Camp in the stone buildings once used to store grain. After
the number of prisoners had been diminished, the North
Camp was used as a punishment area. Over 100 men were
imprisoned in there at the moment, all accused of offences
against the order and governance of the camp. It was a
badge of honour to be locked up in the North Camp, and
Michael and Fitz had both done their time.

They walked across the open cobble-stoned square surrounded by buildings. Frongoch had been a distillery before the war and all the old buildings remained. The chimney of the old distillery towered blackly above them, cast-
ing its shadow through the long summer months and on
into the winter. The first winter had been cold in Frongoch,
the wind whistling down from the exposed slopes of the
hills that surrounded them. Michael and Fitz had often
huddled together in the shadow of the chimney desperate to
escape the biting cold. But somehow they had survived
despite the boredom, the bad food and the wet and damp.

The spring had brought a new freshness and vitality to
the camp. Their lessons had increased as the days length-
ened, becoming more intense and concentrated. Michael

had also noticed a change in Fitz as their imprisonment had endured the second summer. The old joker who took nothing seriously had gone and a new commitment to the cause had emerged, gaining strength from all the others around him. Each night he was sitting with the old Fenians, talking to them about their experiences and how he could become a better soldier for Ireland.

Michael looked at him as they walked across the square to their huts at the other side of the camp. His face had changed too, the softness, almost babylike flabbiness had been replaced by grit and determination. He had lost weight, of course, they all had, but the gaunt features were more than just a consequence of their bad diet. It was as if their days here had hardened him, like soft clay that had been moulded and baked in an oven.

One of the guards called Myers approached them. He was a Scot, who had spent his life in the British Army and had seen action in the Boer War, one of the few survivors of Spion Kop. He leant forward as he passed them whispering through his moustache. 'Got some fags, lads, if'n you want 'em.' He coughed at the end of his sentence, a consequence of a German gas attack in 1915.

'How much?' whispered Fitz.

'Two quid a pack.'

Fitz threw his head back. 'That's bloody daylight robbery. They don't cost more than two shillings and sixpence in Llangollen.'

Myers chuckled. 'Well, mebby you should take a little stroll into town to buy them. You'll have to get past me and the guards, past the barbed wire, past the towers and down the road, but with a bit of luck you might make it there alive.' He coughed again, longer and louder this time.

Fitz grunted. 'You've made your point, Mr Myers. The

usual place at two?'

Myers nodded and walked on, coughing into his closed fist as he did. The usual place was behind the latrines on the far side of the camp. It was the place that all exchanges for cigarettes, tea, uncensored letters and the little luxuries that made life bearable took place.

'You know, Michael...'

'I know what?'

'The finest thing about the English soldier is his corruptibility. It was as true today as it was in Cromwell's time. But where am I going to get two pounds? And me, gasping for a fag too.'

Michael pulled out a letter he had received that morning. 'My sister wrote to me. She sent me a postal order for ten pounds.'

'We're rich, Michael Dowling. And I will take a small donation for the cause of Irish freedom and the freedom of my own lungs from you.'

'Freely given, Mr Fitzgerald.'

'And freely taken, Mr Dowling.'

They marched on back to the long narrow building on the right where they lived. The leader of their hut, an old IRB man called Walsh stood outside the door. 'They'll be wanting to take our photograph.' He pointed to three civilians setting up a tripod camera opposite their building.

'Has the Chief agreed?'

'He has. So clean yourselves up. You two are going to be posing for the British press today.' His Mayo accent was still rich and thick.

'And what are we to be posing as?' asked Michael.

'Upstanding members of the Irish Volunteers. The Chief has decided we must show ourselves as serious men, not a rabble. The Brits are wanting to portray us like animals who stabbed them in the back by rising in Dublin in the middle of war.'

'The Brits have always treated us like animals.' Fitz spat on the ground.

'Aye, so we have to show them we are soldiers. Get yourselves cleaned up.'

They moved past him into their hut. The others inside were getting ready for the photograph; combing their hair, shaving in the sink at the end of the room, putting on their best jumpers, polishing their one pair of shoes. The uniforms, or what was left of the uniforms after the fighting, had been taken from them when they arrived, and they had been issued with a couple of shirts, a jacket and two pairs of trousers. Henry Mertons the prisoners called them, after the tailor who produced all the demob suits for the Brits.

'It looks like we're to take this seriously,' said Michael.

'Aye, we're going to be famous. The men who took on the British Army.'

After twenty minutes, all eight of them were ordered out of the hut and assembled in front of the camera. They lined up as if on parade, shoulder to shoulder, hands down by their sides, fingers pointing down the seams of their trousers.

The photographer raised his head from beneath a dark cloth. 'This won't do, gentlemen, no, no, no.' His voice was squeaky and querulous, like a mouse in human form. 'Much more casual, gentlemen, not like soldiers. Just mingle about as if the camera wasn't here.'

He popped his head back under his black cover and raised the flashbulb.

'Stay where you are,' ordered Walsh, 'you are soldiers of the Irish Volunteer Army. Stand at attention.'

The men stood rock solid, shoulder to shoulder.

The little photographer's head popped out from beneath his cover once more. 'No, no, gentlemen, don't you understand English? I want you to be lounging around, enjoying life. A few of you could even be playing games or chess.'

'There'll be no playing games in my hut,' growled Walsh. 'This is how the men will be shot. Take it or leave it.'

The photographer shrugged his shoulders. 'As you will, but my editor will not be happy.' He popped his head under the cover once more, raising the flash pan and said. 'Smile gentlemen.'

'Anybody who smiles is on a charge,' growled Walsh.

Michael smiled and the flash erupted, blinding them all.

Chapter 29

'There he is, my da, on the left, looking at the camera.'

Jayne recognised him immediately. The same jaunty smile was on his lips, but the eyes were darker now, with a determination that was missing from the earlier photograph. 'Do you know who the others were?'

'He was always pointing them out and telling me. I would have to be a spalpeen to forget. Next to my da, looking down is Patsy Cline. He was killed during the Civil War, may God have mercy on his soul. Next to him is Eamon Curley. He died of the TB in 1929. My da always said it was sleeping out in the fields on the run from the Brits that did it. Look at the man, he's as thin as a rake already.'

'Who's on the right, looking down?'

'That's the man you're after, my da's best pal, Michael Dowling. He often used to talk about Michael. Best man he ever knew, my da said.'

'What happened to him?'

'Nobody knows. There was some falling out, about the Civil War, I think, but my da never talked about it. He and Michael parted ways and Da never saw him again.' She stared off into the fire again, as if speaking to her da once more. 'He often used to wonder what had happened to Michael Dowling, missed him more than anybody else, he did.' She smacked her lips, 'I'd love a drop of tea. Would you be after making some?'

Jayne went back to the kitchen. An old kettle was sitting on the stove. She took a box of matches and lit the fire. It popped loudly but then settled down to burn with a bright blue flame. Filling the kettle from a single tap, she placed it onto the flame.

In the sitting room, the old woman was still in her chair, the album in her lap, staring into the fire. Jayne wondered where she was now. Was she a little girl, sitting on her father's lap, listening to his stories? Or was she older, still listening to his stories, but helping him now?

The clock ticked on the mantelpiece and the fire settled down as a piece of coal collapsed to ash. It broke the reverie of the old woman. 'They didn't mean to do it, you know. Orders.'

Jayne didn't understand what the old woman was saying. Behind her, the kettle whistled loudly like a cock proclaiming the dawn.

'You'll find the tea in a caddie on the shelf. Real Irish tea, none of those teabags with their sweepings from the floor. Four spoonfuls, now, make it good and strong. Just a splash of milk for me, don't drown the tea. And you'll find an old packet of biscuits on the shelf. I fancy a Jammie Dodger, so I do.'

Jayne did as she was told, letting the tea brew for a couple of minutes as she rinsed the cups. She found an old tray on the shelf, poured the tea, adding the splash of milk for the old woman and a much larger gulp for her. She opened the biscuits, putting six on a small plate. Carrying her tray, she strode into the living room.

The old woman was still sitting in the same place, but the album was nowhere to be seen. Instead, on her lap was a bundle of old typewritten sheets of notepaper, wrapped with a rubber band, and another bundle of newspaper clippings, yellow with age.

'He didn't tell the men from the ministry everything

when they asked him. Didn't trust them. Bunch of old pen-pushers, he said. But he wrote it all down. Wanted to tell the truth he said. Kept a lot of newspapers from the time, too. You'll find Michael Dowling in here.'

Chapter 30

The journey down from the mountain was made in silence. Michael sat in the back, grim-faced with the line of his jaw set hard against his skin.

I sat next to him, looking out of the window. The two others sat in front, staring straight ahead.

We had covered the body loosely with stones and earth at the top of the mountain. When we were half-finished, I said, 'That's enough. No point in burying him properly, we want the British to find him.'

We left the tools at the side of the makeshift grave. As they hurried away, back to the waiting car, its engine still running, I looked back at the spade lying beside the mound of earth. The man's foot was still sticking out from his grave, lying next to the spade. It was as if he was still alive, trying to step out from his earth prison.

Michael stopped and turned back, taking a few steps towards the grave and its foot. He wanted to go back and finish burying the man properly. But that wasn't the idea. The orders were clear. Make sure the body is found, Fitz, they told me. We want to put the fear of death into the bastards.

Michael stammered something and then shouted out loud. 'We must help the man out. He's still alive. He's trying to get out.'

I put my arm around his waist and pulled him away. 'Shush, Michael,' I said, 'We've got to go now.'

At first he resisted, then his body went limp and I could

bundle him into the back of the car.

'But the leg, it's...'

'He's dead. I shot him myself. He's dead, Michael.'

'But the leg...'

There was a roar from the engine as the driver stomped on the accelerator, impatient to get away from the top of this mountain.

'He's alive. He's still alive.' Michael shouted back towards the rocks as we drove away, the car fishtailing wildly as we went from the grass of the verge onto the tarmacked road.

'He was still alive,' whispered Michael.

I didn't answer. How could I? I knew the man was dead.

I think it was then that we lost Michael to the cause. A shame. He was the best man who ever fought for Ireland.

* * *

The news came two days later.

Michael was lying on his bed in the safe house on the North Side of Dublin. He hadn't moved for the last two days since the death of the English soldier.

I tried to get him to eat something. 'At least, have a wee bite of bread and tea. You'll be just skin and bones unless you get something inside you.'

Michael ignored me, lying on the covers facing the wall.

When he did move, I saw him pulling out the effects of the officer we had shot.

'Give me a look at them,' I said.

He passed them over quietly.

There wasn't much for a life. A watch. Two letters. A few coins. A notebook. A silver cross. That was all. Not much.

I read the letters. One was addressed to the parents of one of his officer friends but never posted. It described the heroic death of a man in some grubby field in France during the last days of the war. The letter was grubby with fingerprints as if it had been opened, read and closed many times over the last year or so. A letter too awful, too descriptive to ever have been sent. A letter written for the man as much as it had been written for the parents.

The second letter was addressed to their man's sister, and written in a different tone; light, playful even. He missed her terribly, hoped she was well and happy in Bradford and talked of the day soon when he would be back with her in their house. The last line was the most chilling in its happiness. 'Just four weeks and three days left to my discharge, then I will be home with you all.' It was signed with a carefree flourish, 'your loving brother, John.'

I threw the letters on the bed.

'That was his name. John Clavell. I will remember his name, we must remember, Fitz. He wasn't a nameless man, an unknown soldier, but a man with a name and a face and parents and a sister who loved him. A man who had died on top of a cold mountain in an even colder country for a cause that he couldn't understand.'

'There's no point, Michael. He was a soldier like all the other soldiers. Do you think this bastard's generals cared about the millions they killed in France?'

O'Kelly burst in to their room, waving a piece of paper in his hand. 'We've done it. We've won.'

I jumped up, 'Done what? Won what?'

O'Kelly bounded over and jumped on the bed. It shook

beneath his weight. 'It's over. We've won. The Brits have signed a truce. They've surrendered.'

I jumped off the bed and danced around the room.

Michael just sat up in his bed.

'It's over. We've won, Michael. Don't you understand?'

He didn't say anything. Reaching out his hand, he took the letters and the watch and the other effects putting them in his pocket.

I shook him by the shoulders. 'It's over, Michael, we've won.'

'Have we?'

I saw him looking at me, disappointment etched on his face. 'It had to be done.'

'Did it?'

'He was a soldier, he knew the score.'

Michael looked at me, his head tilted to one side. For the first time since the death of the officer his face became animated. 'Don't you see, Fitz, he wasn't some nameless soldier, but a man with a face and parents and a sister who loved him.' He took out the letters and the rest of the effects from his pocket. 'This is all that's left of him, Fitz.'

Chapter 31

Jayne Sinclair turned over the last page of the manuscript and picked up the newspaper clippings. They were yellow and faded, beginning to tear on the creases where they had been folded. A few dealt with killings on the streets of Dublin, a few more with shootings in Croke Park; the British army had fired into the crowd. The last three dealt with one event. The kidnapping and murder of a British officer. His body had been found in the hills above Dublin, shot once in the back of the head.

She didn't have time to read them all now. She would take a photo of them with her mobile and read them later. But one stood out and she looked at it now. It was an article from The Irish Times.

BRITISH OFFICER FOUND MURDERED

LT. JOHN CLAVELL KIDNAPPED AND SHOT.

BODY FOUND IN HALF-DUG GRAVE.

The body of Lt John Clavell of the Kent Fusiliers was found today by a shepherd in the mountains above Dublin. The man, Martin Flannery, had been rounding up his flock when he noticed his dog scraping at the ground near some rocks. Mr Flannery reported that some of the body had been out of the grave when it was found.

Lt Clavell was a decorated British officer, well loved by his men and his fellow officers. He had been kidnapped last week while on a shooting expedition in Wicklow with some friends. The friends had been released but, until yesterday, Lt Clavell's whereabouts was unknown.

Lt Clavell was unmarried but he leaves a grieving family in Bradford, West Yorkshire. The body of the gallant soldier will be transported to Heaton Methodist Church for burial with full military honours on Saturday.

Clavell? The name meant something to her, what was it? Then, it hit her. Clavell was the maiden name of John Hughes' mother. How were they linked? How had a man who was dead married the sister of a murdered British officer? This was becoming more and more complicated. An enigma wrapped in a mystery, shrouded in a conundrum. There must be answer somewhere, but where?

She reached into her bag and pulled out her hand-written notes. John Hughes had been born in Bradford in 1925. How was it all connected? There were some pieces of the puzzle still missing. It was time to pay a visit to Bradford and check out the maternal side of Hughes' family. That's where the answers would lie, if there were any to be found.

She glanced at the time, 10.55. The taxi would be arriving soon.

The knitting needles stopped their clacking for a second. 'So? What d'ye think? You know nobody would publish it. Who wants to hear the ramblings of an old Republican.'

'The world is different now. You could self-publish if you want? I'll research it and send you a few addresses on email.'

'Now what would I want to be doing with e-mails? I don't even have one of those computer things. No, if he's not around to see it, it can stay with me till I die. I might leave it to those people at the Barracks. They would know what to do with it.'

'I think that's a good idea. I'll ask Captain Ellis to contact you.'

'You be doing that, I wouldn't mind meeting the captain again. I'll give him another piece of my mind.'

Jayne heard the honk of a car horn outside. The taxi had arrived. The old woman put down her knitting. 'I suppose you'll be off now.'

Jayne stood up. 'Thank you for everything, Miss Fitzgerald. Your father devoted his life to Ireland.'

'That he did. He may have had to do a few bad things for the cause but he didn't lie about them. He was always straight was me da.' The old woman stood up slowly. 'Me 'oul knees. Gone they are. Too much praying when I was a child.'

They shook hands. Jayne felt the strength beneath the apparent frailness of the woman. She wanted to lean in to give the woman a kiss on the cheek. But she didn't. That would have been too modern, too informal for this woman. A quick shake of the hand was all that was needed.

'Would you mind if I took a photo of a few of the pages?'

'Go ahead. They're just sitting in the drawer minding their own business.'

Jayne put the pages and the newspaper articles down on the settee and quickly shot the ones she needed with her mobile. She could print them out later to show her client.

'Thank you once again, Ms Fitzgerald. You don't know how much this means to me.'

'I hope you find your Michael Dowling. My da never could. Went to his grave hoping he would see him again one day.'

'I hope so too.'

The old lady sat down again, taking up her knitting. 'I won't see you to the door, my knees...'

'Don't worry, I'll see myself out.'

'And don't worry yourself, it will work itself out in the end. It always does.'

Jayne gathered her notes and stuffed them in her bag. She walked to the door, taking one last look at the old woman sitting in the chair by the fire, staring down at her knitting. What did she mean 'it will work itself out in the end?'

The taxi horn blared again.

'Goodbye, Ms Fitzgerald.'

The only answer from the old lady was the clacking of knitting needles. It was as if Jayne had never been there.

She opened the door. The taxi was waiting in the street. A different one than she expected. Perhaps her driver had been unable to make it. At least, he had arranged a replacement for her.

She picked up the bag and closed the old woman's door behind her. She walked to the taxi. Something was wrong, another person was sitting in the back.

At that moment, a strong pair of arms encircled her, her bag was taken, and she was bundled into the back. A burly man got in beside her, sandwiching her in the middle.

'Good morning, Mrs Sinclair. I'm so glad you could join us. We'll just wait for Tony and then we'll be off.'

The front door opened and her bag was thrown inside. A man followed it into the seat. A nod to the driver and they moved off.

'I hope you enjoyed your little talk with Ellen. What did you discuss?'

'None of your business.'

She felt something sharp in her side, just below the breast. She looked down and saw the metal of a gun barrel digging into her ribs. She could smell the gun oil, a sharp, tangy smell like the scraps in a steelyard.

'Now, I was hoping that we were going to have a friendly conversation on this lovely November day. We don't get many days like this in Dublin. I think it's always best to enjoy them. Go for a drive out into the country.'

'I've got a plane to catch. Let me out now.'

Again, the gun jabbed her beneath the ribs. This time, she groaned audibly.

The man sitting next to her was small, almost elfin in appearance, with a head that seemed too large for his body. A bald head with a few strands of hair combed across the top, large ears, a pug nose and the disconcerting habit of pushing his glasses up onto the bridge of his nose each time he spoke.

'There you go again. Here we are having a pleasant conversation and you want to keep shouting. Now that isn't very friendly, is it? Sean over there doesn't like prodding you with his gun. He likes it even less when he has to use it. Makes an awful loud noise it does. Enough to wake up the dead. We wouldn't like that, would we?'

Jayne shook her head.

'Good, I knew the minute I saw you, we were going to get on like a house on fire. Didn't I say that Sean?'

The burly man beside her didn't say a word.

'He's not one for the conversation himself. The strong, silent type is our Sean. Now where was I, Mrs Sinclair? Ah I remember, I was asking a few questions and you were doing the answering.'

The car turned left. They had exited the city now and were into a leafy suburb. She had no idea where they were or where they were going. She shifted her position to the left away from the snub nose of the revolver.

'How is Ellen these days?'

'She's fine. Old but as sharp as a button.'

'Are buttons sharp these days? Must be an English phrase. She was remembering the old days, was she?'

'Look, I don't have to tell you anything.'

The jab of the muzzle in her ribs once again.

'No, you don't, that is true. But Patrick here is available to drive around Dublin for the rest of the day. And me, Sean and Tony, well, we're not busy either. I'm thinking it is you who has the plane to catch, is it not?'

Jayne looked at the clock on the dashboard. 11.20. She was going to miss the flight.

'The sooner you answer a few of our questions, the sooner we can let you down to get your flight. Sean will miss you, though, won't you Sean?'

Jayne felt the nose of the pistol in her ribs once again. The car accelerated away from the traffic lights. The houses on each side of the road were larger now, set back and with large gardens in front and at the side.

Jayne shifted her body to face the small man sitting on her left. She refused to look at the thug with the gun. He was just muscle with just a couple of brain cells to spark him into action.

What was so significant about her research? Why were these people interested in it? And who the hell were they?

Chapter 32

Dublin. November 19, 2015.

David Turner had followed Jayne Sinclair to the terraced house in Ballsbridge. What was she doing here? He watched as an old lady answered the door and let her in. 'Let's sit and wait, Ronnie. She's got her case with her. My bet is she's going straight to the airport after she's finished here.'

'I'll find out who the old lady is. A mate in the Garda can do a quick check.' He picked up the mobile, dialled a number and began to speak. 'He'll get back to me in a minute.'

They sat in the vehicle on the street, watching the door. It felt just like the stakeouts they used to do in Northern Ireland, even the houses looked the same. Sitting. Waiting. Drinking bad coffee. Eating worse burgers. Not speaking, never saying a word. He hated every second of it, just as he hated it now. Patience really wasn't his forte.

The phone call, when it came, was a welcome relief to break the silence. 'Okay, got it. Thanks. I owe you one.' He switched off the phone. 'Her name is Ellen Fitzgerald. Her father was an old Sinn Feiner. She's been arrested a few times, public disorder, breaking the peace, nothing too serious.'

So yesterday a visit to the archives at the Cathal Brugha Barracks and this morning a trip to see one of the Old Guard. What was she doing? Looking into something that happened during the fight against the IRA? He would know more when he got back to England. He would pay one of his more computer literate friends to access the laptop he had stolen before he gave it to the client. Her files would tell him everything he needed to know about what Jayne Sinclair was up to. Until then, he would just sit and watch, and report back on the dot at noon.

Time passed slowly, it always did on a stakeout. As if it had been slowed deliberately to make the waiting even more painful. Sometimes people chatted away the hours, naming favourite movies and their casts, English football teams or talking about past operations and who had been a plonker. But he wasn't much of a talker and Ronnie was even less so. More of the strong silent type. Strange, he always thought the Irish had the gift of the gab.

'Somebody has pulled up outside. Looks like a taxi.'

He leaned forward, looking at the new arrival. It had a taxi sign on its roof but two men had got out from the car and stood by the door of the house, while another remained in the back.

'That's not a taxi, it's a welcoming committee.' He recognised the trademarks of an IRA operation. Using a taxi was the giveaway. What was more innocuous, more ordinary than a couple of people sitting in the back of a taxi?

The door opened a crack and then stopped. The men standing on either side of it, leant back into the wall, waiting for Jayne Sinclair to exit. She stepped out carrying her case and stopped, surprised to see someone sitting in the back of her taxi. The man at the door took her by the arms and bundled her into the back, the other man sat in the front with her case. The taxi began to drive off immediately. It was all over in a matter of seconds. A very professional operation. Anybody who didn't know, would think the woman was just sharing the car with the men, taking a taxi to the airport perhaps.

Turner tapped the dashboard. 'Follow them, Ronnie, but at a distance. I don't want them to know.'

Chapter 33

'Now, you're probably wondering who we are and why we are taking you on a little tour of Sean's hometown?'

'The thought had crossed my mind.'

'Aye, it has a habit of doing that on journey like this. We are what you might call a welcoming committee. We welcome people and ensure they had a wonderfully safe time in our fair city. Don't we, Sean?'

The thug beside her played the big, silent type to perfection.

'We were wondering why an ex-police woman like yourself was visiting our city?'

'How do you know I'm ex-police?' It was time to start asking the little man questions herself. Change the relationship in the back of this car.

'Ah, a little birdie told me. The same wee bird also said you had visited the barracks and the university asking questions. I'll ask again. Why are you here in Dublin?'

'You seem to have a talkative bird there, a parrot perhaps? Or a magpie who likes stealing shiny things from people's hotel rooms? What did you say your name was?'

'I didn't Mrs Sinclair. Let's not deal in names for the moment. I'll ask again, why are you here in Dublin?'

'To see the sights. I'm a tourist like anybody else.' Jayne disliked the little man sitting next to her with his bad breath. She wasn't going to tell him anything.

'And one of those sights is Ellen Fitzgerald, is it?'

'It is.'

'Ah well, Sean there, was thinking that Ellen wasn't in any guidebook he knew of, weren't you Sean?' The big man didn't say a word just nodded his head.

Jayne took her cue from him. Silence is golden.

'Let me lay my cards on the table, Mrs Sinclair.'

The little man opened his hands revealing soft pink palms and long, elegant, fingers. They were the hands of a child.

'Ellen Fitzgerald is important to us. She and her father deserve respect and admiration for all that they have done in their lives. We wouldn't like that legacy to be sullied in any way. Do I make myself clear? Particularly not this year. The year we celebrate the anniversary of one of the greatest times in Irish history.'

Jayne wasn't going to let this little man lecture her any longer. 'Why did you steal my laptop?'

'What laptop?' The little man's eyes opened wider, he seemed genuinely surprised. 'I can assure you Mrs Sinclair, we don't steal people's property, we have our principles,' he said with a sniff of self-righteousness.

A quick flash of eyes in the rearview mirror. 'We're being followed, boss. The white Volvo.'

The little man twisted in his seat, looking behind him. 'Are you sure, Tommy?'

'He's been behind us since we left the old lady. Just one car.'

'The Garda or the Specials?'

'Don't know, boss. Not a car I've seen before.'

The little man turned and stared at her. 'Who are you, Mrs Sinclair? A researcher in family history or is that just a cover?'

The car swung sharply left. She was thrown against the little man.

'It's still there, boss. Three cars back. I'm sure it is tailing us.'

'Pull through the lights up ahead and turn left, Tommy.'

The driver accelerated towards the lights as they turned red. Ignoring the signal, he turned left, forcing a car to stamp on its brakes. A long, annoyed squeal of a car horn followed.

'Turn left at the next road, Tommy. Listen, Mrs Sinclair. I don't care who or what you are, but you are to leave Ellen Fitzgerald alone, is that clear?'

The car swung left again and screeched to a halt again. Jayne was thrown out of the car onto the pavement. Her bag came sailing out after her, landing with a thud against the wall behind her. She sat there for a few moments, rubbing her knee. She dragged herself to her feet gingerly. As she did so, a white Volvo drove past. In the passenger seat, a man was staring at her. She had seen him somewhere before? But where?

Who was he? And why was he following her?

Chapter 34

Dublin. November 19, 2015.

They followed the taxi through the suburbs of Dublin, making sure to keep three cars behind.

'Looks like they're not going to the airport.'

Why had the IRA picked her up? Was it because of the old woman? Or something else? 'Keep following but stay well back.'

'They are bound to spot us eventually with only one car. This lot know what they're doing. We've come back on ourselves. The same junction we were at five minutes ago.'

'Keep after them, drop further back if it will help.'

They followed the taxi for twenty minutes. It kept to the suburbs avoiding the centre of the city, heading east through Rathmines and then south towards Tallaght. Where were they taking her? And what were they doing? All he could see were three heads in the back of the car. Two turned towards each other, one was facing front.

Suddenly, the car sped up, mounted the pavement and turned left through a red light.

'Follow them, Ronnie. Don't lose them.'

They were blocked by an old man driving an even older car. Ronnie glanced to his left and swung the car up onto the pavement, forcing a cyclist off his bike. The car careered down the pavement, one tyre on the road. A woman with a pushchair opened her eyes in fear as the car kept coming and coming straight towards her.

She screamed.

At the last minute, Ronnie swerved back into the road

just before the junction, swinging left through the red light. A bus was coming straight towards them from the right. The loud pitched squeal of brakes. An immense green mass looming closer and closer. He could see the driver forcing himself back into the seat, pushing down with all his might on the brakes.

They were going to be hit. David Turner braced his body back against the seat, preparing it for the shock of the impact.

The crash of metal on metal never came. Just as the bus loomed over them, the wheels of the car gripped the road and they began to surge away, the distance between them and the large green lump of metal known as a bus slowly getting larger and larger.

'They've turned left up ahead. Shall I follow?' Ronnie was as cool as a spring day, still focussed on the car in front.

'Keep after them.'

Ronnie's eyes never left the road ahead, staring at the white taxi, and moving in a slow, controlled manner. He swung the car around the corner. Ahead they could see Jayne Sinclair picking herself up from the ground, her bag lying next to her.

'Shall we stop?'

'No, keep on going. She's out now.'

'Keep after the taxi?'

David Turner thought for a moment. 'No, let them go. No point in chasing after them. The last thing I want to do is piss off a bunch of Micks on their home turf.'

Ronnie seemed disappointed at the decision. He wasn't being paid to fight the IRA, not anymore anyway, but he still missed the adrenalin rush of a car chase.

As they passed Jayne Sinclair, she looked over towards

their car. Let her see him, no point in hiding anymore, she had probably worked out that she was being followed already.

Chapter 35

Dublin. November 19, 2015.

She missed her flight. After picking up her case and wandering around for ten minutes, she had walked into a greengrocer's to ask where she was.

'The airport? Well, you'll be long way from there.' The old man behind the counter gave a little chuckle at the folly of the question. 'It's over on the other side of town. An American tourist, are you?'

Jayne ignored the question. 'Could you call me a taxi?'

'Well, there are no taxi firms hereabouts, but Pat sometimes runs us to the airport if we're flying off on holiday. I'll give him a call.' He picked up the phone and after a long chat about the weather and how the man's son was doing at the university, they talked about going to the airport. The shop owner put the phone down. 'He'll be here in twenty minutes. Could be half an hour, though. With Pat, you can never tell. Now can I be getting anything for you while you wait?'

Jayne suddenly realised she was starving. She hadn't eaten that morning. And after the events in the car, she was desperate to eat something to settle her stomach. 'Do you have a sandwich?'

'That we do. Only egg and onion today, though. That's all that Mrs Clancy made this morning. Her hens must be laying so.'

'Egg and onion would be lovely.'

She sat outside the shop eating her sandwich and waiting for her ride to the airport. What the fuck was going on?

Why had she been kidnapped? All they seemed to ask about was her visit to Ellen Fitzgerald as if it was all that mattered. Had she inadvertently stepped into the middle of something? Or was her client's past somehow caught up with something deeper, something more important? She didn't know. Not yet anyway, but she would bloody well find out. Nobody threatened her. It didn't matter if it was some thug in Moss Side or a small pale man in Dublin.

She took another bite of the white bread sandwich. Egg and onion, an acquired taste but not one she was interested in acquiring. She threw the rest of the sandwich away.

Had her client been truthful with her? Was there more to this than just finding a long-lost father? She thought back to their meeting. The man was old and ill, dying according to his nephew. All her instincts shouted, no they screamed, he was only after one thing. To find out who he was and where he came from. It was like 'Rosebud' in Citizen Kane. An idea, a vague memory, a desire to return to that state of innocence that existed before he was sent to America. It was as if he was returning to his childhood. She had seen the same in her father. He could remember details from growing up in Hulme better than he could remember what he had for breakfast that morning. Or worse. He could remember the name of his teacher at primary school, but he couldn't remember her name. Or her face. It had been three days since she had last seen him, she needed to visit him again.

So what the fuck was going on? Since the start of this case, a brick had been thrown through her window, her computer had been stolen, she had been kidnapped, and now she was certain she was also being followed.

Was it all because some old man wanted to know who his father was? Or was something more involved. MI5?

The IRA? The Irish Special Branch? Had someone seen a Dublin connection to all of this and decided that it needed to be followed up?

Whatever it was and whoever it was, one thing was certain. Somebody was after her and they weren't looking for her dazzling personality

And then one other thought hit her.

Paul's bloody dinner with his boss. She looked at her watch. 12.30.

Shit. Shit. Shit.

Chapter 36

Didsbury, Manchester. November 19, 2015.

It was 8.30 in the evening before she reached home. She had missed her plane and had only managed to get on the 5 pm flight by a mixture of charm and pleading. Of course, it had taken off late and then spent ages circling over Manchester Airport deciding whether to land or not. The captain's voice, with its mellow Irish burr, so relaxing on her flight to Dublin, now became as irritating as a toothache.

'You may have noticed that we are circling the lovely city of Manchester. According to the air traffic control, we are number eight in the waiting list to land. So, I'm afraid we'll be a wee bit late arriving. With a bit of luck and Irish charm we'll have you on the ground in twenty minutes.'

She had rung Paul as soon as she exited the plane. The call went straight to his voicemail. An infuriatingly calm voice asking her to leave a message after the beep.

Of course, it was rush hour in Manchester when she landed, getting a cab had taken years. She had finally rushed back to their house, opened the door and found it was eerily quiet.

Paul had left a short note on the table top in the kitchen.

'I've taken them out for dinner at the Eagle.'

That was all. No threats. No written disappointments. Nothing else, not even a signature.

She went to the fridge and pulled out a bottle of wine and the rest of the chocolate. Not a great trip. Her laptop

215

had been stolen, she had been kidnapped by the IRA, she was sure she was being followed and now, to add icing to the rest of the shit cake, she had managed to piss off her husband. Way to go, Jayne.

She poured herself a glass of wine and took a large chunk of chocolate and popped it in her mouth. This time though, she didn't enjoy the taste. Everything was going wrong. She had left the police force because she couldn't handle the stress of being responsible for someone's life. Dave Gilmour had died because she didn't react quickly enough.

And now, she was responsible for another person, John Hughes. He had less than two months left to live, and she had to find out the answers for him in the next few days.

She put her head in her hands. Why did people rely on her so much? Why couldn't she just have an easy life? Stay at home, be the dutiful wife, cook a bloody dinner for Paul and his obnoxious boss, a Stepford Wives smile pasted across her face.

She could ring Richard Hughes now and tell him she was giving up the case. He would understand, after all, he asked her not to pursue it in the first place. The old man wouldn't be happy but she couldn't help that. There were plenty of other professional genealogists he could ask. People who could do the job just as well as her.

She picked up her mobile and scrolled to the number. As she did so, the cat rubbed its body against her legs, mewing quietly. She reached down to stroke its soft black fur. The message board on the wall caught her eye. A square piece of paper was pinned next to an electricity bill.

LEAVE IT ALONE stared back at her, its black block capitals stark against the white paper, shouting out its message.

How dare some bastard throw a brick through her window? How dare he threaten her? Nobody was going to frighten her. Not the thugs of Moss Side or Salford, and certainly not some bastard who thought he could get her off a case.

She hadn't been scared as a police detective and she wasn't going to be scared now.

She took a large mouthful of wine. She had made progress in this case, she hadn't left it alone. She wasn't going to give up now despite everything. No bastard was going to scare her off.

She thought about ringing Richard to find out the condition of John Hughes, but she couldn't face any more questions that evening.

She grabbed her wine and stomped upstairs to the study, clicked on the desktop computer that perched on a table. It was an old PC and nobody in the house used it anymore, but Paul kept it up-to-date. 'Just in case,' he always said.

She accessed her notes on the case in the Cloud, copying them into a new file on the desktop. She used her mobile to send the pictures she had taken of Miss Fitzgerald's photos and of her father's memoirs to her email account.

Good, up-to-date now. Leave it alone? Fat fucking chance. What next? Time to find out more about John Clavell.

She logged on to the archives of The Times newspaper. What was the date of his killing? She checked her notes, June 8, 1921.

She typed in the date. A page came up. She scanned it and typed the name Clavell in the search section. There it was. An article on page three.

BRITISH OFFICER KIDNAPPED BY IRISH IR-

REGULARS

She read the article. Declan Fitzgerald's memoirs contained far more detail.

She opened the next link.

BRITISH OFFICER'S BODY FOUND

Shot dead. Family in mourning.

Captain John Clavell to be returned to Bradford.

The body of the slain British Officer, Captain John Clavell, was transported yesterday to his home town of Bradford. The coffin was escorted by a detachment of his regiment, the Royal Kent Fusiliers. Captain Clavell's body was discovered in the mountains south of Dublin last Tuesday. He had been kidnapped the week before whilst on a hunting expedition with Irish friends.

The body will be interred with full military honours at Heaton Methodist Church in Bradford on June 18th.

The murder of Captain Clavell occurred three days before the truce was signed between the British government and the so-called Irish Sinn Fein. At one point, it was believed that the murder would affect the negotiations between the Crown forces and the representatives of Sinn Fein but an agreement was finally reached.

All wreaths and notices of condolence should be sent to the family at the Old Dene, Queensbury, Bradford, Yorkshire.

There it was again, the same family name kept coming up. Clavell, not a common name at all. Wasn't there a writer with the same name? She shook her head, 'focus, Jayne,' she said out loud. This was the same surname as the mother of John Hughes. She felt the familiar frisson of excitement down her spine. At least now she had an address to work with.

Chapter 37

The following morning all was not well in the house. Paul had come back late and, from the noise he made banging upstairs and falling over in the bathroom, very drunk. He had stayed in the spare bedroom. She thought about going to see him and apologising but it all seemed too little and too late. Better to let him sleep it off, they would talk in the morning.

But they hadn't, of course. She woke up early and went down for her coffee and breakfast, feeding the cat before herself. The poor thing just mewed contentedly as it devoured its pork and rabbit pate.

He came down later, apparently still not fully recovered.

'Good morning,' she said as he came through the door.

A cold, unshaven stare. No response.

She went back to drinking her coffee. He banged around in the cupboard apparently looking for a mug but actually venting his anger on a piece of inanimate furniture.

She opened her mouth to say the words of apology. She knew the dinner was important to him and she should have been back for it. She thought about telling him the truth about what had happened in Dublin, but the words just wouldn't come out. It was like when she was a copper. The last thing she wanted to do when she went home was talk about work. What do you say over the cornflakes? I saw a dead body yesterday. A pregnant woman knocked over by a car, her brains spilling out on the roadway. Or I nabbed a 12-year-old this morning for thieving. Wanted money for his dealer. Or worse. Nothing happened today. I helped nobody, I did nothing except fill in time sheets and logs and all the time-consuming bureaucracy that comes with being Police. So she had made a conscious decision never to talk about work except with colleagues. Only they knew what it was like.

But this morning she knew she had to make an effort. 'Look, I'm sorry about last night. I screwed up, ok.'

Silence. He just sat there drinking his coffee and reading his paper.

'Are we going to talk about it, or are you going to play silly buggers?'

Silence.

Silly buggers it was.

She was too busy and too stressed to deal with him and his silences right now. 'When you want to talk about it, let me know. In the meantime, I'm going to see my dad.'

She went upstairs to take a shower and get ready. He didn't come and see her. As she was putting on her coat to go out, he finally spoke.

'He offered me a promotion last night. European Sales Manager, based in Brussels. I'm flying there today to check it out.'

'Sounds good, it seems like he's not such a fool after all.' She hoped the backhanded compliment would make him smile.

She was wrong.

'If I take it, we'll have to move to Brussels for three years. It's based there, close to the European Commission.'

'What about my father? What about my job?'

He just looked at her and shrugged his shoulders.

'Is that all you have to say?'

He turned back to his newspaper. She stood there in her

coat and her bare feet. She could hear the clock ticking on the wall. Cheap bastard thing from Ikea. She wanted to throw it across the room. But she didn't. All she noticed was the headline on the paper. 'Celebrity Big Brother. New Scandal.'

She pointed to the door. 'I'm going to see my father. We'll talk about it when I get back.'

'I won't be here. I'll be in Brussels.'

'Well, we'll talk about it when you get back.' She packed up her files and her notes in her bag. 'I'll see you later.'

There was no answer from him.

* * *

'How's the weather today? Mrs Trainor?' Jayne had psyched herself up to be chirpy before stepping into her father's home. Funny, how she thought about it that way. His home with a small 'h' rather than the Home, with all the institutional baggage that the word brought with it. It was his home, probably more so than any other home they had lived in.

'It's good, Mrs Sinclair. He's missed you the last couple of days. Had a bit of a relapse on Wednesday but came out of it again. He'll be happy to see you. He's in his usual place in the annexe.'

'Thanks.' She walked through the fire doors and down the corridor. He was sitting facing the garden, staring out through the large picture windows. She wondered what he did all day. Unlike the others, he didn't seem to spend time watching TV or playing cards. He must just read and stare out of the window, keeping himself to himself.

'Hello, Dad.'

He continued to stare out of the window.

'Hello, Dad,' she said a little louder.

Slowly, he turned his eyes towards her. Vacant eyes, seeing but not seeing. 'Who are you?' A blank look on his face. 'I don't know you.'

She sat down next to him, taking his hand. 'It's me, Dad, Jayne.'

'I'm not your dad. I'm...' The voice trailed off as he searched for who he was.

She gripped the hand tighter. 'Dad, it's Jayne, I've come to see you.'

'Who's Jayne? I don't know no Jayne.' Then a smile spread slowly across his face.

She looked at him and saw the glint in his eyes once more. She slapped his hand. 'Dad, don't mess around. It's not funny.' A tear escaped from her right eye and ran down her cheek.

'Had you going, though, didn't I?'

She wiped the tear away. 'Promise me you won't do that again, Dad. Promise me.' She wiped her face again.

'We are fragile this morning. Lost our sense of humour, have we?' She stared at him. 'Ok, Ok, I promise. No more jokes about Mr Jones.'

Mr Jones was what they called his disease. The Alzheimer's that was creeping up on him, slowly infesting his mind. Mr Jones was another person who had no memory and no past. He was a faceless person, the man in a crowd. When he forgot something, he was having a Mr Jones moment. When a day passed and he couldn't remember what he had done, it was a Mr Jones day. When the frustration got the better of him and he felt the rage coming on, it was the time of Mr Jones.

'Please, Dad. You don't know how much it hurts.'

He touched her hand. 'I promise.' He looked down at her bag, changing the subject. 'How's the case? Have you found the old man's father?'

'Not yet, but I'm getting close.' She took him through the events in Dublin, omitting the theft of her Mac and her kidnapping. He couldn't understand and he couldn't help anyway. She showed him the printout from the Fitzgerald memoirs and The Times article.

He pinched his bottom lip with his index finger and thumb. 'Looks like you have to go to Yorkshire, lass. But have a care when you're there. Tight as ducks' arses are Yorkshire people.'

'There speaks a true Lancastrian.'

'Aye, and proud of it. But that's where you'll find the truth. This Michael Dowling man and the woman are linked somehow. And from the condition of your client, you better go soon. He's worse than me.'

She remembered that she had forgotten to call Richard Hughes. She would do it when she left the home. 'I'll go today, Dad. I've only got three days before I have to report back to him.'

'If he lasts that long. And talking about deadbeats, how's Paul?'

She didn't answer. 'I'd better be off, Dad. The bright lights of Yorkshire beckon.'

'Aye, the unbearable lightness of being in Halifax. Wasn't that a TV programme?'

'Should be if it wasn't.' She picked up his hand, noticing how paper-thin the skin was, translucent like the finest sheer silk. 'It's not good with Paul, Dad. He wants to move to Brussels. A new promotion.'

Her father was silent for a long while. 'You do what you

think is right, Jayne. I've always told you. Do what's right.'

'I got sick of hearing it when I was at school. Like a broken record, you were.'

'It's as true then as it is now.'

'But what's right isn't what's easy.'

'Never was, lass. Never was. And if it were, it wouldn't be right, would it? Stands to reason. So the right thing to do now is...?'

'Go to Yorkshire.'

'That's my girl. You can work out what you're doing when he gets back. Meanwhile, do what's right now.'

She leant forward and wrapped her arms around his thin body.

'Don't go all soppy on me now, girl, not after 42 years, you don't.'

Chapter 38

Bradford, West Riding of Yorkshire. June 10, 1923.

Michael stood in front of the house. Above the door, the numbers 1641 were carved in stone. Funny, he thought, this house was built when England was on the eve of a Civil War just as his home was in the middle of one now. Devalera and the anti-treaty side had announced a ceasefire in May, but he didn't know if it would last. He didn't care about it anyway. Not anymore. He missed Fitz and the friendship they once had. But Fitz was lost to the cause, lost to Ireland, rotting in some jail in Athlone, put there not by the British but by his former comrades.

The same men who had executed so many of their former comrades. Stood them against a wall and shot them dead for rebelling against the Free State. Civil Wars were definitely not civil, pitting brother against brother, Irishman against Irishman. This one was following the lead of all the others, becoming more brutal, more vicious on both sides as time went on. Had history taught them nothing? Apparently not. It had devoured Ireland's leader, Michael Collins, shot dead in some ambush on a quiet country road in the county of his birth, Cork.

He would have no part of them or their killing. And no State could call itself 'free' when it was killing its citizens.

Wars devour their young.

Calm yourself, Michael. Now is not the time to become agitated. Ireland and her troubles are behind you now. They are in the past, you have something else you need to worry about now.

226

He took three deep breaths and walked up the driveway.

It had taken him a long time to get here. After the announcement of the truce with the Brits in 1921, he had fallen apart. The knowledge that if they had waited three days, John Clavell would still be alive. If they had requested new orders from HQ. If he had been moved to another location. If they had decided to do it later in the week, he would still be alive and still breathing.

Instead, he lay in some grave in Bradford, a bullet hole in the back of his head.

Too many ifs clouding Michael's mind at that time. Fitz had urged him to pull himself together, to continue fighting for the cause. But, for Michael, that part of him was dead now. As dead as John Clavell. He had drowned all his belief in a United Ireland in the bottom of a whiskey bottle. For a year he had drunk himself stupid, ending up in doss houses or sprawled out in the gutter, his body aching from the guilt, while Ireland had wrenched itself apart through recrimination and squabbling.

He knew now that he had to go through all that. He had to get to the very bottom before he could rise again.

It had happened one night. He had been drinking in some bar in Dublin Quays. He couldn't remember how long but it seemed like an age and a day. He had staggered out of there, not knowing where he was going or where he came from, the whisky propping him up as he swayed from side to side on the pavement.

He had walked, or staggered, for hours. It was still dark when he stopped in front of a derelict house. The bricks and the charred wood and the dirty wallpaper had been cleared away, but he recognised it straight away. The blackened walls where the flames had eaten the poor life of the family that lived there were still vivid on the walls. And off to one side, a small cairn of bricks marked where the child had lain, her dead hand clutching the silk ribbon.

He stood there for hours. Gradually, the sun broke through the grey shield of a Dublin day and still he stood there. People walked around him. A policeman tried to move him on. But still he stood there, staring at the cairn of stones.

An old woman came out from one of the neighbouring houses. She took him by the arm and led him to her step. 'It looks like you could be wanting a drop of tea.'

She placed a cracked cup in his hands and he slowly raised it to his lips.

It was sweet and warm and bitter all at the same time.

'Did you know the family that lived here?'

He didn't answer, raising the cup to his mouth one more time.

'Well, you may and you may not. But, you can't be standing there all day and night so. What will people think?'

He took another sup of tea. 'I suppose not,' he mumbled.

She reached into her apron. 'Here's sixpence, why don't you go and get yourself something to eat? You're as thin as an 'oul tinker.'

He looked down at his hands holding the cup. They were bony and wrinkled and old. Not hands really, more like claws. She pressed the sixpence between his fingers.

'Thank you,' he mumbled.

'Don't be thanking me. Thank himself.' Her eyes flicked upwards to the grey sky. 'He's the one you ought to be thanking.'

Slowly, he placed the cup down on the step and stood up.

'Thank you.'

He hadn't touched alcohol since. Sure, he had been tempted many a time, but the image of the child's hand clutching the ribbon always strengthened his resolve.

As he got better, he realised that he still had unfinished business. He had to go to Bradford and give the effects of John Clavell back to his family. It wasn't much: the letters, a watch, a notebook, a silver cross, but he had to go. It was almost as if by going he could be absolved for his responsibility in the killing. Not released from it, simply absolved.

It had taken him a long time to work out how he was going to do it. He couldn't just knock on the door and say, 'Here I am. I was involved with killing your son.' And sending the effects anonymously through the post wouldn't have been right. He had promised to deliver them to the man's family. He had to do it in person.

It was reading the letter that Clavell had written to the family about his dead comrade that gave Michael the idea. All he had to do was pretend to be a fellow officer from Clavell's regiment. He already had the name of one man he could use. Charles Trichot. The man was dead, killed in France, but nobody else would know that except him. Adopting his identity would make the initial approach to the family so much easier. Give them the effects and walk away. They would be none the wiser.

It was so simple, yet utterly believable. And here he was, six months after conceiving his plan, walking the driveway to John Clavell's house sober as a judge.

The house was small and solid, in that dark-stoned Yorkshire way. A house like the people; stolid, steadfast, not given to extravagance or frippery. He knocked on the door. A maid opened it almost immediately.

'Could I speak to Mr Clavell?'

She looked at him for a moment, then turned away to

run down the hall, crying.

He was left standing at the door. Not a good start. What had he done wrong? He was tempted to run away, get as far as he could from this house and these people.

An elegantly dressed woman appeared at the door. 'You are looking for my father?'

Michael nodded.

'I'm afraid he passed away two months ago. Can I help you?'

She was beautiful in an austere way. Dressed in black from head to toe, her dark hair stood in vivid contrast to her alabaster skin. There was no hint of make-up, not a trace of powder, rouge or the fashionable lipstick. And in the middle of that naturally beautiful face, a pair of ice-cold blue eyes. They looked through him, piercing him with their knowledge and candour.

The resolve he had spent six months constructing seemed to ebb away in an instant. Once again, he was tempted to run away. Not to answer her question, but turn on his heels and run back down the drive and away from her. It was only her voice that stopped him as she repeated her question.

'Can I help you?'

'I...I... was looking for Mr Clavell.'

'As I explained, he passed away two months ago. Is there anything I can help you with?'

Michael took a deep breath, remembering everything he had learnt on the train coming here. The letter in his pocket the perfect introduction to a man who was already dead. A man whom he would now bring back to life. 'My name's Trichot, Charles Trichot.' He stammered again. Take a breath, Michael, compose yourself. 'I used to serve with your brother, John.' He left the details of where and when they had served together deliberately vague. For a moment, he saw a small spark of hope in those ice-blue eyes and then it died just as quickly as it had sparkled.

'My brother, he died. In Ireland, last year.'

'I know. I knew him there.'

She opened the door wider. 'Pardon me, I forgot my manners. How could I be so rude as to leave a comrade of John's standing at the door? My father would have scolded me for...' At the mention of the word father, her voice trailed off. She recovered herself. 'Please come in.' She stepped aside and indicated that he should enter.

The hall was old fashioned, decorated in a style that had gone out of fashion with the death of Queen Victoria. She led him to a drawing room. It too looked like it had been untouched since the Boer War; heavy furniture, topped with china and bric-a-brac, a black mahogany writing desk in the corner and a large fire roaring in the grate. The room was warm, almost too warm. The young woman rang a bell.

The maid who had answered the door came immediately. 'Tea for our guest, Daisy. I'll take a cup too.'

'Yes, ma'am.' The maid curtsied prettily and exited without raising her eyes to look at him.

'I'm sorry, I didn't catch your name.'

'It's Trichot, Charles Edward Maurice Trichot. A bit of a mouthful I'm afraid. Everybody calls me Charles. And you are?'

'I'm John's sister, Emily.' She stopped talking for a moment and stared into the fire. Then quickly recovered herself, remembering that there was someone else there. 'Did he ever mention me?'

Michael thought back to the evening before John Clavell's death. They had talked about everything that night; his parents, the war, friends who had died or lost their minds, his sister. They had even talked about Ireland. The eyes were still looking at him.

'I forget my manners again, here I am asking questions and you haven't even sat down yet.' She pushed an errant lock of hair back into her chignon nervously. Her fingers were long and elegant. Artist's fingers.

He sat down on the edge of the couch, not daring to make himself too comfortable. 'Your brother did talk about you.' He tried to remember what his prisoner had told him that night. 'He said you were his annoying little sister.'

She laughed. 'That was what he used to call me. His 'annoying little sister'. Even though, we were born quite close together, less than a year separated us.' For a moment, she stared into the fire. 'He always seemed older than me, perhaps it was the war, things he saw, things he did.'

'Wars age us all, turning young men old before their time.'

'Yes, he thought that too. He thought that he was old before his time. You must have known him well?'

'Quite well,' Michael answered slowly.

'You know, you are the first of his comrades to visit since the funeral. I don't remember seeing you there.'

'I couldn't make it. Still on duty.'

'That terrible Irish war. You know, he died three days before the truce. Two weeks later and he would have been safely home here, with Father.' Again her voice trailed off.

'What happened to you father?'

She sat up straighter, visibly trying to control herself. Her voice changed, becoming colder, more detached. Winter descended on those ice-blue eyes. 'Father wasn't the same after John's death. Oh, he tried to keep up appearances, going to the mill, trying to drum up new orders, but his heart wasn't in it anymore. He came home every evening and sat there.' She pointed to a chair next to the couch. 'He started to drink. A few glasses in the evening became a whole bottle and then he began drinking before he went to work. I tried to help him. To stop him, but he wouldn't listen. Couldn't listen. Daisy found him one morning, still sitting there in the chair. An empty bottle of whisky by his side and an empty bottle of pills on the floor.' She stopped speaking and stared into the fire.

'I'm sorry for your loss.' These were the only words Michael could think to say. The words used for such a long time to console the grieving but only alleviating the consolers of the need to express their real emotions.

She stopped staring at the fire and looked directly at him with those blue eyes. The blue shimmering in a water of barely formed tears. 'He never really got over John's death. He was the last hope, you see. My other brother had died in the war, and my father was old-fashioned. A woman's place was in the home, not running a mill. My brother was to take it over when he left the army.'

Michael thought back to the night before John Clavell's death when they had chatted about life and war and memories. 'He told me he was going to leave.'

'We thought he was safe in Ireland. He had survived the war, survived that butchery. A couple of months more in the Army and he would have been home with us. Father would have retired and John would run the mill.'

'What happens now?'

She sat up again, her back becoming straighter. 'Now, I prove them all wrong. I have taken over the management with the help of Mr Thwaites.'

At that moment, the door opened and Daisy bustled in with a tray. Placing it down on the table next to Emily.

'Milk and sugar, Mr Trichot?'

'Both, please. And call me Charles.'

She poured the milk into the china cup, followed by a long stream of dark tea. Michael noticed once again the elegant fingers as they held the sugar tongs, dropping two cubes of sugar into the cup. He stood up and took his tea from her, sitting back into the same place on the couch.

She poured herself a cup adding just a splash of milk. 'Enough about me and my family, Mr Trichot...Charles. You have not come all this way to Yorkshire just to hear about my woes. You are Irish yourself, am I right?'

'How did you know?'

'Your accent, a way of speaking.'

'You have a good ear, Miss Clavell.'

'Please call me Emily.'

He took a sip of tea, giving himself time to remember his story. 'Actually, I was born in Surrey. My father was a vicar there. We moved to Ireland when I was a child and stayed on for my education when my father went back to a new vicarage in Surrey again.'

'Oh, you must be the man John talked about. The man who swore like a trooper but whose father was a vicar. He talked about you often.'

Michael felt his face blush. The story he had found in the letter had been true.

'You shouldn't be embarrassed, Mr Trichot...Charles,' she corrected herself, 'I'm sure I have heard worse down at the mill.'

She had misinterpreted the reddening of his face. 'I'm so glad he talked about me to you,' he stammered, his face reddening even more.

'He talked about you a lot.' She stopped for a moment. 'He said you had been killed in the last days of the war.

Was very upset by it.'

Those blue eyes staring at him again. He had been expecting this. 'Reports of my death have been exaggerated,' he joked.

For a second, her eyes didn't move and then her mouth widened to a broad smile. How beautiful she looked when she was smiling, he thought.

'Who said that?'

'I'm afraid I stole it from Oscar Wilde.'

'So you did.'

'I was injured for a long while. Everybody thought I was dead. A shell, I lost my memory. It was a hard time. A year before I could rejoin the regiment.'

'John was already in Ireland by then.'

'I joined him there.'

'I'm sure he was happy to see you.'

'I think I was happier to see him, to see them all.' Once again, she smiled, a beautiful smile when the ice-blue eyes lost their coldness and became the loveliest, warmest visions he had ever seen.

'Thank you for coming all this way to see me. You don't know how much it means.'

'Thank you for having me. But there is a reason for my journey.'

She leant forward. The eyes staring at him again.

'I came to return these effects of his to you.' He pulled out a small bag from the inside pocket of his jacket.

'But they said everything had been lost when he was captured...'

'It was. After the truce, one of the local IRA commanders gave these things to me before the regiment left the town.'

'You met my brother's killer?'

'It wasn't the man who killed your brother. They said it was outsiders, men from Dublin, who killed him. We never found out their names.' He opened the bag. 'It's not much I'm afraid.'

She took the bag from him.

'There's just four things; a small notebook. Most officers carry them. Used for writing down all the stuff one has to remember.'

She took out the book, inside the spine was a stub of a pencil, the end still had tooth marks. She opened the book and flicked through it. 'John always had the most appalling handwriting. His school often complained about it.'

'Some letters. He kept all of them your family had written.' He turned over the envelope with its return address on the back. 'That's how I knew where to find you.'

She took the letters and placed them beside her. Not looking at them. Not opening them.

'A silver cross.'

'I gave him this to keep him safe. Wasn't much use, was it?'

'He loved the cross. Wore it all the time,' Michael lied, hoping to comfort her. It seemed to work. Her long fingers stroked the cross, feeling its simple sharp lines and the smoothness of the silver.

'The last effect that they gave me was his watch.'

Emily reached into the bottom of the bag. Inside a pocket, she found a box.

'I packed it into a small box. I hope that's ok?'

She opened the box. Sitting there was John's watch. The tears began to flow down her face. 'My father gave each one of his sons a watch before they left for their regiments. 'So you won't be late,' he told them.' She stopped talking.

Michael reached over and handed her his handkerchief.

She wiped her tears away and once again recovered. 'My father thought timeliness was next to godliness. 'Never be late,' he would say, 'punctuality is a virtue.' She stopped talking again. She turned over the watch again and again in her hand.

Michael remembered the day of the execution. John waiting and ready the morning Michael had gone to fetch him. 'He was always on time, your brother. He kept your father's words close to him.'

Tears began to run down her face again. She wiped them away with his handkerchief. Once again, she fought to regain control of herself. 'Thank you for bringing these effects of his. Before, we had nothing. They said there was nothing. But now a little part of him has come back to me. Does that make sense?'

Michael knew exactly what she meant. A little piece of us rubs off on the things we own, the things we hold most dear. 'He's always here with us,' he said finally.

Then she stopped crying and looked at him once more. 'You are right, Mr Trichot. He's always here with us.'

Chapter 39

'Hello, Mr Hughes, it's Jayne Sinclair. How is your uncle?'

'He's a little better, Mrs Sinclair. He's out of intensive care now, but still at the hospital under observation.'

She heard a shout down the phone, followed by a loud crackle.

'Mrs Sinclair,' a hoarse, old voice breathed through the earpiece, 'there's life in the old dog yet. Not much mind you, but still enough to kick these stupid doctors halfway into next week. What have you found?'

Jayne held the phone away from her ear, the voice was so loud. 'I'm glad to hear you sound so well, Mr—'

'Enough of that, Mrs Sinclair. I pay you to research my life not to flatter me. I have my nephew for that. What have you found?'

'Well, there's a lead in Yorkshire...'

'That's where the home was.'

'And where the marriage of your parents was registered. I think I may have found a link to a man called Michael Dowling. He fought during the Easter Rising and your cap badge could have belonged to him.'

'May have. Could have. Should have. Have you found anything concrete, Mrs Sinclair? Or am I paying you for hot air?'

'You're paying me to find out who you are, Mr Hughes, which I am in the process of doing. I am following up leads in Yorkshire and will go there today.'

'Get a move on, Mrs Sinclair. We will be leaving the UK on Monday evening. And I don't need to remind you my health is not as good as it once was.' As if on cue he began coughing, a harsh, barking, noise.

The coughs continued in the background as Richard Hughes came on the phone again. 'I keep telling him you are working on it, Mrs Sinclair, but he refuses to listen. Never listened to anybody else in his life and he isn't going to start now.'

'Are you still leaving on Monday?'

'We are going. He's decided to check himself out of the hospital against the doctor's advice today. We're moving back to the hotel. They won't let him drink or smoke here. Our flights are booked for Monday evening. You have till then I'm afraid.'

'I understand, Mr Hughes. I'll do my best.'

'Thank you, Mrs Sinclair.' She heard more shouts from the background, then the line went dead.

She was sat out in the car park in front of her father's nursing home. Should she go back and pack? She couldn't see the point. All she needed was her notes. Everything else she could pick up in Yorkshire.

She looked all her around her. Nothing.

For a moment a feeling of dread surged down her spine. The awful sense she was being watched, being followed. She wondered if she wasn't paranoid, the shock of being in the back of the taxi, threatened by that little man, had somehow affected her more than she thought.

The carpark was empty, she couldn't see anybody watching her. Her mind flashed back to the face in the other car in Dublin, the white Volvo. Were they following her or the IRA men? She didn't know. Just because you're paranoid, it doesn't mean they're not out to get you. She remembered the old joke and shrugged her shoulders.

'Get a move on, Jayne, you haven't got all day.' Once again, she spoke out loud. She entered the address in the satnav and put the car in gear. If they were following her, then there was nothing she could do about it.

Not yet anyway. But if she ever discovered who they were, she would kick the living shit out of them. After she had asked them, politely, who they were and why they were following her, of course.

Always get the answers before the violence. First thing you learn at Police Training College.

Chapter 40

Time for his noonday call. David Turner pressed the speed dial on his phone, it linked him directly to his client.

'Hello, you're on speaker phone. I'm on the M62 at the moment, following her car.' This time he had attached a Zoombak tracker to the rear of her vehicle. The satnav in his hand beeped reassuringly and a small dot travelled on the M62 slightly ahead of him, showing her car and its route.

'Find out where she's going. Call me back at three pm. I want you to stay in touch more often now. She's getting closer.' The client's voice had changed from being tentative and unconfident. Now, he was the one giving the orders.

'My operative will have broken the code on her computer by now. Do you want me to send you the hard disk?'

'Do that. Call me back at three pm sharp.'

'Will do. I'll call back then with an update. Any further orders, sir?' He was beginning to sound like he was back in the army again. It felt good, playing this client as he had played the officers. The added 'sir' at the end snapped out like an unspoken salute. He could feel the client enjoying it on the other end of the line.

'Good, carry on. Three pm sharp.'

God, he's even beginning to sound like an officer. The connection was cut and a buzzing noise filled the car. Well, he didn't mind taking orders again as long as he was in charge. More orders meant more money. And he was always happy to receive more money.

The small dot on his satnav began to bear left towards the M606. Going to Bradford or Halifax then. He wondered if he would have time for a curry. Loved a good curry he did. Got the taste for it when he was in Singapore, training their army. He often went down to Racecourse Road, eating a mutton curry off a banana leaf with his hands, his fingers stained a bright yellow by the time he had finished. A Bradford curry would have to be pretty good to beat the taste of Muttu's, eaten off a banana leaf with fried chicken and sambal on the side.

His mouth began to water at the thought of it. Come on, lad, concentrate on work, not on food. Do your duty, your stomach can be filled later.

He followed her off the motorway onto the M606. Where was she going?

Chapter 41

Bradford, Yorkshire. November 20, 2015.

The detached house was set back slightly from the road and had evidently seen better days. Above the porch, the numbers 1641 were inscribed on a stone. Perhaps it had been a prosperous farmhouse when it was built, sitting high on a hill above the small village of Bradford.

But the arrival of steam power had changed all that. The many streams in the valley had powered the mills where carding, looming and weaving had been carried out. The mills needed a labour force to man those machines. Houses were built, long rows of back to back houses, like ranks of soldiers on a battlefield. Gradually, the houses reached out up the hill, swallowing up the old farmhouse like a tidal wave flowing over a sand castle. The mills grew more and more dense, each one spewing out dense fogs of smoke, turning the green and pleasant land into something brown and stony and terribly unhappy.

Somehow, the house had survived, surrounded but still standing. An outpost of a gentler, quieter, more rural life in amongst the terraced back-to-backs. The faceless men, women and children of the mills isolated from its gardens and lawns by a high stone wall.

Jayne parked her car at the entrance to the house and walked up the driveway. The front door was old and battered, with green paint peeling from the wood, revealing another coat of brown beneath. She tried the doorbell.

No sound. Was it working? She looked up at the windows. No sign of any life at the curtains. In fact, no sign of any curtains. The house looked and felt deserted. She knocked anyway. 'Hello?' she called out.

A noise came back. Somebody jumping down uncarpeted stairs. The door flew open. A young woman stood in the opening.

'Hello.' Jayne smiled.

'Are you the cleaner? Come on in.' The woman walked away.

Jayne followed her into the house. 'I think there's some sort of mistake...' she said tentatively.

'This way,' the voice shouted from the kitchen.

Jayne stepped over a pile of boxes in the hall. The kitchen was straight ahead. 'I think there's some mistake,' she repeated, 'I'm here about Mrs Clavell.'

'I'm Mrs Clavell.' The young woman stood with her hands on her hips.

'I'm here about Emily Clavell.'

'I think you have the wrong place. My name is Sonia Clavell.'

She must be a relative. 'I should explain. I'm a genealogical researcher.' She handed the young woman a card. 'I've been commissioned by my client to research his past. My investigations have led me to this address.'

The young woman was still looking at the card. 'Well, it's been in the family for a long time. Just sold it recently. You don't know how happy we are. But, as you can see, we're very busy, and if you're not the cleaner...'

'If I could just ask you a few questions. It wouldn't take more than a couple of minutes.' She smiled hopefully. 'It would be an immense help in my researches.'

The young woman looked at her watch. 'Just a few minutes?'

Jayne nodded.

244

'Well, it is time for a cuppa while we wait for the cleaner to come. Would you like one?'

'Lovely.'

'No biscuits, I'm afraid. Roger ate the last of them this morning.'

'Roger?'

'My Lab.' As if on cue, a large black Labrador, tail wagging like a regimental drummer, bounced into the kitchen, sniffed at Jayne and went to its owner. 'He's hungry again. I'll put the kettle on if you can get the dog food down from the shelf. What did you say your name was?'

'It's Jayne, Jayne Sinclair.'

'Well, Jayne, how can I help you?'

Jayne reached up for the bag of dog chow on the shelf. Roger immediately switched his attention from his owner to her. 'Where should I put this?'

Sonia Clavell poured a stream of hot water into a teapot. 'The bowl is somewhere on the floor where he left it.'

In the corner, Jayne spotted a bright green bowl. She filled it full of dog chow with one hand, pushing Roger away with the other. When she stepped away, he dived in, wolfing down huge mouthfuls of dried food.

'Roger, manners...' shouted Sonia.

The dog stopped what he was doing for a second, looked back over his shoulder at his owner and then went back to inhaling food.

'I give up.' Sonia handed over a hot cup of tea. 'There's milk on the table. Help yourself.'

Jayne poured a splash of milk into her tea and smelt the rich aroma. 'Where to start?' she said aloud to herself.

'The beginning is usually the best place.'

She liked this no-nonsense woman. 'I'm looking for the father of my client. He was adopted in America from the

Ilkley Children's Home.'

'When was that?'

'In 1929.'

'A long time ago. Why don't you ask at the home?'

'Unfortunately, it burnt down in the 1930s.'

'So he wants to find his relatives.'

'Right.'

'Where do I come in?'

'I don't know. His mother was Emily Clavell. She died in 1928 and he was put into the home in early 1929, we think.'

'Emily Clavell? The name rings a bell.'

'The census has her living in this house with her parents, and two elder brothers in 1911. One brother was killed in the war and the other died in the fighting in Ireland in 1921.'

'I didn't know there was any fighting in Ireland.'

Jayne passed over the photocopy of The Times article. 'See his address is given as this house.'

Sonia read the article. 'Poor people, losing a son like that.'

'Do you remember anybody of that name?'

The young woman thought for a moment. 'No, but I wouldn't, it's my sister who's the family history expert.'

Right on cue, there was a loud knock on the door. 'At last, the cleaner is here.' Sonia put down her tea and answered the door. She came back with a broad smile on her face. 'Speak of the devil. You're in luck.' She stepped aside to reveal a taller, more careworn version of herself with short hair and glasses. 'This is my sister, Annie.'

While Sonia made more tea, Jayne explained what she was looking for to Annie. At the mention of Emily Clavell's name, her face lit up. 'My great aunt. She was my grandmother's younger sister. Twelve years younger, actually. Our side of the family inherited this house from her when she died in 1928.'

'But she was married, why didn't the husband keep the house?'

'I don't know. My grandmother didn't talk about her much. Some family scandal. They were all devout Methodists, you know.'

'Do you have any old pictures or anything like that?' Jayne asked hopefully.

'I don't think so. Everything was lost or thrown out by our mother. She was a stickler for tidiness. You wouldn't believe it, looking at the place now, would you? She wasn't able to keep it up in the end. Too much for her. We tried to get her to move into sheltered housing but she wasn't having it. This was her home and this was where she was going to stay till the end of her days. Her church was around the corner and the shops were close by. This was her life and she wasn't going to change.'

Jayne felt deflated by the news. It looked like she was never going to get to the bottom of the case. It was Saturday now, she had to report to John Hughes before he left on Monday. What was she going to do?

'The only thing we still have from the old days is a family bible. As I said, they were devout Methodists. It's got all the births and deaths in it from 1850 odd. Would that help?'

Jayne sat up straight. 'That would be brilliant. At least, it would give me background to your family.'

'Hang on, it's here somewhere. Sonia, have you seen the Bible?'

'It's in the box of old books. I was going to give it to the Oxfam shop. It's out in the hall.'

Jayne followed Annie out there. They moved aside boxes full of old lampshades, bits of crockery, old pots and pans, finally getting to the bottom where a box of old books lay.

'It should be in here.'

They took them out one by one. Old recipe books were on the top, followed by Reader's Digest Specials. At the bottom, they found a black cover with gold lettering on the front. *Holy Bible.*

'Why would my sister want to throw this out? Sometimes I despair of her.' Annie brought out the old book. She opened the inside cover. In elaborate gothic writing, the inscription read;

This holy book belongs to Nathaniel Clavell and his family. May the Lord keep them and watch over them. Followed by a date, MDCCCLVIII.

'1858,' said Jayne. 'The inscription was written in 1858.'

There followed a list of names, dates of birth and death, written in a variety of inks and styles of handwriting. 'See, there's Emily.' Annie pointed to the middle of the list. 'Emily Clavell. Born 27 April 1894. Died 4 Dec 1928.'

'The other names are your descendants? Who is this?' Jayne pointed to the last name on the list. 'That's Mary Clavell, a distant cousin. She was the last person to live here full-time. A sad story really. Her fiancé was a pilot who died in the war, and she never married afterwards. Went a little doolally, don't you know.' Annie made a circling signal next to her head. 'Lived in this house all alone until three years ago. It all became too much for her and she went into an old folks' home out in Haworth.'

'Bronte Country?'

'It is. The home's called 'Wuthering' funnily enough.'

'Would she have any old photos or family documents?'

'I talked with her when I was researching the family. She had some things but not many. Didn't show them to me. As I said, went a bit strange after the war, she kept expecting her fiancé to walk through the door one day.'

Jayne thought of her father and his moments.

'Anyway, she wasn't much help. Kept remembering the grand balls she had gone to as a child and talking of the fiancé who was killed. It was as if he was still alive.'

'Can I go to see her?'

'If you wait till three pm, I'll take you there.'

Jayne looked at her watch. 11 am. She would have to kill four hours. 'You said you researched your family history?'

'We were quite a prominent family in the area. Had one of the first mills.' She sighed. 'But it's all been lost now. This house is the last one left and even then, it's not worth very much.'

'Did you get far in your family history?'

She smiled proudly. 'Took it back to 1723. We originally came from around here. Farmers who made it lucky during the industrial revolution.'

Jayne thought for a moment. 'So, if you were a prominent family in the area, births and family events would have been in the local newspapers.'

'Of course, that's how I found out about the mill we owned. You don't know how many hours I spent down at Central Library.'

Jayne stood up and rushed into the kitchen. 'Thanks very much for the tea, Sonia. Sorry, got to rush, I've had an idea.' She picked up her bag and coat. 'Thanks Annie for all your help, you don't know how much it means to me. I'll be back at 3 pm. We can go and visit Mary then, ok?'

Annie nodded. 'Fine, but I don't know if it will be any use. She's not really with us if you know what I mean.'

The two sisters stood in the hall as Jayne opened the door and ran to her car. Then she ran back to them. 'Er, Central Library is where?'

'It's called something else now. You know what councils are like, always changing names, I think it's just to keep their signwriters busy. But it's down in the centre of town, opposite the town hall. Just head straight downhill. You can't miss it.'

'Thanks once again.'

She got in the car and backed out of the drive. She didn't notice the Audi that pulled out and followed her down into the centre of Bradford.

She looked at her watch. 12.15 pm. The library probably closed at five on a Saturday. She drove quickly, shooting through a series of lights which were luckily all green.

After fifteen minutes, she saw a sign for the centre, drove past a rather ugly block of university buildings on the left, followed the road as it bent right, and a minute later was at the edge of a jumble of functional sixties buildings surrounding a beautiful old town hall. A sign for the library was on the right.

She parked the car in one of those municipal car parks modelled after medieval dungeons but twice as dour. Sixties town planners had so much to answer for. If she had her way, she would have them all paraded in front of the people whose lives their stupid decisions had blighted, letting them throw eggs and rotten tomatoes at the assembled idiots. A sort of modern version of the stocks.

She rushed up the steps to the library. A sign led her to the local studies library. She approached a severe middle-aged woman standing behind a desk.

'Do you have old editions of the *Bradford Telegraph and Argus* for 1924?'

The woman smiled condescendingly, imparting her knowledge as if reading from the Bible. 'It didn't exist then. The T&A wasn't formed until the amalgamation of the Bradford *Daily Telegraph* and the Bradford *Daily Argus* in 1926.'

At least, she was on the ball. 'Could I have a look at those papers in 1924?'

She reached behind her, scanned the boxes of microfilm for the right dates and handed Jayne two of them. 'There's a free reader in the corner.'

Jayne pulled out her notes from her bag. Everything had to be by hand until she bought herself a new MacBook Air. Who had stolen her previous one? The IRA? But they said nothing about it in the car. The people who were following her? She didn't know. Too many things were strange about this case. As if she were investigating in a sea of treacle being held back by the arms and legs.

She shook her head. 'Concentrate, Jayne.' The old man sitting at the microfilm reader next to her looked across, as if she were the village idiot.

Jayne ignored him, loading the Bradford Telegraph microfilm into the machine. She checked her notes. According to her initial search, the marriage was registered anytime between October and December 1923. She quickly whizzed through the reader until she hit a new paper dated October 1st.

She scanned each page looking for a clue or a headline that would give her the answer. She knew it was a long shot, but if the family were prominent mill owners then the marriage of a daughter should be given some space.

The paper covered everything; the price of wool,

worsted and finished cloth. The latest scores at Headingley, Yorkshire were bowled out for 124. A man arrested for stealing threepence. A woman found dead in her home, smoke inhalation from a faulty heater was the verdict. Even international news got a look in. Wars in China, Ramsey McDonald's treaty with the Soviets, the Australian immigration policy condemned by the League of Nations.

This was going to take ages, she thought. She had three whole months to search, from October to December, and she didn't have time.

She pressed the button to advance to the next page. It was a new paper with a date of Monday, October 6. She scanned through the headlines and, near the back, she finally found what she was looking for. On page 24 was a group of pictures headed, 'This week's weddings.' Beneath it, photographs of happy couples, in their best wedding outfits, were laid out like cards on a table. Beneath each picture were the names of the happy couple and a brief description of the wedding.

She checked each picture. No mention of an Emily Clavell.

She quickly whizzed the microfilm forward to a week later. The same again. Wedding photos on one of the pages near the back. This time page 26. She stared at the pictures of the couples, each one smiling into the camera, wondering if they truly enjoyed their married life. For a second, she thought of Paul. He must be in Brussels now. She hadn't heard from him today, not even a call when he was at the airport. She would talk to him tonight. Let him settle into his hotel first.

She scanned forward to the next Monday, October 20. There, in the most prominent place at the top of the page, was a headline, Local Girl Marries, and beneath it her beaming bride, Emily Clavell.

Next to her was a man, smiling contentedly into the camera. He had put on weight but she recognised him immediately.

Chapter 42

Bradford, Yorkshire. June 1923 - September 1924.

He didn't know the exact moment he fell in love with Emily Clavell. Probably because there was no exact moment. Instead, it was a process of forgetting, of losing himself in his new life and becoming entwined with hers, that gradually formed itself into love. A realisation that he could no longer live without this woman in his life.

After their first meeting, he had stayed in Bradford, taking rooms in a pleasant house on Ash Grove run by an old Irish woman, Mrs Flaherty. He told Emily he needed to stay to resolve some family business but, in reality, he didn't know why he remained in this city. It was dirty and dark and depressing. But there was just a feeling that he had to be here, at this time. And what do we have to go back to in Ireland? Nothing except war and killing and death.

He finally found out why he had stayed when one day over tea Emily had spoken to him directly.

'You are a man of the world, are you not Mr Trichot?'

'I wouldn't know about that, Miss Clavell.'

'Please call me Emily.'

'Only if you will call me Charles.'

'Charles, let me be direct.'

'Ah, I've heard about this Yorkshire directness.'

'My brother told you about it?'

He didn't answer. Silence implied the memories were too painful to talk about.

'I'm sorry. Sometimes, I forget and talk about him.'

He remained silent. She carried on. 'What I have to ask you is quite an imposition, I know, but, if you hear me out, I have to speak my mind. I owe it to those who work with their families and me. Please excuse my directness.'

'For a direct woman, you are taking a long time to ask your question.'

She stopped speaking and looked at him. Her mouth broadened into a lovely smile. 'You must stop teasing me, Charles. Not when I have something important to ask anyway.'

'Ask away, Emily. I'm all ears.'

She settled herself and took a small sip of tea from her china cup. He couldn't help but notice the way a stray tendril of hair hung down from her chignon, caressing her neck.

'As I was saying, you are a man of the world. I have never left Bradford. This is all I know.' She raised her hands, indicating the room in which they sat. 'It strikes me that if we are to survive at the mill, and I am determined that we are, we must develop new markets for our cloth. Relying on what we have done in the past is no longer good enough.'

'You are thinking how can you develop your business?'

'I am. Last week, we lost another customer. Apparently, the Post Office was uncomfortable dealing with a woman.'

'So how can I help?'

'I would like you to help develop the business and create new markets for us. I can manage the day to day running of the company, I've been involved in it all my life, but it seems the modern world cannot handle a woman being in charge.'

He thought long and hard about her offer. Here was an opportunity to right the wrong he had done her family, to atone for his mistakes and, perhaps, make her life a little better.

'Do you have a problem working with a woman too, Mr Trichot?'

'No, no, of course not. I would be happy to help you in any way I can, Emily.'

Her shoulders relaxed and she sighed audibly. 'Of course, you will be paid.'

'I have one condition, Emily.'

Immediately, her shoulders tensed and she sat upright on the settee. 'And what is that, Mr Trichot?'

'I should very much want not to be paid. It's the least I can do to help you and your family.'

She thought for a moment. 'With the loss of the Post Office contract, our finances are not in the best of shape, so I do appreciate your offer. But I have one condition of my own, Mr Trichot.'

'And that is?'

'We look into our relationship three months from now. If it is proving mutually satisfactory, then I insist that we begin to pay you a salary for your work.'

He raised his cup of tea. 'To our new relationship.'

She raised her cup in return. 'May it prosper.'

'May it prosper,' he repeated.

* * *

The months flew by. He spent most of his waking hours with Emily, planning and organising the future of the mill.

He was amazed at her energy and drive, the way she knew every single one of her workers, greeting them each morning with a word or two or asking after the health of a relative. He was amazed at her enthusiasm and her desire to keep the business open and flourishing.

He threw himself into the work, making sure that he was the male face of the business, but deferring to her on all decisions.

Their first major contract came after two months. It was for uniforms for the newly formed Garda Siochana, the police force of the Irish Free State. He had obtained the contract through an old friend who had risen through the ranks of the new government. The irony of the situation was not lost on him. The saviours of the mill and all those who worked there were the same people who had been fighting her brother and his army.

He was in no doubt that she saw the irony too, but the future of the mill and its workers was far too important to let fear or anger or remorse cloud her judgement.

On the day of the signing, she had sat opposite him after the representatives from the Irish Ministry had left. 'With this contract, we will be able to take on new workers. We are secure for the next two years.'

'I think even better than that. The cloth could be used for police forces everywhere. It's hard-wearing and re-silient. I'll start contacting the British police forces tomorrow. We must be able to expand now that we have the machines up and running.'

'I've seen a new American loom. It's three times faster than our old machines, and uses less labour.'

He held up his hands. 'We shouldn't run before we can walk.'

She laughed. 'You're right. We mustn't over-expand. It's just that, for the first time, we seem to be out of the woods, our future is more secure than it ever was and it's all down to you and your work.'

For a moment, he stared into her blue eyes. So open and honest and trusting. The image came back to him of the hill above Dublin, a car's engine idling in the distance, the smell of cordite in the air and a body lying on the coarse earth. Not just anybody, the body of her brother.

She reached out and touched his arm. 'Are you all right? Your face has turned white. Almost as if you've seen a ghost.'

'It's nothing,' he stammered, 'just thinking about what we have to do next.' He stood up. 'I should get started on collecting the names of the Chief Constables...'

'Are you sure you're feeling well? You don't look good. You've been working too hard.' A broad smile crossed her face. 'We'll go out on Saturday. Take a day off. A picnic at Bolton Abbey. Have you ever been there?'

He shook his head.

'Then, it's decided, we must go. I'll ask Mr Rawlings, and Mrs Hopkinson from the mill to join us. We must all celebrate our success.'

He stood up and walked to the fireplace, As he did, the image of a smoking gun, a body lying stretched out on the ground, blood slowly seeping from its head, and above, high in the sky, the sad trill of a lark ascending, intruded into his mind.

He shook his head and looked down at her face looking up at him.

A beautiful face, open and honest. Emily's face. A face he longed to hold in his hands.

* * *

The preparations for the day out to Bolton Abbey proceeded quickly. On the day, there were eight people altogether and three cars. He drove one of them, with the picnic hampers, Emily and the maid, Daisy. The factory manager, Mr Rawlings drove the other, while one of the foremen was the driver of the third.

They headed across the rolling dales of Yorkshire, through countryside that reminded him of the area around the Shannon. But here everything was ordered and organised: neat dry-stone walls bordering fields inhabited by fat white sheep. The roads were well-made and well-maintained, not like the dirt tracks of Ireland. And, above all, the houses were solid and compact, secure in the solidity of their grey stone. Unlike the hovels and white-painted walls with their thatched roofs of his own country. The land may look the same but the people on it were very different.

They reached the Abbey and immediately began to unpack the picnic baskets. Emily walked up to him. 'Today, you are to do nothing, Mr Trichot. Today is a day for enjoyment and games and relaxation.'

'I thought you were going to call me Charles.'

She looked over her shoulder and smiled. 'You're right, it is definitely a Charles day.'

He smiled back. 'And it shall be an Emily day too.' He looked across at the others fussing over the laying of the rugs and the placement of the food. 'Hang the English formality, for one day at least.'

She took out a hamper from the back of the car. 'Sometimes you surprise me, Charles.'

He took it from her and together they walked to join the others. 'And how do I do that, Emily?'

She looked down at her feet. 'Oh, just something I've

noticed. Sometimes, you talk about the English as if they are another people, not your own people.'

Before he could answer, Mr Rawlings came rushing up. 'Here, let me take that from you. It's got the beer and the pies in it this one.'

Mr Rawlings wrestled the hamper and hurried back to where Daisy was laying out the food on the rugs. Emily had joined her and was helping. He stopped and lit a cigarette. He would have to be careful in the future.

The rest of the afternoon went beautifully. The sun had shone down on them. The pies and sandwiches had been eaten. Bottles of Mackeson had been drunk by the men and cups of tea for the women. Games had been played and won and lost.

After a while the others had wandered off to explore the ruins of the Abbey. Only himself and Emily remained sitting on the rug. He was smoking a cigarette and she drinking her umpteenth cup of tea.

'We make a good partnership, Mr Trichot.'

'I believe we do. But I thought it was a Charles day?'

'We make a good partnership, Charles.'

'Thank you, Emily. With a bit of luck, we should get the Yorkshire police contract. I've a meeting with the Chief Constable on Wednesday.'

'Remind him that he used to know my father. They were old school chums.'

'On such close friendships, the British Empire was built.'

She laughed. 'I suppose it was.' She looked around her at the ruined buildings, collapsed stone and half fallen arches. 'You know this was once a thriving monastery, full of monks and food and life.'

He tried to imagine the monks singing the mass, following their rituals, walking through these now ruined cloisters.

'Look at it now, a few beautiful ruins…'

'Things change. Nothing is permanent.'

She turned to stare at him. 'Not even happiness?'

'Happiness least of all. A fleeting moment, as soon as one realises it has happened, it's gone.' He blew on the end of his fingers.

'Yes, a mayfly. Alive for a day and then gone forever.'

He sat up and leant on his elbow. 'You're very thoughtful today, Emily.'

'It's just...it's just that nothing lasts forever,' she stammered. 'I thought we were a happy family with our futures settled: John would run the mill when father retired and I would get married, have lots of children and live happily ever after. Such childish dreams.' She shrugged her shoulders. 'Then, the war came and all was changed, all changed.'

He went to comfort her, to touch her arm, stopped for a moment and then went ahead, touching her elbow.

She didn't move away.

'We can't change the past, Emily. Just make a better future.' As he said those words, it was as if a weight had been lifted from his shoulders. There was no point atoning for a past he could never change. What had happened, had happened. All he could do was work to create a bright future. For both of them.

She looked up and he could see a tear forming in her eye. 'It's just sometimes, it's so hard to forget.'

He nodded his head. 'I know. The past intrudes on our lives. A thief of the future.'

He looked down at the tartan pattern on the rug. He could feel the soft cotton of her shirt beneath his fingers and the promise of an even more delicate skin beneath it. It was now or never. Time to speak to her, tell her the truth. She would hate him, but at least, he could stop the pretence, stop the lies.

But she spoke first, interrupting his thoughts.

'I'm going to be a direct Yorkshirewoman again, Charles.'

'If you are going to tell me to you want to pay me for my work, the answer is still no. Perhaps, if we get this police contract...'

'It's not that.' She stared directly at him. 'We make a good partnership, don't we?'

'We do, silk and steel. I'm the silk.'

She laughed and then recovered herself quickly. 'I want to be serious for a moment so please don't interrupt me because I think I'm only going to be able to say this once.'

He placed his finger across his lips. 'I won't say a word.'

She sighed loudly, sat up and turned towards him. 'We make a good partnership. We work well together and complement each other. Over the last months, I think we've grown closer, been honest and open with each other, hiding nothing...'

His head went down, so she couldn't see his eyes. He would have to tell her soon, he couldn't keep maintaining the lie much longer. She deserved to know the truth, his truth.

She carried on speaking, rushing the words as if this were the only way she could finish what she had to say. '...Well, it strikes me we should make our relationship more permanent. As permanent as anything could be in this world that's full of change. Look, Charles, damn it all, what I want to tell you is I think I have fallen in love with you. There I've said it...'

She looked down at the tartan rug.

He was stunned. She feels the same way I do. I've loved her from the moment I set eyes on her, loved every inch of her, every smile, every frown, every word she's ever spoken.

And then the memory came back to him. The body lying on the ground, blood seeping out from a hole in his head. Not a body, her brother. But that was the past. He couldn't change it. It was done, over, finished. All he had was here and now and her. Nothing else mattered. He looked up at the broken walls of the once-great Abbey. Nothing was permanent, it was all in the past.

'Forgive me, but didn't you hear what I said? I'm asking you to marry me.'

In that moment, he realised the truth meant nothing, all that mattered was here and now. He sat up, took hold of her hands in his and said, 'I've loved you from the first moment I set eyes on you. I would love to be your husband if you'll have me?'

His face broke out into the broadest smile. She threw her arms around his neck and hugged him close to her. 'Let nobody ever part us, Charles. Let us stay close forever,' she whispered in his ear.

'Aye up, what's all this then?'

The factory manager was standing over them both, hands on his hips, his moustache bristling.

'We're to be married, Mr Rawlings.'

'Well, lass, it's about bloody time. I thought you'd never get round to asking him.'

Chapter 43

Jayne adjusted the focus on the microfilm reader, making it as sharp as she could. She squinted her eyes. It was the same man, she was sure of it. The same man who was in the photo of the prison camp in Frongoch. The man whose name was Michael Dowling. He looked a little older, the hair had a few grey streaks through it and the eyes were set deeper, but it was the same man.

She read the caption beneath the photo: Miss Emily Clavell married Captain Charles Trichot at Heaton Methodist Chapel on Saturday, October 18.

The man who had been involved in the killing of John Clavell was now married to his sister. What a strange story. How had they got together? How did he meet her? And why did he pretend to be somebody who was dead? She thought back to Declan Fitzgerald's memoirs. Hadn't Michael Dowling been given the personal effects of the British officer they had shot? Fitzgerald wrote of the promise Dowling had made. Had he returned the effects personally, masquerading as a dead British officer? But then to fall in love and marry the sister? She supposed stranger things had happened. Was it love or was it a strange sort of guilt? Atonement for the death of her brother?

She would never know. The past often gave us dates and times and events but it didn't leave much trace of people's feelings. The reasons why they acted as they did. We could know the past but never really understand it.

She checked the clock on the library wall, 3.30. Time to

drive back to see Annie.

At least now, she had a name for John Hughes' father. Michael Dowling. So John Hughes' real name was not John Trichot, as on his birth certificate, but John Dowling.

She was making progress. She rolled the spool to the end and shut off the microfilm reader. The librarian received the boxes back like a priest holding the chalice at Mass.

'One other thing, if I may?'

The librarian pushed her glasses back on to the bridge of her nose and sighed audibly.

Jayne wasn't going to be put off by such an obvious display of petulance. 'Do you have any records for the Ilkley Children's Home?'

'Well, if we did, they wouldn't be here.'

'Where would they be?'

'In Wakefield, with all the other records.'

This was becoming annoying. Jayne used her best police detective's voice, usually saved for the most recalcitrant criminals, but in this woman's case, she would make an exception.

'Please don't waste my time or that of the other people waiting here.' She pointed to the queue that had begun to form behind her. 'Get on your desktop and check out the archives from the central database. You do know how to do that, don't you?'

The woman immediately began to type on the keyboard in front of her. 'There are no records for the Ilkley Children's Home in any of our databanks,' she said finally.

Jayne smiled. She already guessed that would be the case, but she needed to be sure. 'Thank you for your time and patience. Have a nice day, won't you?'

She left the library and rushed down the steps. Time to

see Annie and visit the old lady in her home in Haworth. It might be a wasted trip but you never know, one always had to cover all the bases. The old lady might have heard some family gossip or stories that could add a background to the report she would give John Hughes.

She checked her watch. If she finished the interview with the old lady at 5 pm, she could be back in Manchester by eight at the latest. A quick call to John Hughes and she would deliver her report to him on Sunday morning, plenty of time before he flew back to the States.

She might even be able to visit her father in his home after the meeting. Sunday was always the worst day for him. Throughout his life, it was the day on which he was busiest: mass in the morning, followed by a couple of hours in the allotment and then out with her. Until she was one, they spent every Sunday together, while her mother stayed at home. Visiting museums, walking in the Peak District or just driving out into the Cheshire countryside. It was a time she loved.

Thinking back to her childhood had suddenly given her an urge for the comfort of chocolate. She checked through her bag.

Nothing, not even a square of Dairy Milk. She stepped off the pavement to cross the road to the multi-storey dungeon otherwise known as a municipal car park, then stopped. Wasn't there a shop next to the Library? Perhaps they would have some? She turned back quickly.

A black Audi came out of nowhere on her left and accelerated towards her, coming straight at her.

She could see the hard black bonnet, four round circles against a metal grill. Getting closer and closer.

She threw herself backwards against the wall, banging her elbow on the hard concrete. The black Audi raced past.

266

She felt the wind lashing her hair across her face.

'Fucking idiot,' she shouted after the speeding car.

She tried to see the face of the man driving. But the rear window blocked her view. She checked the number plate 64AGD1. Didn't recognise it. She would ask Rob to check who it was with the DLVA later. The bloody driver should be off the road.

A swirl of white to her left, dancing in the breeze. Her notes had spilled out from her bag and were flying across the road.

'Fuck, fuck, fuck,' she said as she ran to chase after them.

It was only later she realised that her need for chocolate had probably saved her life.

Chapter 44

He leaned forward and switched off the dash cam. He had just missed her but he wouldn't miss again.

This was the moment he really enjoyed. The time before a killing when his heart slowed down and his mind became truly focussed. A killing machine with all the heartlessness of a snake.

He remembered the first time. The Iraqi, a stupid man who had been caught in a roundup of suspects. In the wrong time and the wrong place.

The man was stupid because he got angry at the questions they asked him, shouting, what was he doing there? Why was he under arrest in his own country? What had he done wrong?

He had felt the same slowing of his heart rate, the same awareness of his breathing, a stillness in his mind as he had reached out and seized the Iraqi's windpipe in his fingers, squeezing it and squeezing it and squeezing it without saying a word. The Iraqi had struggled for a few seconds but then went limp as the hand cut off his oxygen supply.

The others had done nothing. They just stood around and watched. For him, time had stood still as he watched the man's eyes, silently screaming for help, pleading for him to stop.

But he didn't.

Eventually, somebody had pulled him off and pushed him out of the cell. He sat in the corner of the jail as the Iraqi's body was carried out, wrapped in an old grey blanket.

'Dump it in an alley,' said the officer, 'it will be seen as just another murder by the Sunnis. Put a couple of rounds through the head before you go.'

It had finished him in the regiment though. Lack of control they said. They didn't care that he'd killed somebody, just that he'd killed without being ordered to do so.

Afterwards, it hadn't stopped him killing. Only now, he decided when and where he was going to kill.

If the client paid, he killed.

If the client didn't pay, he killed the client.

If somebody angered him, he killed.

If somebody was in the wrong place at the wrong time, he killed.

If it pleased him, he killed.

The client had made it very clear on the phone call at three pm. Despite all of Turner's precautions, he persisted in giving his instructions in the open, without using the code words.

'She's getting too close. Terminate her. Make the death appear accidental.'

Not a warning. Not a brutal killing. An accident. Another one to add to his collection of snuff movies, The client seemed to enjoy giving the order. But he would be the one who enjoyed the execution. Again he chuckled at the double entendre in the words.

He liked creating 'accidents'. They were the pinnacle of his profession. Killing somebody with a shot through the head or a stab in the heart was easy. Any thug could do that. But killing somebody and making everybody else believe it was an unfortunate accident, there was a skill there.

Professionalism, not mere brutality.

He had missed her the first time. He wouldn't make the

same mistake again.

Time to dump this car and acquire a new one. She still hadn't spotted the tracker so she would be easy to pick up again.

Next time, he wouldn't fail. This was getting personal.

Chapter 45

The journey to pick up Annie had been uneventful. She had been checking in her rear view mirror all the time to see if she was being followed. Was it an accident in the city centre, another useless or drunk driver? Or was it something more than that. All the time she had been working this case, she had the feeling that she was being watched. Had John Hughes set somebody to spy on her? She wouldn't put it past the old bastard. The brick through her window, the theft of her laptop, the kidnapping, and now being nearly run down by a crazy driver, there were too many coincidences for her liking. She didn't believe in coincidences. They were merely events that you hadn't found a reason for.

She was determined she was going to find out what the hell was happening. She parked outside the old house again. The door was open and Annie waved from the window. A white van with Oxfam written on the side was parked in the driveway.

'Won't be a minute. They are just taking away the last of the stuff,' shouted Annie.

Good, time to make a few phone calls. First, she needed to find out who was the driver who had almost knocked her down. She picked up her phone and dialled the number. 'Rob, it's Jayne again.'

'Have you got my chocolate already?'

'Not yet, Rob, but I need you to do me another favour?'

'Oh aye, what is it this time?'

'Can you run a check on a car for me?'

'Another bar of chocolate?'

'Two bars this time. You always were a cheap date.'

'Give me the number.'

'A black Audi. 64AGD1'

'Ok, I'll run it through the computer and get back to you.' For a moment there was a silence on the other end of the phone. 'Are you right, Jayne? You sound a little agitated.'

She decided to be open with Rob. 'I'm ok. Just think I'm being followed. I want to check who it is.'

'Just because you're paranoid...'

'Doesn't mean they're not out to get you. I know, heard it before, Rob. Check it as quickly as you can, please.' She added the please, realising that he no longer worked for her.

'At your command, my lady. But take care out there, one slip and the bastards can get you.'

The line went dead. One slip and the bastards can get you. Had she slipped up again? Had she missed something? Was somebody else going to die because she screwed up?

She shook her head. Don't think like that, you're not police any more. You're a researcher looking into somebody's ancestry. Not a copper dealing with thugs and dealers.

She tried to call Paul to tell him where she was. Again, she got his voicemail. This time, she left a message. 'Call me back, Paul, as soon as you get this. We do need to talk, the silence can't go on.'

Finally, the client. The phone rang three times before it was picked up. She heard Richard Hughes' smooth voice loud and clear. 'Mrs Sinclair, good to hear from you.'

'Is Mr Hughes there?'

'We're back at the hotel. My uncle is sleeping at the

272

moment.'

There was something in Richard Hughes' voice that irritated Jayne. A hint of triumph perhaps. 'Could I speak to him?'

'I don't want to wake him. The doctors have given him a sedative. Have you any news?'

'If he comes round, you can tell him I've discovered the real name of his father. It wasn't Charles Trichot at all. It was a man called Michael Dowling. He was using Trichot's name.'

'Why?'

'I'll explain when I see you. It's too complicated at the moment and I have a lead I need to follow up.'

'Where are you going?'

'To see a relative of Emily Clavell.'

'Mrs Sinclair, that's great news, I'll let my uncle know when he wakes up.' There it was again, that smirk in the voice.

God, they are an unsavoury family. Perhaps, that's what money does to you.

'Keep in touch, Mrs Sinclair. Let me know what you find. ' The phone line went dead, not even a goodbye or a take care.

Annie slipped into the seat beside her. 'Calling your client?'

'He's not very well. I don't think he has long left to live.'

They drove out to Haworth on the B6144. As they neared the town, everything they passed seemed to echo the names of the famous family that had lived in the Parsonage. Heathcliff Road, Bronte Gardens, the Heights Tearooms, even a Bronte fire station. She imagined a windswept Heathcliff sliding down a silvered pole in a bright yellow pair of trousers.

'Why are you smiling?' asked Annie.

'It's a bit of an industry, isn't it? All this Bronte stuff.'

'When the mills closed they had to have something to cling on to. Around here, it was Heathcliff and Catherine. The place is just here on the right.'

Jayne steered the car into the car park. The Home was a modern, rather faceless red brick building with PVC windows. It looked clean and antiseptic. They stepped into the reception area.

Annie spoke to the receptionist. 'We're here to see Mrs Clavell.'

'Is she expecting you, dear?'

'I don't think so. A last minute call. We were in the area. My friend has come a long way to see her.'

'Another visitor from America? She will be excited.'

Jayne stepped forward. 'A visitor from America?'

'About a month ago. She doesn't get many.' She flicked through her book. 'I remember him. Nice man.' She stabbed the book with her finger. 'See, name of Hughes.'

'Hughes? John Hughes?'

Her finger followed a long column of visitors to the home. 'No. Right surname, but this man was a Richard Hughes.' She looked up from her ledger. 'You don't sound very American.'

'I'm from Manchester.'

'Well, I guess that's far enough.' She sniffed. 'I'll just call to her room.' She picked up the phone and dialled a number. 'Mary, it's Glenys here. Glenys from the reception desk, you remember me, we met this morning. You have a visitor. What's that? Yes, I know you don't have many visitors. Can they come to see you?' She listened to a small voice on the other end, before putting the phone down. 'She'll see you but only for fifteen minutes. Noel Edmonds is on the telly and she doesn't want to miss it. The Room is 423, just down the corridor on the left.'

They pushed through the fire doors and the familiar smell of boiled cabbage, antiseptic and old people stung Jayne's nose.

They found the room quickly. Annie knocked on the door. 'It's your cousin Annie Lightowler. Can we come in?'

They heard a squeak from inside and Annie pushed open the door. The room was small but tidy. In one corner was a washbasin and hot water tap, a single bed lay opposite it and a wardrobe and dresser on the far wall. In between, they could see the back of a high chair. A small head turned to greet them. 'Hello, I'm Mary, who are you?'

'I'm Annie, your cousin and this is Jayne.'

'Are you looking for Tarzan? You won't find him here. But I remember going to see him when I was young. Johnny Weissmuller he was. We loved it when he swang through the trees. I waited every time for his little leather front to swing up too, but it never did. More's the pity.'

'Jayne has come from a long way away.'

'Are you from America too?'

'No. I'm from Manchester.'

'Went there once, didn't like it, too many Mancunians. I think that's what they call themselves, isn't it. Mancunians. Sounds like something you catch at the vets.'

'Jayne would like to ask you a few questions, if that's okay?'

'Are you going to be asking me the same ones the American did?'

'I don't know, what did he ask?'

'About Emily and her husband. Terrible story, that. Makes me shiver thinking about it. Such a scandal.' Her thin body wriggled theatrically in her red chair. She turned to Annie. 'You're Alf's daughter, aren't you? Don't see much of you these days, nor your sister. Have you sold that bloomin' house yet? Hated the place I did at the end. Loved it when we came back from India in the thirties though. It was beautiful then, and we had servants to keep it clean. Can't keep it clean now, too big, too dirty.'

'We've just found a buyer, Aunt Mary.'

'Good. I hope they can keep it clean. It deserves to be clean.'

Jayne interrupted. 'I'd like to talk to you about Emily if I may.'

'Oh, I never met Emily. She had already died before we came back from India. That's where I was born of course. In Madras, it was in 1922, I think. At least that's what it says on the birth certificate.'

'When did you come back to England?'

'It was 1931 or maybe 1932. I can't be certain, I was so young you see. I can still remember my Indian Ayi though. A lovely woman with a stud and ring through her nose. You know, I saw a young girl with something exactly like it on the telly yesterday evening. I don't know why she would do something like that to her face, it's so—'

'You were telling us about coming back to England,' Jayne interrupted.

'Was I? That's right, I was. We came back because Father retired and we'd inherited this house when Emily died, so we had somewhere to live. I was a late baby. He was already 53 when I was born. Died when I was seven, Mother remarried again, of course. Well, she had to, didn't she? Who was going to take care of us if my father wasn't there?'

'I'm sorry, I have to ask you about Emily. Is there anything you remember about her?'

'That's exactly what the young American chap asked. He wanted to know about her husband. Sordid scandal, it was. I gave him the photographs I had. I found them in the attic one day. Somebody must have put them there, probably Emily.'

Jayne held her breath. 'You gave him the photographs?'

'There were only two of them.'

Jayne's head sunk beneath her knees. Had she come this far only to find the evidence had already been taken by Richard Hughes? A wave of disappointment washed over her. It had all been a waste of time. Richard Hughes knew all about the family, he even had pictures of the wedding. Why had he asked her to go on this wild goose chase.

She thought back over her conversations with him. Each time, he had seemed to be giving her encouragement, he was actually trying to stop her. She understood finally why he had asked her to fake her investigation in the lobby of the Midland Hotel.

She looked at the old woman, sitting next to her in her chair. 'It's okay, Mary. You did the right thing.'

'I'm so glad I did. I didn't like him at all. He looked like Noel Edmonds but he never looked me in the eyes. Don't like men who don't look you in the eyes.'

'Thank you for seeing us anyway.' Jayne stood up. 'I won't keep you from your programme.'

'My fiancé was like Poldark, you know. I mean his body was like him. I do like a firm stomach, don't you? None of that flabby stuff. Men are far too flabby these days.'

Jayne thought of Paul. 'I know exactly what you mean, Mary.' She looked across at Annie. 'Well, we must be off. I have to drive back to Manchester tonight.'

'See you again. You will come again, won't you?' There wasn't a pleading in the voice, more a questioning, a testing.

'Of course, I will. I'd love to come and see you.'

'And I promise, I'll be back more often, Auntie. I haven't been a very good relation, I know,' said Annie.

'I do understand. We old people have lived too. How the busyness of life sometimes overtakes what's important. The funny thing is, now I have so much time on my hands, and so little to do.' She stared into the air.

'I will be back, I promise.' Jayne nodded her head and walked towards the door.

Mary awoke with a start from her memories and said, 'I didn't give him the letters. Didn't like his eyes, never looked you in the face. Always darting to one side or the other. Shifty man. I don't like shifty men, never have, never will.'

Jayne turned back.

'I like you, though. I like the way you look at people. Straight and straight-forward. I like that. None of that darting here and there. You'll find the letters in a bundle in the wardrobe in the biscuit box. There's a few articles from the time too. Shocking scandal it was.'

Annie walked across the room to the wardrobe and after a few seconds brought out an old Huntley and Palmers tin box. 'This one?'

'That's it. Her letters are on the bottom.'

Annie opened the box after a short struggle. She reached in a took hold of a small stack of letters. The paper of both the envelope and the letter was a light cream with enough weight to suggest it was expensive. The dark ink of the address had changed into a deep maroon with age.

Jayne opened the first one and began to read.

278

October 18, 1924.

My darling Emily,

Thank you for a year of perfect happiness. It's our anniversary today and, as I promised, I will write to you every year to celebrate our love.

I know I'm not good with words, I should be telling you how much I love you every day but I don't. The words stick in my mouth, dancing on my tongue and sometimes get swallowed up by my infernal shyness.

But I hope you can see by the way I look at you that I love you very much. The way your hair glistens in the light. The way you bite your bottom lip when you are thinking. The way you brush that lock of hair that I love to kiss, from the nape of your neck.

Sometimes, when we are together, I can't stop staring at you, counting my blessings of the day we met.

This time next year, with luck and the help of the Almighty, we will have a new addition to our happy family. A visible symbol of our love and our life together.

But today, on our anniversary, I just want to celebrate one person.

You.

Thank you for all the joy you have brought me. I was in a dark place and now all I can see is light.

I love you more than life itself.

Your husband,

Charles

The room was silent. Eventually, the old lady spoke. 'I

often dreamed of having that sort of love with David. But it wasn't to be. The war took him away from me. Never met anybody the same again. I couldn't face having my heart broken.'

'I think we all dream of that kind of love,' said Jayne. 'Shall I read the next one?'

'Do, the baby has been born in the next one.'

Chapter 46

Happiness, real happiness, never lasts.

And he had been happy, every day filled with the joy of living, working and being together. The arrival of their son had been the culmination, the visible proof of their love for each other.

He went into the hospital, Bradford Royal Infirmary, and found her lying in bed with a bundle of lacy clothes in her arms. Hidden in that bundle was the smallest, reddest face he could ever imagine. A button nose, the longest eyelashes and already his father's telltale smirk plastered across his face as if he were reimagining some joke that had been told to him in the womb.

'How are you?'

'Tired and sore. I don't think he wanted to come into the world at this moment.'

'Aye, he's like his dad, happy to sleep and do nothing, surrounded by you.'

She handed over the bundle of clothes to him. He took them carefully, afraid he might drop his new son on the carbolic soaked floor. The baby smiled up at him

'Look, he's smiling. He knows it's his da.'

'It's probably wind.'

'Shush, woman, he definitely knows it's his da.' A small hand had snaked out from beneath the clothes and encircled his thumb, holding on to it tightly. Then, the little face creased up and a long wail issued from a toothless mouth.

'He's hungry. Pass him over to me,' Emily said. 'I'll feed

him, so you must go.'

'Can't I stay?'

'No, the nurses will be shocked. A man staying in the room while I am feeding the baby, they will be gossiping about the scandal from here to Haworth. How's the mill?'

'All's fine. Everyone sends their love and they can't wait to meet the young lad. We've started on the Yorkshire police contract. First delivery is on Wednesday.'

'Good, good.'

'I'll come back this evening.'

'I'll wait for you. We'll wait for you,' she corrected herself. 'And please bring some Fry's. I've a craving for chocolate for some reason.'

'I thought the cravings were supposed to stop now.'

'You know me, I never follow anybody else. I've my own way. And one other thing…'

'What's that?'

'I've been thinking…'

'Like you do when you've just had a baby.'

'I've been thinking, we should change the house. Get rid of all the old furniture and buy something new, more modern. With the baby, it's time for a change.'

'Well, we can afford it with the new contracts. Why not?'

She smiled. 'Why not? We can't live in the past all the time. Not with this little present.' She held the baby up. It opened its toothless mouth wide and a wail like a police siren echoed through the room.

He kissed her on the forehead. 'I'd better go before he brings the place down.'

The following years passed so quickly, it was like being in a race where the only other competitor was time. John, they had given the Christian name of her brother, had grown so quickly. Learning how to crawl and then walk as if he had known how to do them both for years. He began to speak at a young age, haltingly at first but then in a flood. New words and sentences gushed from his little mouth, not always in the right order but holding meaning for him, annoyance crossing his face when his mother or father was unable to decipher what he wanted.

The mill was doing well too. Their decision to concentrate on one just segment, the production of police uniforms, had paid off. As other factories were closing across the city, they were expanding, becoming the main supplier of uniforms to most of the forces in England.

It was a lucrative operation, with their mill the only one in the city operating round-the-clock. When everybody else was closing or laying off workers, the police forces all over the country were expanding. The terrible miner's strike of 1926 and its aftermath meant that their business grew even more as the numbers of police were increased to deal with the perceived threat to the established order.

He thought of the irony. Here he was, a man who had been ready to kill policemen in his youth, having to meet them each week to understand their needs and confirm their orders.

It meant he had to travel, of course, throughout Britain, seeing the country in its rage and despair, and also seeing its richness and beauty. How could both exist at the same time? He didn't have the answer. All he knew was that every time he travelled away, the absence of his wife and his son bit deep into his heart.

The arrival of their son had made their relationship even stronger as if here was a link that bound them tighter together like a steel chain. His absence didn't make the heart grow fonder, it made it grow weaker like a plant deprived of water, withering on the ground. He wanted to be with them both all the time, enjoying his new life and the life he had created.

He knew it couldn't last, of course. Such happiness never lasts.

The end when it came was as sudden as it was unexpected. He was on a business trip to Glasgow to sign a contract for the delivery of police uniforms. The trip had gone well but a sudden flurry of February snow had him stuck in the city for two days longer than he had wanted.

When he had finally managed to get a train to Bradford, nobody was waiting for him when he arrived at the station. Often, Emily brought little John to greet him as he descended from the train. It was one of the great joys of his life to see the boy run down the platform to meet his father, his little legs taking him closer and closer to his waiting arms.

But there was nobody this time. No car waiting. No Emily. No John.

He took a taxi home. As it pulled up to the front door of the house, he looked up and just one light was shining from a window. The rest of the house was in darkness. An immense wave of dread and foreboding washed through his body. Had something happened? Had the boy been injured? A fall?

He paid off the taxi and rushed to the door. Nobody came to greet him as he shouted his arrival. The house was in darkness as if mourning a terrible loss. Where were the servants? Why didn't they meet him when he came through the door?

He rushed into the living room to find Emily sat on the chair in front of the fire. The same chair she had sat in all those years ago when they first met.

She didn't look at him as he entered the room.

'Emily, what's going on? Where are the servants? Where's John?'

'I've sent them away.' Her voice was dull, a monotone as if coming from the depths of a black well.

'Why? What's happened? Has he been injured?'

She sat staring into the fire, before slowly turning her head towards him. He could see she had been crying. 'Why didn't you tell me, Charles? If that's your name...'

He tried to charm his way out of her question. 'Tell you what?' He stepped towards her. 'I don't know what you mean.'

'Stay where you are,' she commanded.

He stopped walking forwards. 'Emily, please tell me what's going on. There must be a terrible mistake.'

She turned back to stare into the fire. 'There has been a mistake and it's all mine. All my fault. I should have known it was too good to be true.'

He advanced towards her again. 'Emily, you're not making sense...'

She glared at him and he stopped moving towards her.

'While you were away in Glasgow, we had a visit from one of your old comrades in arms, Captain Forsythe. You do remember him, don't you?' The last sentence was delivered with a savage irony.

His shoulders slumped and he stood there.

'Obviously not. He was on leave from the Royal Kents in India and visiting his sister in Leeds. She was excited to tell him about an old comrade who had married and was living in Bradford. Imagine his surprise when he found out the name of this old friend.'

He just stood there, letting her words sink in, fear rising from the centre of his soul.

285

'He paid me a visit two days ago. Showed me a picture of the real Captain Trichot, the man who was killed in 1918. It only leaves me with one question. Who are you?'

Chapter 47

Haworth, Yorkshire. November 20, 2015.

Jayne finished reading the third letter. 'He's begging her to forgive him.'

'He lied about his name, pretending to be that officer,' said Mary.

Jayne scanned the letter again. 'Here's the passage again.' She read out loud. 'My real name is Michael Dowling. I was a member of the Irish Volunteers and I was with your brother when he died. He asked me to pass his effects on to his family. That's why I came to visit you.'

Annie looked shocked, 'That means...'

'He was one of the people involved in the death of her brother. No wonder she couldn't bear to be with him anymore.'

'There's one more letter. You should read that next.'

Jayne picked up the last letter. She didn't really want to read it. It was like looking into somebody's private thoughts and secrets. She thought she had become used to that as a police detective but this was different. Too personal, too searing.

Despite herself, she pulled the yellowing sheet out of the envelope.

Dear Emily,

I hesitate to call you my wife anymore, because I know that our life together is over. I don't blame you at all. If I had experienced the same pain as I have given you, I would not forgive me either.

I understand your pain. I just wish it wasn't me who had given you so much hurt.

I know now you will never forgive me. As you said, how could you share your bed with a man who had killed your brother?

I know the wrong that I have done you. I wish I could go back in time and re-write that day. But I can't. What's done is done, and I must live with the consequences.

I have just one last favour to ask you. If you have an ounce of compassion left in your heart, please grant it to me.

I would like five minutes to say goodbye to our son, John. Just five minutes to give him one last kiss and say goodbye.

Please say that you agree.

After that, I will vanish from both your lives, never to see either of you again. That is my promise.

Please, I beg you from the bottom of my heart, grant me this time with my son.

Yours

Michael Dowling

Chapter 48

The servant showed him into the sitting room. She hadn't said anything to him as she opened the door, gesturing for him to go in. He had followed her as she led him through the old house to a back room they never used.

'I'll bring the boy,' she said coldly.

'Is Emily here?' He hoped to see her one last time, to try to explain, to hope against hope that she would listen to him and forgive him.

'The mistress has gone out. Shall I bring the boy?'

He nodded. That evening when he had returned from Glasgow seemed so long ago but it was only two weeks. He had told her everything. The truth had come gushing out of him like oil from a well. Once he had started talking, it seemed he would never stop. All the time she was just sitting there, watching him with her sad, blue eyes.

When he had finished, she had simply turned to him and said, 'You must leave here. Leave John and me. Never return.' That was all. No tearing of hair. No anger. No screaming and kicking and punching. Perhaps, if she had done any of these things, it would have been easier for them both. It was the way the anger and the disappointment were bottled up in her that killed them both, leaving him with no hope at all.

The maid returned a minute later and pushed the boy into the room, closing the door behind him, leaving them alone.

John stood near the door for a few seconds before he

recognised his father and ran to greet him.

Michael opened his arms and the boy ran into them. He picked him up and swung him around. 'You're getting heavy, little feller.'

'I've got a train set now, Mrs Gayle lets me play with it if I eat all my dinner.'

Michael placed him gently back down to the ground. 'You must eat everything if you want to grow big and strong, John.'

'Like you, Daddy?'

'Yes, as big and strong as me.' He let his son feel his biceps. It was something the child loved to do.

Then, Michael held the boy close, wrapping his arms around the small body, feeling the ribs sticking through the chest and the little heart beating wildly in the chest.

'Daddy, you're hurting me,' said a small voice.

'Sorry, John, Daddy doesn't know his own strength sometimes.' He took a deep breath. This was going to be difficult. He had practised what he was going to say many times but still wasn't sure he could do it.

He took another breath and held the child at arm's length. 'Listen, John. Daddy has to go away for a long while.' He paused to let his words sink in.

Eventually, John replied. 'Does that mean you won't be able to play anymore?'

He nodded his head. 'I'm afraid it does, John. I have to go, you understand. Daddy doesn't want to, but he has to go. Do you understand?'

John nodded his head slowly.

'Before I go I want to give you two gifts.'

The boy's eyes brightened. 'Are they toys?'

'Not really, but you must keep them safe wherever you are. Promise?'

The young boy pointed to his heart. 'Cross my heart and hope to die.'

Michael took a book from his pocket. 'A long time ago a good friend gave me this book as a present to remember him. I'm giving it to you today so you will be able to remember me.'

'But I can't read yet, Daddy. Sometimes, Mrs Gayle reads to me. I like it when she does that.'

'Don't worry, you can read it when you are old enough.' He remembered the day Fitz had given it to him all those years ago when they were young and innocent, still studying at UCD.

'You can have it, Michael,' he had said, 'haven't I just won a treble at the races. I can buy a whole library if I wanted.'

The inscription was still there, written in the bright ink Fitz loved, slightly faded now as time had eaten into the words.

He closed the book and handed it over to his son. 'Keep it safe, John. Take it with you wherever you go.'

'I promise, Daddy.'

'The next gift is something you can wear.' Michael produced the cap badge of the Dublin Brigade from his pocket. As he held the small bronze button in his hands, he thought back to those days in the GPO. The smell of smoke and oil and cordite came into his nostrils and the image of the dead child's hand clutching the ribbon, the same age as his son, leapt into his mind.

He pinned the badge on the lapel of John's coat. 'A very brave man gave me this.'

'Did he die in a war like Mommy's brother?'

'He did, John. He died in a war. So when I'm not here, you must be a brave little man and look after your mammy.'

He took the boy by the shoulders. 'Look after her, won't you, John?'

'I will, Daddy.'

Michael felt a film of tears form over his eyes. His vision was beginning to blur but he couldn't let the lad see him crying. He couldn't do that to his son.

He pulled the boy close to him and hugged him tightly. One last time. One last hug. Just the one. Holding on as if he would never let him go.

'You're hurting me, Daddy.'

He let go and stood up. Trying not to look at his son, hoping the little boy wouldn't see the tears in his eyes.

He walked to the door and took one last look behind him. The boy, his son, was standing in front of the fire, holding the book to his chest and looking straight at him.

'Goodbye, John.'

'Goodbye, Daddy,' were the last words he heard as he closed the door.

Chapter 49

Jayne finished reading the letters.

'Do you think she allowed him to see his son again?'

Jayne reached into her bag and produced the book and the picture of the cap badge. She opened the book to the flyleaf and read the inscription again. 'I'm sure he did. That's how the boy was in possession of this book when he went to America.'

'Looks like you have found his father,' said Mary. 'That's all I have. Four letters. You might find more in the attic at my old house, but I doubt it. Emily died in late 1928 from pneumonia we heard. But, judging from these letters, she may well have died from a broken heart.' She folded all the letters back into their envelopes. 'It was 1931 or 1932 before we came back to England from India. My father said he always intended to adopt the boy but by the time he could visit the orphanage, the young man had already been sent to America. I remember him saying that it was probably for the best.'

'I wonder what happened to Michael Dowling?' asked Annie.

Jayne was staring into mid-air. 'I have a hunch. I'm not certain but it could be the answer.' She stood up. 'I'm sorry, but I have to go back to Manchester and see my client now. They need to hear this story from me in person. I'll drop you back at home if you'd like.'

'That would be perfect.'

Jayne gathered her things, carefully putting the book

and the picture of the cap badge back into the plastic folder in her bag. 'Thank you for everything, Mary. You've solved it all for me.'

Mary was flustered, brushing a stray white hair from her forehead. 'Take the letters. Your client should have them. What am I going to do with them?'

'I couldn't...'

'Take them. They will mean far more to him than they do to me. Come again, won't you. I've enjoyed your visit. And you too, Annie.'

'I will Mrs Clavell.' Jayne pointed to the door. 'Sorry, it's such a rush but he's old and very ill. He needs to hear this from me.'

Mary shooed both of them out of her room. 'Go, go. Go. I've missed far too much of Noel Edmonds anyway. I like to watch it from the start when they've got all the suitcases.'

Jayne and Annie closed the door behind them. They rushed down the corridor, saying a quick goodbye to the receptionist and ran to Jayne's car.

'You don't have to take me home. I can get a cab.'

'Don't worry, it's on my way.'

She put the car in gear and drove to the exit of the car park, signalling left. A quick look and she pulled out into the main road.

She didn't see the dark blue BMW.

Didn't hear the whine of the accelerating engine.

Didn't recognise the danger she faced until it was too late.

It came out of nowhere, crashing into the side of her car with the scraping crunch of metal on metal.

Her head was rocked backwards and hit the headrest behind her. In slow motion, she saw Annie's body fly to the left, the seatbelt straining across her chest, her head hitting the glass of the door window.

The car was revolving now, the countryside and hedges moving quickly past the windscreen. There was a puff of white smoke. Her body was enveloped in the soft embrace of the airbag as it inflated from the steering wheel.

Then the car stopped revolving and flipped over. Once. Twice. Coming to rest at the side of the narrow road.

She was looking straight into a hedge over the top of the dashboard. But everything was at a strange angle. A tree was growing straight at her, the thin leafless branches intertwined in front of her in a pattern she couldn't understand.

Off in the distance, she could hear the sound of an engine revving.

Getting louder now.

Closer.

Closer.

Another crash. More scraping of metal against metal. The car flipped over again and her body launched up to hit her head on the fabric covering the roof.

Annie was next to her, hanging loosely from her seatbelt.

Her voice screaming. No, not her voice, somebody else's voice. Annie's voice. Loud, sharp. A face covered in blood. Annie's face.

Then silence.

She heard the car door opening. The metal struggling to stay wedged into the car.

Got to wake up.

Got to wake up.

A hand reaching in and grabbing her head. Somebody had come to help her and Annie. She felt her seatbelt being unfastened. They were going to help her out of the car.

Must wake up.

Must get out.

She felt a strong hand grip behind her neck.

Get me out.

Get me out.

The hand tightened its grip and her head was forced forward, banging against the edge of the door.

Help me.

Help me.

Again, her head rocked backwards against the back of the seat. The hand tightened its grip, wrenching her forward onto the hard metal surface of the door. Blood gushed from a cut above her eye and flowed down her face.

Her eyes.

Don't blind me.

Don't blind me.

She was thrown back against the headrest of her seat, her neck snapping at the sudden movement. The hands gripped her throat, thumbs digging deep into her Adam's apple. She couldn't breathe.

Got to do something.

Got to do something.

For a second, the man relaxed his hold on her throat, fiddling with something on his jacket.

A camera.

He was filming her.

Filming her death.

She summoned up all her strength and thrust her elbow sideways. It met the soft flesh of a groin. She pushed the point of her elbow in deeply, hearing a sharp intake of breath as the man doubled over, kneeling in front of her.

She smashed her elbow down on the crown of his head. A small empty patch took the force of the blow. He's going bald, she thought, losing his hair. Her elbow crunched into his head, sending a shock up her shoulder.

She wiped the blood away from her eye. He lay on the ground at her feet, his head resting on the ledge of the door. She grabbed the door handle and wrenched it closed.

His head was trapped against the jamb. She felt the impact echo through her arms. She pulled the door, again and again, and again, feeling the metal thud into the soft flesh covering the skull.

She slammed the door until her arms were exhausted and she no longer had any strength.

A man's body lay across the sill of the door, blood pouring from his head.

Not moving now. Not saying a word.

In the distance, she could hear the high pitched whine of a police siren. Somebody must have called them.

It was a time she loved. The whirring red light. The roar of the police car engine. The metallic voice of dispatch. And, above all, the anticipation. What lay ahead? What would happen in the next twenty seconds? Would she be able to handle it?

But normally she was in the car rushing to the aid of a victim. This time, she was the victim.

Annie moaned next to her, blood pouring from a cut on her head. The man was still lying across the open door.

The siren got louder and louder, an annoying noise she thought, too annoying. She heard the sounds of running feet.

She finally let go of the car door and all went dark.

Chapter 50

She opened her eyes.

Green walls. A neon light above her. The smell of perfume. A lovely perfume. A woman's perfume.

Somebody was leaning over her, adjusting something on her wrist. 'Where am I?'

'Bradford Royal.' The face was brown but the accent was Yorkshire with the 'ds' pronounced as 'ts'.

She tried to lift herself up. Strong hands pushed her back onto the pillow.

'You've had an accident. Concussion. You need to lie quietly.'

Jayne moved her head. Her brain seemed to move more slowly, sloshing around in her skull. A sharp pain lanced between her eyes. She let out a groan.

'See, stay still. You need rest.'

She lifted herself up from the pillow. 'Annie...'

'The other woman is fine. She's sedated at the moment. She's got a fractured tibia and clavicle, but she'll be ok. The other man wasn't so lucky. He's got a fractured skull, still in intensive.'

'My things...?'

'I've put them in the wardrobe over there. There's nobody else in this room at the moment. So enjoy the peace and quiet. Rest, that's what you need.'

Jayne tried to get up despite her throbbing head. 'I need to get to Manchester...'

The strong hands pushed her back on the bed. 'You're

298

going nowhere in that condition. I'll get a doctor to see you soon.'

'What time is it?'

The nurse looked at the watch hanging from her uniform. 'Two twenty-five.'

Jayne looked out the window. The sun was shining and she could just see the fingers of a branch reaching out to the sky.

'It can't be. I left the home at five o' clock.'

'You've been out for over a day. It's Sunday.'

'What? I have to get up, go to Manchester...'

Once again, the strong hands pushed her back on the bed. 'You must stay in bed. You're in no condition to leave this hospital.' Her voice oozed professional calm.

'I've got go.' She struggled against the hands pushing her down.

The voice was calm and authoritative. 'You can't go now. The police want to interview you about the accident.'

Jayne lay still. Quick flashes snapped through her brain. The sound of metal on metal. A car engine revving. The touch of those cold fingers on her neck. The pain as her head hit the door. The crunch of metal on a human bone as the car door struck his head, again and again and again.

'I'll go and get a doctor. He'll give you a sedative. Just lie here quietly.'

Jayne nodded her head slowly. The good little patient.

As soon as the door closed, she sat up in bed. A searing pain stabbed between her eyes and out through the back of her head. She swung her legs over the edge of the bed and attempted to stand. Something was holding her back. She looked down at her hand. A tube went from the back of her hand to a bottle above her bed. She peeled off the plaster and pulled out the catheter.

More pain.

She gritted her teeth, gingerly resting her feet on the floor. She stood up and immediately, the world began to spin. Grabbing hold of the end of the bed, she steadied herself. Who had tried to kill her? And why? She had a pretty good idea now. There could only be one reason.

She took two faltering steps to the wardrobe. Her bag and her clothes were inside. She reached in and took them out, nearly collapsing with the pain in her head.

'Sit down, I need to sit down,' she said out loud. But then she remembered the nurse. Can't let her find me. Need to get to Manchester.

She slid into a skirt and pulled on a jumper over her hospital night gown. As it slid over her face, she felt the fabric catch on the bandages above her eye, making her wince.

She tottered to the sink in the corner. The face that stared back at her was pale and wan, the white of the bandages standing out against the blue of her eyes. 'Well, you're not going to win Miss World. Not this year anyway.'

She pulled on her jacket, feeling the pain in her shoulder shoot through her body. Once again, her head began to throb. Steady, Jayne. Just take a moment.

The pain subsided. She looked at her shoes. High heels. Can't risk them. She slipped her feet into some hospital slippers, grabbed her bag and hobbled to the door. Opening it a little, she peered out into the corridor. That particular hospital smell of pure antiseptic and strong cleaning solvent hit her nose. Outside, two nurses were rushing into the ward opposite. There seemed to be some kind of emergency. The desk at the end of the lobby was empty.

She opened the door and stepped out into the corridor. Holding on to the wall, she edged her way down towards the lobby. The lift doors were closing. She shouted at a man inside. What came out of her mouth was a sharp squeak. 'Please hold the door.'

The lift opened. She hobbled into the lift and nodded thanks to the man. As she did so, a sharp pain hit her again, shooting through her right temple.

'You look worse for wear. Just had an operation?'

The man was making small talk with her. Please let him shut up. She forced a small smile. He looked back towards the door, staring at the stark metal.

The lift slowly descended. Too slowly. Quicker. Quicker.

Finally, after what seemed like an age and a half, the doors opened onto a busy lobby. People were hovering all around, rushing here and there.

She navigated her way cautiously through them, nearly bumping into an old man in a wheelchair but narrowly avoiding him.

She stepped through the doors. The cold November air hit her like smelling salts. She stopped, gathered herself and stumbled on.

A taxi rank. Open the door. Sit inside.

'Where to, love?' Another broad Yorkshire accent.

Where was she going? Manchester. But where in Manchester?

'Where to, missus?' repeated the taxi driver.

And then it came to her. 'The Midland Hotel, Manchester.'

The taxi driver sucked in his cheeks. 'It'll cost ye. Have to charge both ways. Gotta get back to Keighley tonight.'

She reached into her bag. Where was her purse? Had she left it in the hospital? No, there it was. How much was in it? Enough.

'Hello love, let's say 100 quid both ways. Off the meter, ok?'

She nodded her head. She felt so tired, so very tired. Must stay awake.

She felt the car pull away from the curb. 'Don't mind if I put the radio on, do ye? Always good to have a bit of music on a long trip.'

She nodded her head again. Must call John Hughes. Tell him I'm coming. But then she thought about the accident and all that had happened to her since she took this case. Her hand closed around the phone.

She felt tired, so tired. She could hear the sound of Smokie on the radio, but it seemed so far away.

She closed her eyes and for the second time in less than a day, her world went dark.

Chapter 51

Midland Hotel, Manchester. November 22, 2015.

She woke as the taxi driver shook her shoulder. 'We're here, madam. The Midland Hotel, Manchester.'

Her eyes flickered open. 'What time is it?' she muttered.

He checked his watch. '3.45, madam. You've been asleep the whole journey.' His head began to wobble in that wonderful way South Asians do when they are concerned. 'I could take you to a hospital, if you want, you don't look well.'

'I'll be fine.' She reached into her purse and paid him one hundred pounds, adding another twenty as a tip.

'This is too much, madam. One hundred is enough.'

'Keep it. It will pay for the petrol on the way back.' She grabbed her bag and staggered out of the car, holding onto the side of the taxi for balance as another wave of nausea threatened to overwhelm her. Got to keep going. She pulled out her phone and made a call. She hoped they would come soon or she wouldn't be able to make it through this.

She let go of the taxi and staggered up the steps, through the marble-lined lobby of the Midland. The place stank of money and opulence. Where else would Rolls have met Royce? Must focus. Don't allow my mind to get distracted.

She limped into the lift and pressed the button for John Hughes' floor. Just ten more minutes and then I can check myself back into the hospital. The nurse was right. I need to sleep. A deadening surge of tiredness filled her body. She leant against the side of the lift as it rose. Beneath her feet, she noticed a carpet with one word on it. Sunday. Was it Sunday already? She hoped John Hughes hadn't left for the airport yet. She must talk to him in person. Tell him the story. Test her hunch.

The lift jerked to a stop. She walked gingerly out, down the carpeted corridor, holding on to one wall just in case her legs gave way.

She pressed the door button. Almost immediately it opened. 'You're here, finally, take these cases down to our car.'

She stepped into the suite, Richard Hughes had his back to her, putting some papers in a briefcase. 'Get a move on, porter, we haven't got all day.' Slowly, he turned his head. The look of surprise on his face was wonderful. For the first time in her life, Jayne actually saw a mouth drop.

He recovered quickly. 'Mrs Sinclair, you're here.'

'Well spotted, Mr Hughes.'

John Hughes wheeled himself slowly into view. In a weak voice, he said, 'I knew you wouldn't let us down, Mrs Sinclair.'

'You're looking pale, Mr Hughes.'

'Better than you look, Mrs Sinclair. And I've got Leukaemia.'

For a moment, another wave of nausea washed through Jayne's body. She closed her eyes and began to feel herself fall.

'Where's your manners, Richard? Bring Mrs Sinclair a chair.'

Jayne heard the pad of feet on a deep carpet, followed by the touch of wood against the back of her knee. She opened her eyes and dropped into the chair. That felt better. Much better.

Focus.

Focus.

John Hughes was speaking.

'Sorry, I missed that.'

'I was saying Mrs Sinclair, you look like you have been in the wars.'

'I had an accident. You should see the state of the person who caused it.' She looked straight at Richard Hughes. 'Not a pretty sight.'

'See, Richard, I told you. A woman after my own heart.'

'We need to leave for the airport, Uncle...'

'We'll go soon. Mrs Sinclair has to tell us what she found first.' He nodded at Jayne, indicating that she should start.

Jayne took a deep breath. 'The name of your father wasn't Charles Trichot. It was Michael Dowling.'

'You told us that on the phone,' interrupted Richard. He was immediately shushed by John Hughes.

'Michael Dowling was a student at University College Dublin, reading history. He was also a member of the Irish Volunteers who took part in the Easter Rising.'

'A fighter. I knew my father had to be a fighter.' John Hughes hit his knee with his fist. It was the most animated Jayne had ever seen him.

'He was captured and imprisoned at the end of the Rising, serving time in Frongoch prison in Wales before being released in 1917.'

Richard Hughes stood up and stood behind his uncle.

Jayne continued speaking. 'He joined the IRA as it was known then, becoming an organiser for them, travelling the country as a representative of HQ. His best friend at this time and comrade in arms was Declan Fitzgerald.'

'The DF of the inscription in the book?'

Jayne nodded. 'At one point, his active service unit captured a British officer called John Clavell. They executed him two days before a truce was called in Ireland.' Jayne realised her words were becoming blunter.

'Clavell? But that's the surname of my mother on the birth certificate.'

Jayne fought with the pain that stabbed though her head. She touched the bandage above her eye. 'He was her brother.'

'My father shot him?'

'I don't think he did. The actual killing was carried out by Declan Fitzgerald. But your father was certainly involved.'

John Hughes was silent now staring at her. Richard Hughes was hovering behind him.

'I think your father, Michael Dowling, had become sickened by the killing and the war. After the truce in July 1921 and probably during the Civil War in late 1922, he travelled to England. He seems to have assumed the identity of a man who had been killed in France in 1918.'

'Charles Trichot.'

'That's correct.' Jayne could feel herself getting stronger now as if the telling of her tale had somehow infused her with a new energy. 'He met the sister of the officer who had been killed...'

'Emily Clavell. My mother.'

'Perhaps he assumed this identity to return some personal effects of her brother to Emily. We'll never know. Anyway, they fell in love and married in 1923.'

'The marriage certificate with the name of a man who died in 1918. I was born in 1925, the year after the wedding. That explains it all.'

'Not quite, Mr Hughes. Apparently, Emily Clavell found out the real identity of her husband...'

306

'When was that?'

Jayne reached down and pulled the letters from her bag. 'In late 1927. These letters make it obvious she couldn't stand to be with him anymore. They separated in early 1928 when you were two and a half years old.' Jayne opened the book given to her by the old man a week ago. It felt much longer than a week.

John Hughes was silent. A single tear dropped from his eye and rolled over the brown wrinkle on his face. 'I don't remember anything,' he whispered.

'You were too young, Mr Hughes.'

'What happened to my father?'

Before she could answer, Jayne heard the rap of something metallic and hard against a wooden table. 'Well done, Mrs Sinclair. You have solved the mystery.' Richard Hughes was standing behind his uncle, a dark steel-blue pistol nestling in his hand. In front of him on the table was a long knife. 'I knew some of the details, but I hadn't worked out all of them.'

John Hughes slowly turned his head towards his nephew. 'Richard, what are you doing?'

'What I should have done years ago, Uncle.'

'Put the bloody gun down. Don't be more of an idiot than you already are.'

Richard Hughes began to laugh. 'Uncle, I've put up with your insults all my life. Do this Richard. Do that Richard. You're a fucking idiot, Richard. Don't waste my time, Richard.' Then the laughter stopped and the man bared his teeth. 'NOT. ANY. MORE,' he screamed at the top of his voice.

The old man shrank back into his wheelchair.

Then the smile appeared again. The voice was calm and measured. 'This time, Richard is going to do what he wants.' He picked up the knife with his left hand. 'You see, Mrs Sinclair pulled out a knife here and stabbed you through the heart, Uncle. You were arguing about money after you refused to pay her for her work. She was angry and the accident had created an imbalance in her mind. I was forced to shoot her. Otherwise, I would have been stabbed too. I'm distraught because I have taken a human life.'

'You won't get away with it, Richard.'

'Oh, I will Uncle. This time, I will. You're very quiet Mrs Sinclair.'

Jayne lifted her head. 'I'm listening to you. You seem to have it all planned out.'

'You can answer a couple of questions for me before I shoot you.'

'And if I don't?'

'I shoot you anyway. At least, you live for a couple of minutes longer.'

'Ask away.'

'What happened to David Turner?'

'So that's his name. I never did know. He's lying in Bradford Royal Infirmary, in a coma. When he wakes up, he's going to tell the police everything.'

'Everything? I doubt it. He'll be paid well to keep quiet. Uncle's money will see to that.'

'You seem to have forgotten his phone. The police will check the last calls on that phone. I'm sure your number will be there.'

For the first time, Richard was not looking so confident. The smile painted on his face, began to look less smug.

'By the time they do that, I'll be in Costa Rica enjoying a life of wine, women and song, wasting all your hard-earned money, Uncle.'

Jayne glanced towards the door.

'Nobody is coming to rescue you, Mrs Sinclair. There's just you and me and Uncle here. In five minutes, of course, the place will be swarming with hotel security when I call down to tell them what I've been forced to do.'

Jayne glanced again towards the door. 'You had one other question, Richard?'

Richard thought for a moment. 'What happened to Michael Dowling? I never found out. Did he vanish? Become a drunk? Another victim of the Great Crash of 1929?'

Jayne shook her head. 'I don't think so.' She turned to the old man. He was sitting in his wheelchair, his face pale and uncertain, looking for the first time a very old and very tired man. 'Mr Hughes, or I should say, Mr Dowling, you told me you had a picture of your family when you graduated in 1949?'

'What's that got to do with anything?' said Richard Hughes.

'Humour me for a minute.'

'It's your last minute, use it as you will.'

'Could you show it to me?'

'Richard, it's in the folder, get it—' He stopped mid-sentence, realising that he was no longer able to give his nephew orders.

Richard Hughes smiled. 'One last service, just for you, my dear uncle.'

Keeping the gun pointing steadily at Jayne, he edged around the table and reached for the folder. 'Is this the one you meant?'

'That's it.'

He slid it across the table to Jayne. She picked it up, opened it and pulled out a black and white photo. She smiled as she looked at it.

'That was taken when I went to college on the GI Bill. My mother and father are on either side. The boy next to me is Richard's father.'

'What's the point of all this, Mrs Sinclair?'

'May I?' She pointed to the bag at her feet.

'Keep your hands where I can see them.'

Slowly she reached into the bag and pulled out her clear folder. She picked out one of the photographs of Michael Dowling and Declan Fitzgerald and the other prisoners taken in Frongoch so long ago when they had been young men. She passed it across to John Hughes.

He looked at it. Old eyes peering into the photograph, bringing it to life with his stare. 'It's him. It can't be him,' he whispered. The photo fell from his old fingers and drifted down to rest next to the wheel of the chair.

Richard rushed over to his uncle's side and picked up the photograph. As he did so, the old man brought his stick down across the back of his head.

Jayne leapt up from her chair and dived over Richard, knocking the gun upwards.

A loud bang.

Smoke filled the air around her head. She tried to breathe through the stench of cordite. Richard's arm was coming down. His knee was beneath her body forcing it on her.

She crushed her body closer to him, knocking his leg away. His right fist came down on her head, right on top of her old wound. A stab of burning pain shot through her skull. She fought to keep conscious. The fist came down again, harder this time.

Must hang on to his arm.

The fist struck down again. She moved her head at the last moment and the elbow hit her shoulder. Her left arm went dead.

He's too strong. Can't do this.

The gun was coming up. Close to her face. She smelt the cordite. Could see the round barrel with its drift of smoke, the scent of metal shavings from a lathe.

No. No. No.

She twisted the barrel and there was another explosion.

Chapter 52

Buxton, Manchester. November 24, 2015.

He saw her reflection in the window first, turning immediately to greet her. 'You look like you've been in the wars, Jayne.'

She had been released from the hospital after two nights under observation. The bandage that had once swathed her head was now reduced to a rather fetching pink plaster above her eyebrow. She still had a headache, though, kept under control by the helpful assistance of a bucketload of aspirin. 'You could say that, Dad.' She sat down beside him. 'How have you been?'

He put out his hand and let it waver. 'Ups and downs, you know how it is.'

'The nurse said that yesterday wasn't good.'

'Was it? I really don't know. Sometimes, I wonder if it would be better to just end it all.'

'Shush, Dad, who would I talk to then? Who would I visit?'

Her father laughed. 'You could try visiting a hairdresser.' A wrinkled hand reached out and mussed her hair.

The doctor had cut a chunk of her hair away as he stitched up the cut on her forehead. 'Is it that bad?'

'A butcher could have done a better job.'

They both laughed. It was good to be here with him, like this, like now, like the old days. 'I solved the case.'

'Of course, you did, I never expected anything else from my daughter. Is that where you got this?'

She nodded. 'Remember the client? Mr Hughes?'

'The one who was looking for his father?'

'That's him. Well, I found the truth for him. Turned out he was a volunteer in the Irish War of Independence. He married the sister of a man who had been shot. They had a son, my client, but then split up. Unfortunately, she died soon afterwards.'

'Of a broken heart?'

'Nobody knows. But she must have been distraught. They both loved each other very much. The boy was put in a home and later adopted by an American couple. Now here's the strange twist to this life.' Jayne paused.

'I'm waiting...'

'The American was my client's real father.'

'What? How?'

Jayne shook her head. 'I don't know. He must have arranged it through the orphanage. I guess we'll never know the real truth since all the records were destroyed in a fire in 1932. I believe he was a resourceful man, though...'

'That means he never told your client who he was...'

'True. John Hughes grew up believing he was adopted. It was one of the things that spurred him on, made him the man he is today.'

'Why didn't his father tell him the truth?'

'I don't know, we'll never know. Guilt perhaps. Or having to explain the truth about the death of John Clavell and the end of his relationship with the boy's mother. I suppose as the years went by, telling the truth became harder and harder until it became insurmountable. And of course, he may have always meant to tell John Hughes, but his death occurred before he revealed his secret. Whatever it was, John Hughes grew up not knowing who he really was.'

'It happens to a lot of us. How'd you get the bump? And don't tell me you hit your head.'

'I hit my head on a car door. Or rather my head was hit for me. John's nephew became worried about my investigation, concerned I would discover new relatives to share his uncle's fortune, he wanted all the money, felt he deserved it after all the years suffering the abuse of his uncle. So he arranged to have me...injured.' The lie came out easily for Jayne. She hoped her father didn't notice.

'What happened to him?'

'He's in a hospital now. Gunshot wound to the shoulder. He'll be charged with attempted murder.'

Her father's eyes narrowed. 'Attempted murder of whom?'

Jayne pointed to herself.

He shook his head. 'I thought when you left the police...'

Jayne laughed trying to defuse the situation. 'You know me, Dad, I attract trouble like honey attracts bees. The irony is I never found any other relatives, not close ones anyway. An aunt and a few cousins. Richard Hughes would have inherited everything anyway according to my client's will.'

'He just got too greedy. And now he's got a hole in his shoulder and a prison sentence to serve.'

'And John Hughes is changing his will. He's forming a trust to help other people, orphans and adoptees, find their parents.'

'So some good has come of having a daughter with a head as hard as a rock.' Her father went silent for a moment. 'How's Paul?'

'Still in Brussels.'

He sighed. 'You know what I mean, Jayne.'

She looked down at her bag. 'If I'm honest, not good, Dad. He wants us to move to live there. He's got a new job.'

'And you, what do you want?'

'You know, Dad, he's never asked me that.'

A large hand, freckled with the dark spots of age, touched her shoulder and ruffled her hair. 'What do you want, Jayne?'

Chapter 53

Didsbury, Manchester. November 24, 2015.

She turned on the light in the kitchen, throwing the new mail on the kitchen top. Outside was a typical Manchester day in November. Dark. Dreary. And wet. Very wet.

She opened the fridge and took out a bottle of Rioja. She needed something deep and earthy this evening. She checked her collection of chocolate, it was getting smaller, time to be replenished. She took out a bar of the Valrhona and put it beside the wine,

Who was she? What did she want?

Questions her father had asked and she knew needed answers. Her and Paul were dead. They had been dead for a long time and both knew it, but pride and a sense of duty to each other kept them together, despite the fights and the bickering. He would never have the courage to break up, she knew that. This move to Brussels was just his way of forcing her to decide, to make a decision.

She opened the wine, pouring herself a large glass. It was exactly what she needed; the sweet sun of Spain mingled with the fruit and tannins of the grape in her mouth. She snapped off a chunk of the chocolate. The two together, sheer bliss. For a moment, she was transported back to Madrid. A happier time for her and Paul, eating and drinking one evening in the Mercado, loving the noise and bustle of the place, enjoying their closeness.

She put down the glass and reached for her wallet, taking out a slim sheet of paper. There was the name of an obscure English bank at the top followed by the By Appointment logo. Beneath it lay her name and a figure repeated in words. 50,000 pounds. Fifty Thousand Pounds. Her client had been generous. John Hughes, or John Dowling as he now called himself said she deserved every penny.

'Freedom,' she said out loud to the kitchen. The money gave her freedom to be who she wanted. To live where she wanted. To do what she wanted. She would call Paul later and tell him she wasn't going to move to Brussels. He would be unhappy but he would accept her decision. It was what he wanted too, he just wasn't able to make the call.

She put the cheque down on the counter top. She would have to sort out the house with him, of course. She knew he wouldn't mind her staying here. Eventually, when they got divorced, they would have to sell it and divide the proceeds but until then it would be hers.

She opened the letters in front of her. Most were bills; water, electricity, gas, another demand from the BBC to pay the licence fee. She couldn't remember the last time she watched TV.

She picked up the last letter. Her name was handwritten in a lovely shade of mauve ink on the cover, Jayne Sinclair. No title. No Mrs. She liked it. A harbinger of the future.

The letter smelt vaguely of lilacs. She opened it, taking out the expensive writing paper inside.

Dear Jayne,

My name is Carroll Gordon. You don't know me but I obtained your name from a mutual friend.

I have rather a strange request for you. I would like you to trace an object not a person. An object with a history and a meaning to both me and my family. An object stolen from us last year which had been in my family's possession since the expedition to sack Peking in China in 1860.

If you would like to hear more, please call me on 0275 657 4398 at your convenience.

I do look forward to working with you to find the thief. And the object?

It was a chicken. One of the animals from the Astronomical Calendar at the Imperial Palace, removed from Peking in 1860 by my ancestor.

regards

Carroll

Jayne reached out to open her computer, realising that nothing was there. She would have to buy a new one with John Hughes' money. A top of the range MacBook Pro perhaps. Treat herself.

She looked back at the letter. It intrigued her. She would definitely take this case on.

In that moment, Jayne Sinclair knew who she was with startling clarity.

She was a Genealogical Detective, solving mysteries from the past, helping people in the present.

The thought brought a smile to her face. The cat rubbed its body against her legs and miaowed. He must be hungry again.

She raised the glass of wine to toast herself. 'Here's to a brighter future, coming from a bright past,' she said out loud.

The cat ignored her and miaowed again.

If you have enjoyed this book by M J Lee, please leave a review on Amazon. It's always great to hear feedback.

If you would like to hear more about M J Lee and his books, go to his website at www.writermjlee.com, his Facebook page at writermjlee or his twitter feed at, you guessed it, writermjlee.